"Haven't you considered the possibility he might be innocent?"

Jessie hated to talk about Aidan's father after last night, but the phone call had changed everything.

"Innocent? How can you even suggest that?" Aidan shot her a look of disbelief. "You were there for the trial. You were on the jury that convicted him!"

"I know this is going to sound crazy, but several times during the trial I had this feeling that your father was innocent. We were instructed to judge by the evidence, not by our emotions, but if his lawyer is going to appeal, maybe there's something we didn't hear about...something that will shed new light on the case."

"He just has expensive lawyers who know how to get an appeal," Aidan said cynically. "He's hurt people, Jessie."

His bitterness frightened her. Maybe it was better to drop the subject—for now.

Dear Reader,

Four more fabulous WOMEN WHO DARE are heading your way!

In May, you'll thrill to the time-travel tale Lynn Erickson spins in *Paradox*. When loan executive Emily Jacoby is catapulted back in time during a train wreck, she is thoroughly unnerved by the fate that awaits her. In 1893, Colorado is a harsh and rugged land. Women's rights have yet to be invented, and Will Dutcher, Emily's reluctant host, is making her question her desire to return to her own time.

In June, you'll be reminded that courage can strike at any age. Our heroine in Peg Sutherland's *Late Bloomer* discovers unplumbed depths at the age of forty. After a lifetime of living for others, she realizes that she wants something for herself—college, a career, a *life*. But when a mysterious stranger drifts into town, she discovers to her shock that she also wants *him!*

Sharon Brondos introduces us to spunky Allison Glass in our July WOMEN WHO DARE title, *The Marriage Ticket*. Allison stands up for what she believes in. And she believes in playing fair. Unfortunately, some of her community's leaders don't have the same scruples, and going head-to-head with them lands her in serious trouble.

You'll never forget Leah Temple, the heroine of August's *Another Woman*, by Margot Dalton. This riveting tale of a wife with her husband's murder on her mind will hold you spellbound...and surprised! Don't miss it!

Some of your favorite Superromance authors have also contributed to our spring and summer lineup. Look for books by Pamela Bauer, Debbi Bedford, Dawn Stewardson, Jane Silverwood, Sally Garrett, Bobby Hutchinson and Judith Arnold...to name just a few! Some wonderful Superromance reading awaits you!

Marsha Zinberg
Senior Editor

P.S. Don't forget that you can write to your favorite author

c/o Harlequin Reader Service
P.O. Box 1297
Buffalo, New York 14240
U.S.A.

THE Model Bride

PAMELA BAUER

Harlequin Books

TORONTO • NEW YORK • LONDON
AMSTERDAM • PARIS • SYDNEY • HAMBURG
STOCKHOLM • ATHENS • TOKYO • MILAN
MADRID • WARSAW • BUDAPEST • AUCKLAND

Published May 1993

ISBN 0-373-70548-4

THE MODEL BRIDE

Printed in U.S.A.

ABOUT THE AUTHOR

Award-winning author Pamela Bauer has gained fans around the world for her heartwarming family-oriented stories. *The Model Bride* is a family story with a twist. The McCulloughs have been torn apart by infidelity and murder, but Jessie Paulson's love for Aidan McCullough and her dogged determination to uncover the truth manages to reunite his family and set them all on the road to a brighter future.

Family is very important to Pam, who lives in Minnesota with her husband, Gerr, and their children, Amy and Aaron.

Books by Pamela Bauer

HARLEQUIN SUPERROMANCE

Don't miss any of our special offers. Write to us at the following address for information on our newest releases.

Harlequin Reader Service
P.O. Box 1397, Buffalo, NY 14240
Canadian address: P.O. Box 603,
Fort Erie, Ont. L2A 5X3

CHAPTER ONE

"MOMMY, I CAN'T SEE."

At the sound of the muffled, squeaky voice, Aidan McCullough glanced over his shoulder. Standing behind him was a little girl bundled up in a bright pink snowsuit, a white woolen scarf wrapped around the lower half of her face. Next to her was a young woman in a down-filled coat, her arms laden with packages.

Immediately Aidan stepped aside, gesturing for the two of them to take his place in front of the plate-glass window. The young mother smiled gratefully at him and murmured something about how kind he was.

Kind, but lacking in common sense, Aidan thought as he shivered with cold. Without a hat, gloves or overshoes, he was hardly dressed to be outdoors for more than a minute or two. Yet here he was, standing in the sleet on a cold, gray November afternoon, gazing into the large corner window of Braxton's department store.

All along downtown Minneapolis's Nicollet Mall, holiday shoppers crowded the sidewalks to view the display windows the local merchants had adorned with Christmas scenes. Sugarplum fairies danced around miniature trees, mechanized characters skated on glass mirrors and toy soldiers marched past gingerbread villages, much to the delight of children and adults alike.

Aidan wasn't delighted. He was chilled to the bone and irritable. He hated the cold, especially when it caused tiny little ice crystals to form on his mustache. He shrugged deeper into the turned-up collar on his leather jacket as a sudden gust of wind thrust tiny pellets of freezing rain down his neck.

"How come they're not moving?" Again the child's voice cut through the crisp air, and Aidan's eyes moved to the three people in the display window.

Unlike the other windows, Braxton's corner showcase had no special effects or mechanized figures that owed their movement to the genius of electronic wizardry. Instead, live models pretending to be mannequins posed inside. A man in a Santa Claus suit sat on a large thronelike chair, and two women dressed as elves stood at his side.

"They'll move in just a few minutes," Aidan heard the child's mother answer. "As soon as the fairy dust falls."

Like most of the shoppers, Aidan knew that at the stroke of every hour and half hour metallic flakes—or fairy dust, as the Braxton's staff preferred to call it—descended upon Santa and his elves. During the five-minute shower, the mannequins came to life, bringing smiles and cheers from the people on the outside looking in. As soon as the fairy dust settled, however, the models once more became mannequins, assuming poses that kept them motionless for the next twenty-five minutes.

Aidan glanced around and saw that the live mannequins had drawn their usual crowd of onlookers. There weren't as many as there had been the other times he had visited the window, he noted. Of course, anyone with a lick of sense would be inside the heated department store shopping in comfort instead of standing outside in the bitter cold waiting to catch a glimpse of Santa in action.

Only it wasn't Santa who had lured Aidan to the window. It was one of the elves. Although, Aidan thought the long-legged blonde with her hand on Santa's arm could hardly be called elfin.

Dressed in a pair of red tights and a green satin bodysuit embroidered with sequins, she didn't resemble the elves Aidan remembered from any of his childhood stories. He guessed she and her brunette co-worker were probably just as great a draw as the jolly old man himself. *What warm-blooded man wouldn't want to feast his eyes upon two such gorgeous-looking creatures?* Aidan thought cynically as his glance strayed to a couple of businessmen who, judging by the looks on their faces, obviously agreed.

Although both of the elves were attractive, it wasn't the brunette Aidan found intriguing, but the blonde. It was her hair that had initially caught his eye, falling in a long, straight curtain and catching the light in such a way that it shimmered, much like the gold tinsel on the Christmas tree in the corner of the window.

She was good at her job, he thought with reluctant admiration. Not once since he had been standing here had she so much as moved a muscle. She stood peering over Santa's shoulder, a sassy grin on her face as though she were sharing some secret with the bearded old man. There was something about that grin that made Aidan ignore the possibility that he could get frostbite if he lingered much longer in the cold.

She reminds you of Kate, a little voice inside his head taunted him. Aidan dismissed the thought as Braxton's clock struck four and a glittering shower of flakes fell from the ceiling.

Like wooden soldiers come to life, Santa and his elves moved with jerky motions, their expressions exaggerated at the sudden realization they were ambulatory. The small crowd outside watched with delight as the trio entertained them with their discovery. Aidan's eyes followed the blond elf, admiring her graceful movements as she held up toys for Santa to inspect.

Every child outside cried Santa's name, hoping to draw his attention with the wave of a mitten. As if on cue, all three models faced the window shoppers.

As the blond elf looked in Aidan's direction he found himself pulling his bare hand from his jacket pocket and waving. For only a moment their eyes met, and he thought he saw a flicker of recognition. Did she remember that he had stopped on several occasions during the past week?

All too soon the metallic dust settled at the mannequins' feet and once again all action inside the window ceased. Santa dropped back down onto the velvet chair, his eyes on the list of toys in his hand. The dark-haired elf was again at his side, her attention focused on a teddy bear. The blonde, instead of looking over Santa's shoulder, stared straight out at the crowd, her gaze becoming distant as though she saw nothing but the wilderness of the North Pole.

Reluctantly the crowd dispersed, and Aidan, too, took a few steps back. Instead of following the others indoors, however, he positioned himself so that he was standing directly in the blonde's line of vision. Then he smiled and watched for some response from her.

When she gave no indication that she had seen him, he shrugged his shoulders and gave her a helpless look. Still she didn't so much as bat an eyelash. He was about to walk away when a group of teenagers approached the window.

"Hey! Look at her." A youth with a lightning streak shaved out of the side of his head waved his fingerless, gloved hand at the blonde. "She's pretending she can't see us." He made several comical gestures in an attempt to get her to move.

"The babe's gotta be made of ice," another boy with a ponytail muttered. "How could she resist a handsome dude like me giving her the treatment?'' He, too, was making faces, trying to get her attention.

They continued to clown around, hoping to distract the lovely elf, but to no avail. Finally one of the four raised a finger in an obscene gesture, but as he was about to thrust it up against the glass, Aidan deftly slid between him and the window.

With his back to the showcase, he was able to block the youth from the elf's range of vision. ''Next time you want to wave at the lady, use all of your fingers,'' he warned the scruffy-looking youth, who muttered an expletive before sauntering away. The other boys followed him.

Aidan turned, expecting to see some sort of emotion on the model's face, but there was none: no recognition in her eyes, no softening of her features in gratitude. He saw only the faraway look that had been on her face all afternoon.

As he gazed at her stonelike features he felt a stab of disappointment. What had he expected? That he would be rewarded for his chivalry?

The tiny voice in his head said, *She's really not like Kate at all.*

After a few more minutes of studying her, he came to the same conclusion. Except for the curtain of blond hair she really didn't resemble Kate, he thought. There was self-control etched in the well-defined mouth, confidence in her posture and determination in her eyes. Kate could never have stood in front of a crowd of people and pretended to see no one.

So why was it, then, that every time he looked at this model he thought of Kate? He didn't want to be reminded of her—especially not now. Getting through the next few weeks would be difficult enough without seeing someone who stirred memories of a woman he would much rather forget. Without so much as a backward glance, he left the window.

"THE ONLY GOOD THING I can say about this job is that at least it's steady work for eight weeks." Devony Dixon groaned as she slowly rotated her dark head in a circular motion, her fingers kneading the tense muscles at the base of her neck.

"It's not so bad. I think it's kind of fun seeing the expressions on the kids' faces when we start to move." Jessie Paulson pulled out the hairpins holding her red felt cap in place and shook her blond hair loose.

"It may be fun to you, but I ache," Devony complained.

"That's because you haven't been doing the yoga routine I showed you." There was a slight note of admonition in Jessie's tone as her blue eyes met Devony's dark ones in the dressing-table mirror.

"Yoga may work for you, but my limbs weren't made to bend and twist like some Gumby doll's." Devony stretched her arms up over her head and grimaced. "Besides, I jog every morning. That's all the fitness I can handle."

"Yoga is more than physical fitness. It's a way of soothing your spirit," Jessie responded, her fingers searching for the zipper on the green satin bodysuit.

"Well, this spirit prefers to soothe itself without contorting any muscles."

"All right, all right. I get the message," Jessie said goodnaturedly, slipping out of the elf costume. If there was one thing she had learned about Devony, it was not to push her into doing anything she didn't want to do.

"Can you believe the number of people there were outside the window today?" Devony asked as she bent to remove her green satin slippers. "Christmas is still six weeks away and already there's a crowd."

"It must be the sales," Jessie commented thoughtfully.

"It would take some pretty big markdowns to get me out of the comfort of a warm house on a day like today."

Jessie chuckled. "Where's your holiday spirit?"

"Where it should be. In my living room."

Jessie grinned. "I noticed your friend with the flash cards was back. You didn't break your pose, did you?"

"Just for a second, but that was only because that guy in the long underwear was standing right next to him."

"There was a guy in long underwear out there?" Jessie asked with a lift of her brow.

"You mean to tell me you didn't see that man who was wearing the big furry cap with the long earflaps and the eyes that blinked on and off?"

"I must have missed him."

"How could you? He was so weird looking." She shook her head in disbelief, then sighed. "I wish I could tune everything out the way you do."

"You can. It's a form of meditation...like yoga," Jessie said with a sly grin, which drew a playful groan from her friend. "The trick is not to make eye contact with anyone."

"This guy's eyes weren't my downfall," Devony retorted. "He wasn't wearing any pants—only a pair of red long johns. And he wore the biggest, clunkiest rubber boots I've ever seen."

Jessie laughed. "Then you should have avoided looking at him altogether."

"I couldn't. He pressed his face up against the glass until it looked like the belly of a snail." She shuddered at the thought.

"All I can say is I'm glad he was on your side of the window," Jessie said with a toss of her head, peeling off the red tights before slipping on a pair of navy leggings.

"Why is it that the odd ducks are always trying to get my attention and the hunks are always trying to get yours?" Devony posed, her hand at her waist.

"I wouldn't call four teenaged boys making lewd gestures hunks," Jessie answered.

Just then the memory of one tall, dark and handsome man gallantly blocking her view of a particularly obnoxious teenager popped into her mind. It was the first time she had wanted to acknowledge anyone's presence. Somehow, this man had been different from the other men who frequently waved at her through the window. As soon as he had turned his back to her and started to walk away she had regretted not smiling at him. One smile certainly wouldn't have cost her her job and she had been grateful for his intervention.

Several times during the past week she had noticed him outside the window. Jessie knew that with the tiniest bit of encouragement he would have found a way to speak to her. The way his eyes had studied her made it obvious.

Whoever he was, she had found his presence distracting. Even though it was nice to know that chivalry was not dead, she didn't need anyone looking at her with such blatant interest, especially someone who looked as though he could have been one of the photos on Devony's Hunk of the Month calendar.

"Well, that about does it for me," Devony announced, interrupting Jessie's musings. "I'm out of here." She gathered up her belongings and slung the strap of her carryall over her shoulder. "I'll see you tomorrow night, right?" She looked at Jessie for confirmation.

"About tomorrow night..." she began.

"Jess! You're not backing out of my party, are you? You promised you'd come." Devony gave her a look intended to make her feel guilty.

And it did, which was why Jessie's face wore an apologetic expression. "I want to, but I only found out last night that my niece is coming down for a few days."

"Which one?" Devony stood with a fist thrust impatiently on her hip.

"My sister Carla's daughter Melissa. Apparently she's been suffering a few growing pains, and Carla thinks a change of scenery will lift her spirits."

"She's a teenager. Certainly you don't need to stay home and baby-sit her on a Saturday night?"

"Devony, she's family. I can't just abandon her because you're having a party," Jessie scolded her friend gently. "Besides, I want to spend some time with her. It's not easy being fifteen."

Devony groaned. "Luke is never going to forgive me. He's only coming because he thinks you're going to be there."

Jessie couldn't suppress a smile. "Your brother will be disappointed for approximately three seconds, and then as soon as he sees you've invited Vicki Watson he'll forget that I was even supposed to be there." Jessie knew that Devony's brother was probably the biggest flirt in the state of Minnesota, and as long as there were unattached women in the room he would never be lonely.

"But I was hoping it would be a chance for the two of you to get to know each other better."

Devony fancied herself as the consummate matchmaker when it came to her friends. Besides modeling, she worked part-time at a dating service, and as much as Jessie hated to admit it, she did have a knack for matching personalities. Unfortunately Jessie wasn't interested in being matched with anyone at the moment—especially not her friend's brother.

"There'll be other opportunities."

Devony shot her a dubious glance. "Not if Vicki gets her way there won't be." She sighed. "Oh, well. I can always hope she catches that flu that's going around and she doesn't show up."

Jessie chuckled. "She's not that bad."

Devony made an exasperated sound. "I don't know how you can say that. You're talking about someone who has a brain the size of an after-dinner mint."

Again Jessie chuckled. "Well, you'd better hope she doesn't get the flu. She's taking my place while I'm on jury duty," she told Devony, straightening the collar on her chambray shirt.

Devony groaned. "What? I have to *work* with her, too? Come on, Jessie. You can't do this to me."

"I don't have a choice, Dev. When jury duty calls, one must go," Jessie said with a helpless shrug.

"Can't you get a postponement? That's what my sister did. She told them she was in the middle of a special project at work. It was six months before she got another notice."

"I don't think they consider modeling in a display window worthy of a postponement," Jessie said dryly. "When I called the court clerk all I got was a lecture about how jury duty is both a privilege and an obligation of living in a democracy."

"Yeah, well now you know why I never registered to vote."

"You don't vote?"

"No, but obviously you do, or else you wouldn't be faced with the prospect of a week in court."

Jessie stared at her in surprise. "You'd give up your right to vote just so you wouldn't get called to jury duty?"

"In this business I can't afford to turn down any bookings just to go do my patriotic duty. Besides, there's never anyone worthwhile to vote for," she added.

Although Jessie had often expressed similar feelings regarding the candidates for office, she would never have considered not voting in an election. Patriotism had been strong in the small town where she had spent her childhood, and she had been raised to value her freedom of choice.

"Well, it's too late for me to unregister myself now. I'm going to have to go and put in my time," she said with resignation.

"Be prepared to be bored," Devony warned. "When my sister finally did go she spent all five days in a room with a bunch of strangers doing absolutely nothing. They never even used her on a jury. She just had to be there in case she was needed."

"That would be all right with me. I could bring my embroidery along and work on the tablecloth I'm giving my grandmother for Christmas."

"Maybe you'll get on some fascinating criminal trial," Devony suggested, her eyes widening. "Like a serial killer or some guy with Mafia connections."

Jessie shuddered. "I don't think there's much chance of that happening in Wright County."

"Oh, that's right. You don't live in Minneapolis anymore. In that case, it probably will be boring." Her face fell in disappointment.

"I'm not expecting 'L.A. Law.' Chances are I'll end up sitting in the waiting room along with the other alternates working on my embroidery."

"Yeah, and in the meantime, I'll be stuck back here in the window with Miss Vicki."

"We'd better get going before they turn out the lights on us." Jessie reached for the garment bag with her elf costume tucked inside. "Fred's probably wondering what's happened to us."

Fred was the night watchman who stood guard at the employees' entrance. At one time he had been a professional wrestler, but now his major interest in life was working with troubled youths at an inner-city recreation club during the day.

"Good evening, ladies. Is your work done at the North Pole for this evening?" he asked with a wide grin as the two models approached the store entrance.

"Another day, another dollar, Fred," Devony said, smiling.

"Ain't that the truth," he agreed with a shake of his head. He got up from his desk and unlocked the door with a key from the circular ring at his waist. They were just about to enter the parking ramp when he snapped his fingers.

"Wait, just a minute." Fred turned back to his desk and reached for a package. "I almost forgot about this. Jessie, this is for you." He gave her a long, skinny white box tied with a red ribbon.

"What's going on? I thought you said you weren't dating anyone," Devony commented, looking at the box curiously.

"I'm not." A puzzled frown knit Jessie's brow. "Where did this come from?" she asked the security guard.

He shrugged. "Can't say, myself. It was here when I came on duty."

Jessie stared at the package until Devony said, "Well, open it up and see what it is."

Cautiously Jessie tugged on the red satin ribbon. Inside the box was a single long-stemmed rose made out of white chocolate.

"Ooh! It's not only pretty but it's edible. Who's it from?" Devony demanded as Jessie lifted the flower from the box.

Jessie rustled through the tissue paper until she found a tiny card, then read it aloud. "This is only candy, but if you'd smile at me I'd send you the real thing."

"That's it? No name?" Devony grabbed the card from her hands as Jessie slowly shook her head. "It must be from someone who tried to make you smile in the window. But the question is, who?"

Although many men passed the window each day and attempted to get her to smile, the first image that leaped into Jessie's mind was that of a tall, dark stranger wearing a leather aviator jacket.

"Fred, are you sure this is for me?" Jessie turned to the guard.

He shook his head. "Like I said, it was here when I came on duty. All I was told was some man dropped it off with instructions that it be given to the blond elf in the window."

Again the image of the mustached man who had stepped in front of the unruly teenagers came to Jessie's mind. There had been something provocative in the way he had looked at her that now caused a tiny shiver to dance up and down her spine.

"Maybe it was the fellow with the long johns and this was supposed to be for you," she said to Devony, attempting to make light of the gift and put the handsome man's face out of her thoughts.

"I don't think so," Devony responded dryly. "He was hardly the candy-and-flowers type. Besides, Fred said it was for the blond elf.'' She playfully tugged at Jessie's pony-tail.

"What do you suppose I should do with it?"

"What do you mean? Aren't you going to take it home and eat it?"

"Devony, it came from some stranger. Maybe it's not safe to eat."

"Look, it's hermetically sealed by the candy manufacturer.'' She held up the rose for Jessie's inspection. "And I see no needle holes anywhere. I bet your grandmother would like it."

Jessie took the rose from her hands and stuck it back in the box. "Fine. I'll take it home," she told her in a tone that revealed none of the agitation swirling inside her.

"I'd say you've got yourself a secret admirer," Devony pronounced with a grin.

"Judging by the number of people gathering outside that window, I'd say you've got more than one," Fred seconded in an authoritative tone.

But the only face that kept recurring in Jessie's mind belonged to a man whose grin seemed to imply a shared secret. He had looked into her eyes provocatively, as if he could see behind them and into her head.

Was it any wonder she couldn't cast aside the image of his ruggedly good-looking face? It had been a long time since any man had been able to make her feel all squiggly inside with just one interested glance. Until today she had thought she had become immune to the charms of handsome men.

Well, she didn't need the kind of feelings such thoughts produced. When she stopped for gas on her way home she tossed the chocolate rose into a trash can near the pumps.

COMPARED TO MINNEAPOLIS, Delano was definitely small-town. It boasted one high school, a post office, a nursing home and a business district that couldn't quite compete with the city's shopping malls but which took care of most of the locals' needs. It was a close-knit community where smiles and friendly greetings were commonplace.

Jessie's grandmother's home was located in the center of town not far from the main street. It was a big, old two-story house painted white, with a gabled roof and a veranda that ran the length of the front. For Jessie it had always been a special place, holding fond childhood memories of many a summer holiday with her grandparents. Even a small town like Delano was an exciting city to a farm girl, and Jessie had loved to walk up and down the main street, stopping for penny candy at the drugstore or an ice-cream cone at the drive-in.

Tonight when she stepped inside her grandmother's house she was greeted by the familiar aroma of freshly baked bread. Automatically her eyes sought the spot on the counter where her grandmother set warm baked goods to cool on a wooden cutting board. She saw two golden brown loaves sitting there.

Jessie smiled to herself as images of her grandmother bent over the table, her snow-white curls tucked beneath a hair net, popped into her head. Even though the body was frail beneath the apron and the fingers bony as they curled around the rolling pin, she still managed to make the most delectable pastries Jessie had ever tasted.

With Melissa expected in the morning, Jessie guessed that her grandmother had spent all of today baking the wonderful delicacies everyone in the family had come to expect. Jessie couldn't resist opening the pantry door.

"What are you looking for?" a scratchy voice called out as she was surveying its contents.

"Looks to me like someone's been doing some baking," Jessie remarked in a warm, affectionate voice. "Lots and lots of baking... Let's see, we have *berlinerkranser,* butter rings, *lefse.*" She tried to make her voice remonstrative, but failed. How could she blame the sweet woman for doing something that gave her so much pleasure?

"Just a few things for Melissa's visit," her grandmother replied, heading toward the refrigerator. She opened the door and started to remove several items, including a plate of leftover roast beef.

"Gran, what are you doing?"

"I'm making you a sandwich. You must be hungry. You don't get a proper dinner break at that job you have." Still wearing her housedress, she automatically reached for the pink apron hanging on a hook at the end of the cabinets.

"I don't need a sandwich, Gran." Jessie took the apron from her hands and hung it back on the hook. Steering her away from the refrigerator and toward the wooden table, she said, "As delicious as I know that homemade bread is, what I'd really like is some *lefse* with butter and sugar."

"I'll make us some coffee." Her grandmother immediately headed for the kettle on the stove.

Jessie again had to steer her toward the table. "If you drink coffee this late, it'll keep you awake. Why don't we have some hot chocolate?" She eased the elderly woman down onto a chair. "You sit and I'll get it," she said in the firm voice she had adopted the day she had moved in with her grandmother six months ago. If there was one thing Jessie wouldn't allow, it was for her grandmother to wait on her.

Even at eighty years of age, Gran insisted on putting together a buffet of food and serving it to anyone who entered her house. In her typical Norwegian way, she was always prepared to set a generous meal on the table for company no matter how short the notice.

Jessie set the table in the manner her grandmother preferred. Good china, polished silver and cloth napkins—even for a late-evening snack of *lefse* and hot chocolate.

"You must have spent most of your day in the kitchen," Jessie commented as she spread butter and sprinkled sugar on the *lefse*.

"*Ja,* I wanted to make sure we had enough to eat when Melissa gets here."

"There'll be plenty, Gran," Jessie reassured her, wishing that her grandmother hadn't spent so much time preparing food that was probably not going to be eaten. Knowing how her niece worried about her weight, Jessie thought it was unlikely that Missy would do justice to her grandmother's supply of baked goods.

"Teenagers eat a lot. I remember that from when I had three of my own," she said with a nod of her head. "And Melissa has a hearty appetite. It comes from growing up on a farm."

Jessie wasn't so sure she agreed, but simply said, "Whatever we don't eat we can send home to Carla."

"I'm surprised your sister's not coming down with her. Nothing's wrong, is it?"

Jessie avoided her grandmother's eyes as she answered, "No, what makes you ask?"

"It's not like Carla to put Melissa on the bus and send her to visit all by herself."

"Gran, Melissa's going to be sixteen in a couple of months. I think Carla thought it would be a good experience for her to come down alone. She can do a little Christmas shopping and spend some time with us."

"But she's going to be missing school."

"Only a couple of days," Jessie answered, then quickly changed the subject before her grandmother probed any further into the reasons for Missy not being in school. "I thought we'd take her over to the Como Park Conservatory in St. Paul. We could show her the poinsettias, then have dinner at that restaurant you like over on Snelling Avenue. What do you think?"

Jessie was relieved when her grandmother was easily diverted to talk concerning their plans for the weekend. Later, as she prepared for bed, Jessie wondered why she had agreed to her niece coming. It wouldn't be easy keeping Melissa's problems from her grandmother, and with Jessie having to report for jury duty, she wouldn't have a lot of time to spend with her niece. She probably should have told her sister it wasn't a good idea for Melissa to come down.

But if there was one thing Jessie never did, it was turn her back on her family. It gave her a warm feeling to know that her family turned to her whenever there was a problem. But as she began her yoga meditation, she wondered what it would be like to be able to cry just once on someone's shoulder herself.

Assuming the lotus position, she pushed such thoughts aside and turned her senses inward, concentrating on the Manet print hanging on her bedroom wall. One by one the stressful thoughts drifted away, and her body relaxed as she meditated.

But something prevented her from finding her moment of peace.

It was the memory of a man with a dazzling smile and dark eyes...eyes that seemed to see right through to her soul.

CHAPTER TWO

"I SWEAR, THE MALL of America is *the* very best place in the whole world to shop!" The words practically exploded as they tumbled off Melissa Collins's lips. "You are so lucky! To think, you can just get in your car and drive to the largest shopping mall in all of the United States!"

After two days of her company, Jessie had become accustomed to hearing her niece speak in extremes. If something wasn't the absolutely, most wonderful experience of Melissa's life, it was probably the most disgusting thing to ever happen to her.

"So you think you'd like living in a big city like Minneapolis?" Jessie asked as they deposited their packages on the kitchen table.

"Are you kidding? It would be the very best thing that could happen," Melissa gushed as she carelessly slung her suede jacket over the back of a chair. "Do you realize that we were at the mall all day and we still didn't get to see every shop?"

"My feet feel as though we did," Jessie said, grimacing as she kicked off her shoes. Besides shopping, they had spent part of the afternoon at Camp Snoopy, the mall's indoor amusement park, where Missy had somehow managed to talk her into riding the Paul Bunyan flume, the ripsaw roller coaster and the screaming yellow eagle.

For Jessie it had been a fun day, especially seeing the reaction on her niece's face as they shopped in what seemed like hundreds of different stores. Even without the holiday decorations the mall would have held Melissa spellbound.

"I'm glad you were able to get so much Christmas shopping done, but I wish you could have looked for something for yourself," Jessie commented as Melissa peeked into bags, reviewing her purchases.

"It doesn't matter."

Jessie took both of their coats and went to hang them in the front hall closet. When she returned, Melissa was standing with the refrigerator door open, staring at its contents.

"I think Gran's already turned in for the night. Would you like me to fix you something to eat before you go to bed?" she asked.

Melissa grabbed a can of diet soda and shoved the refrigerator door shut. "Uh-uh. I just wanted something to drink."

Jessie noticed a plate covered with plastic wrap on the counter. "It looks like Gran left us a snack. Are you sure I can't tempt you with some of these cookies?" She removed the transparent plastic and set the plate down in front of her niece.

Melissa shook her blond head. "Don't want any," she said, focusing her attention on the soda can in her hands.

Jessie took a cookie from the plate, licking the powdered sugar from her fingertips in the process. "I really wish you'd tried on that red dress we saw at Bloomingdale's."

Melissa shrugged. "There wasn't any point. It probably wouldn't have looked good on me. I don't have the right kind of figure to wear a dress like that."

"I wouldn't say that," Jessie corrected her amiably. "One thing modeling has taught me is that you never know how any piece of clothing is going to look on you until you try it on.''

Melissa took another sip of her soda, then said, ''I wouldn't have any place to wear it. It was the kind of dress girls wear to the Christmas dance at school.''

''You're not going?''

''No.'' She kept her eyes on the soda can, her fingers tracing its colorful patterns. ''It's boy-ask-girl, and no one asked me.''

From the tightness of her face Jessie could see that her niece was reluctant to talk about the subject, and decided not to press her about her social life. ''Maybe we'll go back to the mall another night and you can try on some glamorous dresses just for the fun of it,'' she said lightly.

''Trying on clothes isn't exactly fun when you're overweight, Auntie Jess.'' This time there was no mistaking the unhappiness in her face, and Jessie's heart ached for her.

''Melissa, you're not overweight,'' she stated firmly, her eyes automatically scrutinizing her niece's figure.

''Every time I get on the scale I'm at least twenty pounds heavier than my friends,'' she protested.

''I hope you're not comparing yourself with anyone who is short, because when you're tall you can carry more weight. That's one of the advantages of being our height. We can eat lots more than the short girls.'' She gave her a conspiratorial wink.

Melissa responded with a dubious look. ''That's easy for you to say. You're five foot ten and small boned. Look at me. I'm five foot nine but I'm built like a football player.'' She looked down at her slender figure scornfully.

''A football player?'' Jessie repeated emphatically. ''You're hardly built like a football player.''

''Well, I'm not skinny.''

"No, and you shouldn't want to be. With your bone structure you need to weigh more than someone with a small frame." She tried to say this convincingly, but Melissa wasn't buying what she was selling.

"Yeah, sure," she drawled sullenly.

"Besides, thin isn't healthy." Jessie got up to get a glass of milk.

"How can you say that? You're a model. You make a living out of being thin."

"That doesn't mean I'm willing to sacrifice my health to get a job," she said, sitting down again. "Maybe the high-fashion models in the glossy magazines are all still pencil thin, but it's different here in the Midwest. Take a look at the print ads in the Sunday paper and you'll notice there's quite a diverse group of people being photographed."

"The only time I see anyone overweight is in those ads for big women's sizes," she scoffed.

"You're not overweight," Jessie declared emotionally.

Melissa gave her a look that said she thought she was only saying that to be nice.

"You're not!" Jessie repeated, wondering what she could say to this lovely creature to penetrate her tough adolescent armor. "When I look at you I see someone with eyes that most models would love to have. They're perfectly shaped and the most beautiful shade of blue I've ever seen. And I bet they're the first thing people notice about you."

"Now you sound like my mom. She's always trying to boost my confidence by telling me I have perfect teeth," she said irritably. "Well, my beautiful eyes and my perfect teeth didn't get me a spot on the cheerleading squad this year."

Jessie gave her shoulder a gentle squeeze. "I'm sorry that you didn't make cheerleading. I know how much you wanted to be on the team."

"Yeah, well, so did every other girl in school, which meant they were able to pick the cutest and tiniest ones to be on the squad," she grumbled. "They should have just hung up a sign that read No One With Thunder Thighs Need Apply."

"Missy, you don't have fat legs!"

"You haven't seen me in a pair of shorts lately," she said, her voice filled with self-derision. "It's probably a good thing I didn't make cheerleading. I would have looked like a hippo next to all the other girls."

Jessie reached for her hands. "Listen to me. Just because you're not petite and small boned doesn't mean that you're a hippo," she said firmly.

Melissa's response was a grunt of disagreement.

Jessie could see that the conversation was quickly getting out of hand. When Carla had said that Missy was having trouble with her self-esteem, Jessie had thought she'd be able to boost her niece's confidence with a few positive remarks. Now she could see that to a fifteen-year-old girl, compliments from an adult didn't carry the same weight as comments from her peers.

She opted for another tactic. "I know it probably seems like cheerleading is the greatest thing that could happen to a high school sophomore, but trust me, one day you'll look back and see how unimportant it really was."

Melissa snatched her hands away from Jessie. "If you're going to tell me I have to put the whole miserable experience behind me, you can save your breath. My mom's already lectured me a gazillion times about all the other neat clubs and activities I could get involved with." There was a defensiveness in her voice, and Jessie could see her quickly retreating behind her shield of self-defense.

She felt an enormous rush of sympathy for her niece. Being taller than most of the girls and nearly all of the guys at school was not a pleasant experience for any girl. Jessie knew it wouldn't do any good to tell Melissa that it had taken her twenty-one years to become comfortable with her height.

"I wasn't going to lecture you," she said gently. "I was simply going to tell you that I never made the cheerleading squad, either."

Melissa looked up. "It probably didn't matter because you were already so popular. Everyone at school still talks about you."

"You couldn't be more wrong," Jessie told her. "I was terribly self-conscious of my height when I was your age. There was only one boy in my entire class who was taller than me, and he went with the shortest cheerleader in school."

"You're still the biggest celebrity to graduate from our high school."

"I'm hardly a celebrity." Jessie almost laughed at the thought.

"Compared to the rest of the people living in Harding you are. No one could even come close to having as exciting a life as you do."

"Missy, my life is hardly exciting," she said dryly. "It's get up, go to work, eat, sleep...just like everyone else."

"But, Auntie Jess, just working in a big city like Minneapolis is exciting. I mean, you have all the shops and so many places to go and things to do. You have a shopping mall with an indoor amusement park and fourteen movie theaters. We don't even have one movie house in the whole town of Harding."

Jessie understood her niece's sentiments. When she had been her age, she had shared many of the same feelings regarding small-town life. It was only after she had lived and worked in the city for five years that she decided to move in with her grandmother, far from the hustle and bustle of the metropolitan area.

"The city is wonderful, but there's something to be said for small-town living." Jessie tried not to sermonize, but she could see that she was tuning out her young niece.

"You're sounding like my mom again," Melissa said a bit sullenly, pushing herself away from the table. She reached for her packages and Jessie knew that the communications door was going to be slammed shut in a moment.

She reached over to touch Melissa's forearm. "Look, I'm sorry. I don't mean to lecture you. I know you're going through a rough period and I wanted to—"

She didn't get to finish because Melissa cut her off. "Did my mom tell you the real reason why I'm not in school this week?" she asked, anxiety coloring her face.

"I know about your suspension from school," Jessie said gently.

"Oh, no! This is so embarrassing." Melissa's face twisted in pain and tears welled in her eyes. "How could my mom have done this to me?" She turned her back to Jessie, who was wondering the same thing. Why had Carla let her daughter believe that Jessie didn't know anything about her suspension from school? Melissa's next words answered that question.

"I wouldn't have come down here if I had known you knew about all that stuff." With the back of her hand she swiped at the tears streaming down her face.

Jessie reached for her shoulders to gently turn her around. "It's nothing to be embarrassed about. We're family, Missy. Your mother and I are sisters."

Melissa slumped in her chair, her eyes downcast. "I know, but you're so sophisticated and glamorous. You're the last person I wanted to know about the stupid thing I did at school.''

Jessie was quiet for a moment, wondering what she could say to ease the strain between them. ''We all do some pretty stupid things when we're teenagers, Missy,'' she said softly. ''I know I did.''

Melissa sniffled and hiccuped. ''I bet you didn't do anything as dumb as stealing candy bars from your high school.'' She kept her head bent, her fingers scrounging through her pockets in search of a tissue.

''Oh, I don't know. I think taking my father's car when I didn't have my driver's license was a pretty dumb mistake.''

That brought Melissa's head up. ''You really took Grandpa's car for a drive when you didn't have your license?''

''I really did,'' she confirmed soberly. ''I was the same age as you—fifteen—and I didn't even have my learner's permit. And to make matters worse, I got caught speeding.''

''Are you sure you're not making this up?'' Melissa asked, eyeing her suspiciously. ''Mom says you were always a goody-two-shoes in school—that you were never in any trouble.''

''Your mom doesn't know about this. I was lucky enough to get stopped by a highway patrolman who knew Grandpa. When he saw that it was me and that I was crying, he didn't write me up a ticket. Instead, he made me do volunteer work in the emergency room at the hospital in Brainerd. He wanted me to see what kind of shape accident victims were in when they had been speeding.''

''Did it stop you from speeding?''

''Yes, it did. The punishment fit the crime. What about yours?''

She nodded solemnly. "It's going to be hard to go back to school. Everybody knows what I did."

Jessie was quiet for a moment as she contemplated her niece's situation, then said, "You're right, it is going to be tough, and I wish there was something I could do to make it easier for you. I know you can get through this."

Missy gave her a skeptical glance.

"You can," Jessie repeated, getting to her feet. "Haven't you heard that old saying, 'When the going gets tough, the Paulsons get going?'"

Missy cracked a smile. "I'm glad you said that and not, 'Tomorrow's another day.' My mother always says that when I'm upset." She rolled her eyes.

"Speaking of tomorrow, I'd better get to bed. I have to report for jury duty at eight." On her way out of the kitchen, Jessie gave her niece a gentle hug and said, "I'm glad you're my niece."

It was only after she had reached her room that she murmured, "Thank goodness, tomorrow is another day."

"JESSINA KAY PAULSON."

The name was read as though she were being chosen for a starting lineup position at a football game rather than an interview for a jury.

"So much for sitting around doing nothing all day," Jessie murmured to herself as she tucked her embroidery hoop back into her canvas bag.

As soon as she had arrived at the Buffalo courthouse that morning she had been instructed to fill out a questionnaire. After only a brief waiting period the court clerk had begun pulling names and she had been assigned to the panel of forty citizens to be interviewed for jury duty.

"Somebody said they're selecting jurors for a criminal case." The words were said quietly at Jessie's side, and she looked down at the petite middle-aged woman who had followed her toward the exit. The woman was soft-spoken and looked about as uneasy as Jessie was feeling.

"I was hoping I wouldn't have to get involved in a case," Jessie admitted as they slowly filed out of the waiting room.

The older woman sighed. "I wouldn't mind a civil suit, but criminal cases are another thing. The defendants are usually so creepy looking. It gives me the willies just thinking about it."

Jessie suppressed a shiver. "Maybe if we're lucky we won't get chosen. After all, they called forty but they only need twelve."

"Well, I guess somebody has to do it," the woman said with a smile of resignation. Before they could say anything else, a court officer was herding them toward the courtroom.

Jessie's feelings of uneasiness grew when someone murmured, "I heard the guard say it's a murder case." Another person commented that he had a friend who had been selected for a trial that had lasted for several months, prompting a chorus of groans to spread throughout the small group.

Jessie's apprehension grew as they moved toward the courtroom where an officer stood holding the door open. Before stepping inside, she stopped for a drink of water from a fountain protruding from the wall.

It was as she straightened that she realized she was being watched. Jessie's heart skipped a beat as she glanced across the corridor and recognized the man who had so gallantly deterred the obnoxious youths last Friday in front of Braxton's store window.

As their eyes met Jessie saw the surprise on his face. He hadn't expected to see her any more than she had expected to see him. She wondered what he was doing at the courthouse in Buffalo, Minnesota. She had assumed he lived in the city.

A grin spread slowly across his face as he tilted his head in an attitude of appraisal. She recognized the flirtatious gesture—she had seen it often enough. All it would take was for her to smile back and he would be at her side in a minute. She could tell him thank-you for chasing away the obnoxious teens ... find out his name. ...

When the officer holding open the courtroom door cleared his throat, Jessie mentally shook herself. The last thing she needed to be doing was flirting with a total stranger. Annoyed with the tiny rush of pleasure his attention had provided, she hurried into the courtroom, but not before she had given him one last look.

It wasn't long after Jessie had sat down that the court clerk instructed everyone to rise. A short, bald man in a black robe entered the courtroom and took his place at the bench. He told everyone to be seated, then banged his gavel. *Just like in the movies,* Jessie thought as she glanced around the courtroom, only the middle-aged businessman sitting beside two attorneys at the defendant's table was no actor.

He was on trial for murder, and she, Jessie Paulson, might be one of the people who would have to find him guilty or innocent. She listened attentively to the judge's instructions regarding the jury selection process.

It was a lengthy procedure, one that lasted well into the afternoon. When the eleventh juror had been selected and Jessie still hadn't been interviewed, she thought she might get the reprieve she had been praying for.

She was wrong.

As her name was called for the second time that day, she felt another rush of anxiety. Having heard the interrogation of her counterparts, she was not looking forward to the process.

For a moment she thought she might be one of the peremptory challenges, for the two defense attorneys were conferring as she walked over to the jury box. From the looks on their faces it was obvious that they weren't thrilled with her selection.

But then the attorney who had been doing most of the questioning for the defense began to interrogate her. In an effort to uncover any biases or prejudices she might have, he questioned her about such subjects as whether she had ever been sexually assaulted and why she wasn't married. Jessie felt as though *she* were on trial, instead of being interviewed to sit in judgment of the person accused of the crime.

In answering the questions regarding her knowledge of the murder case, she was able to respond honestly and without hesitation. Fortunately, Jessie had been away on a booking in Chicago when news of Kathleen Daniels's death had become the front-page headline of the local newspapers and the lead story on the nightly television news.

All Jessie remembered about the case was that the young woman had been found dead in a cornfield near Howard Lake, her body partially clothed and half frozen. Citizens of Howard Lake and the small towns in that area had been shocked to think that a woman had been murdered so close to their peaceful communities. The reason many of them had settled in rural Minnesota was to get away from the city, where crime continued to rise as the population grew. It was only after police arrested a Minneapolis businessman in connection with her death that Howard Lake was able to return to the quiet place it had always been and folks were able to sleep at night.

Now that man, a sixty-two-year-old financier, sat at the defendant's table in the courtroom. Despite the expensively tailored suit, he didn't look that different from any of the locals Jessie saw in the restaurants around town.

"Ms. Paulson, would you call yourself a feminist?" Will Lepley, the defense attorney, demanded.

"If by feminist you mean do I believe that women should have the same economic, political and social rights as men, then I have to answer yes to that question," Jessie responded, annoyed by the hint of a smirk on the lawyer's face.

"And have you participated in any of the candlelight vigils the local feminists have sponsored at the state capital... you know, the ones to protest violence against women?"

"No."

"What about NOW? Are you a member of the National Organization for Women?"

"No."

The attorney spun around, his finger on his chin, as though contemplating some great dilemma.

"Tell me, Ms. Paulson. Taking into account your feminist views, do you believe you can be impartial in a case involving a man accused of committing a violent act against a woman?" He stared at her as though he doubted whether she could be impartial about anything.

Ever since the interviewing process had begun, Jessie had suspected that he was selectively disqualifying women on the basis of their feminist beliefs. So far, the only female jurors he hadn't moved to strike were all over the age of fifty. None of the men selected had been subjected to such a thorough questioning, and Jessie found herself annoyed by his attitude.

She knew then that if she were to tell him there was entirely too much violence against women and that it was hard to be impartial when day after day women were being abused by men, she'd be dismissed and allowed to go back to the jury pool to do her embroidery. A few hours earlier she might have taken the opportunity.

The thought of being part of a murder trial made her insides skittish, yet she didn't want to be regarded as some frustrated old maid who hated men, which was how Mr. Lepley was trying to depict her. It had never been in her nature to shirk responsibility or to take the easy way out.

In an honest and forthright manner, she said, "I've always considered myself to be a fair person, Mr. Lepley. I abhor violence, whether it be against men or women. I do believe I can hear the evidence in this case and react to it impartially."

Jessie could see she hadn't convinced either of the attorneys for the defense, as they once more conferred in a huddle. When they were finished, Mr. Lepley requested that she be challenged for cause.

The prosecutor protested, which resulted in a verbal battle between the attorneys. The resolution came when the judge intervened and Jessie was approved as the twelfth juror. Like it or not, she was going to hear all the details of the murder of Kathleen Daniels. Unfortunately, she wasn't any happier with the decision than the defense attorneys.

The following morning she took her place in the jury box along with eleven other solemn-looking citizens and the judicial process officially began.

While the district attorney gave his opening statement, Jessie studied the defendant. He was impeccably dressed in a dark gray suit with a white shirt and a subtle blue tie. Despite being sixty-two years old, he was very youthful looking, his dark hair only frosted with traces of silver. He reminded Jessie of her father, a thought she immediately pushed out of her head. She wanted to feel no emotion for the man seated at the defendant's table; the judge had instructed the jurors to be impartial until all the evidence had been presented.

The courtroom was filled to capacity with curious spectators and eager news reporters, all waiting to hear the details of what was becoming one of the most publicized cases in Minnesota history. Again, Jessie felt uneasy. Deciding the fate of a man accused of murder seemed like such an enormous responsibility. She was beginning to wish she had been excused after the interview.

Sitting beside her was a silver-haired woman twisting a handkerchief in her fingers. On the other side sat a portly gentleman with his arms folded across his chest. Jessie thought how unlike "L.A. Law" this courtroom scene was. Although the district attorney was articulate and polished with his opening statement, he lacked the drama and passion that captivated audiences every week on television.

When it was the defense attorney's turn to address the jury, Jessie noticed that Mr. Lepley was not the man to rise to his feet. Instead, his younger partner took his spot in front of the jury box, and as soon as he began to speak Jessie understood the reason. He was as eloquent as he was handsome. As Jessie listened to his opening remarks, her eyes again moved to the defendant.

Automatically her gaze shifted to the row of spectator seats and her heart skipped a beat. Sitting behind the defendant was the same man she had seen in the corridor yesterday—the man who had chased away the teenagers from Braxton's window. Only now he was wearing a dark blue suit with a white shirt and tie. He was seated in the front row and was looking at her.

Jessie felt herself color under his scrutiny, then quickly looked away from his penetrating stare. Who was he and why was he in the courtroom? She couldn't resist another quick peek at him and noticed he wasn't holding a reporter's notepad in his hands. When his eyes met hers, a little shiver of pleasure ran through her and she forced her attention back to the attorney for the defense. Much to her dismay, she realized that her mind had wandered away from his opening address and she had missed part of his oration.

For the rest of the morning she forced herself to block out the spectator seats, but every time the defense attorney spoke, her eyes automatically moved in the defendant's direction. When they did, it was impossible not to notice the man who had flirted with her outside the courtroom. Today, however, there were no sexy smiles on his face. Quite the contrary. Perhaps the facts of the case had sobered him somewhat. The defendant, Thomas McCullough, had been having an affair with the murder victim, a woman much younger than himself.

Jessie deliberately looked toward the court stenographer and pretended she hadn't seen the man looking in her direction. When the prosecution called the medical examiner to the witness stand, Jessie forced herself to forget about him and focus on the coroner, Leroy Jacobs.

He was a bluff, pompous man who reminded Jessie of a professor she had had at the university—a man she had disliked immensely. Unlike the defendant, who elicited sympathy, this man evoked antagonism in Jessie. A very large man, he had an intimidating posture that defied anyone to question his professional opinion.

As the district attorney questioned him, Jessie listened carefully, her uneasiness growing as photos of Kathleen Daniels were introduced as evidence. To Jessie, who had never seen pictures of a corpse, the photos of a body that had been dead for three days were repulsive. What was even worse was the testimony of the medical examiner.

"Dr. Jacobs, will you please tell us in your professional opinion what the cause of death was in Ms. Daniels's case?" the district attorney demanded.

"Asphyxiation," came the blunt reply.

"The police report indicates that she was found with a plastic bag over her head. Are you saying that the autopsy you performed confirmed the initial assumption that Ms. Daniels was suffocated?"

The coroner nodded. "That's right. There was no sign of any disease or injuries."

"What about drugs or alcohol?"

He shook his head. "None. I did the toxicology tests myself and I found nothing."

Despite the loud, authoritative voice, Jessie could see that the coroner wasn't totally at ease on the stand. His hands gave him away. He buttoned and unbuttoned his suit coat numerous times, he scratched his jaw, he rubbed the back of his neck.

As Jessie listened to the district attorney's line of questioning she felt sick in the pit of her stomach. The combination of graphic photos and detailed descriptions of how Kathleen Daniels had died was a hideous experience, one she would not soon forget. Not once during the testimony did she look at either the defendant or the stranger sitting behind him. She simply sat staring at the medical examiner, using every bit of self-control she possessed to maintain her composure.

When the judge announced they would adjourn for the day, Jessie nearly cried out in relief. As she left the courtroom she couldn't help but glance toward the front row of spectator seats. The man who had chased away the teenagers at Braxton's looked about as sick as she was feeling, and again she wondered who he was and why he was at the trial.

But it was only when she was back at her grandmother's that she found her answer. As she was making a cup of tea she caught a glimpse of the front page of the newspaper. It was lying on the kitchen table, and despite the instructions to jury members to avoid reading about the trial until it was over, she couldn't help but notice the picture on the front page.

It was the defendant, his attorneys and three other people—all of whom had been in the courtroom. But it was the man with the mustache that had Jessie picking up the newspaper and reading the caption below. It read ''Financier Thomas McCullough was accompanied to the courthouse today by his wife, Helen, and their two sons, Aidan and Sean.''

CHAPTER THREE

As THE JURY FILED into the courtroom Aidan's eyes were on the tall, graceful blonde in the navy blue dress. Every day since the trial had begun he had watched her walk in and take her place in the jury box.

He had learned that her name was Jessina Paulson. Having seen her in Braxton's store window, he already knew that she was a model. What he hadn't known was that she was twenty-six and divorced. The divorced part rattled around in his mind like a window shade clattering in the wind.

She looked totally out of place with the group of average-looking citizens comprising the jury. Today her blond hair was pulled back from her face and secured with a barrette in a very simple style. Nothing fancy, no mousse or sculpting spray, yet sophisticated. She wore very little makeup, only a hint of rose dusting her cheeks and a pale shade of pink glossing her lips.

With the same composure she displayed as a store mannequin, she sat motionless, listening to the testimony of the witnesses without any expression on her lovely face. He wondered what thoughts were running through her head, what she thought of the trial proceedings thus far.

Although Will Lepley had done an excellent job of cross-examining the state's witnesses for the past week, anyone with half a brain would have to concede that things were going exactly the way the prosecution wanted. Eyewitnesses had seen Aidan's father force the victim into his car the night she was murdered. A red leather skirt and a white silk blouse had been found tucked under the front seat of his father's car—the same clothes a neighbor had testified to seeing the victim wearing that night. And the forensics expert had verified that fibers found under the victim's fingernails matched those found on his father's cashmere coat. It didn't take a legal eagle to see that the D.A. had a convincing case.

Nor did it help that his father had no alibi. Despite all the witnesses Will Lepley had put on the stand attesting to his father's outstanding character, what it all boiled down to was this: would the jurors believe the testimony of a sixty-two-year-old man who had been cheating on his wife or the slick presentation of evidence by the district attorney?

Truth should be all that was needed to acquit any man. He wanted to believe that if his father took the stand and told his story honestly, the jury would believe him. Aidan wondered just what the truth really was. To say that he believed wholeheartedly that his father was innocent of any wrongdoing would only be a lie. But then he had never been objective when it came to his father's relationship with Kathleen Daniels. How could he be? A thick knot of anger colored his perception thanks to unresolved differences that had been shadowing their relationship for four years.

Yet, regardless of the anger between them, Aidan couldn't quite connect the father he knew with the killer the district attorney had described. Fathers didn't commit murder—at least, not the father he remembered. How could a man who refused to kill bugs and spent two hours wandering around in the freezing rain in search of his son's lost puppy harm anyone?

Aidan wished the happy childhood memories could chase away the anger still lingering inside him. There was no point in denying it. It flared whenever he thought of his mother and the unhappiness his father had caused her. It was there whenever he thought about the reason he had left Minnesota four years ago. He wasn't sure if he could ever loosen the knot inside his heart.

Automatically his glance moved to Jessina Paulson. His insides unclenched a little as her compelling and vivid blue eyes met his for a brief moment. For the hundredth time he found himself wondering why *she* had to be on the jury. It was one thing if he chose to walk past Braxton's window and gawk at her, quite another to be thrown together under such circumstances as his father's murder trial.

Although they hadn't been exactly thrown together. She had acted as if he wasn't even in the courtroom, looking right through him in a way that was slowly driving him wild.

It was a shame she was so good-looking, he thought irritably. There was no room for her in his life, yet here he sat, wishing he could find out more about her—what she was like, why her marriage had fallen apart, what was going through her mind at this very moment. Did she think his father had killed a woman in cold blood?

He steepled his fingertips in front of his lips. With or without his approval she was about to play an important role in his life. He only hoped that beneath that cool facade there beat a warm heart.

"YOU CAN KNOW A MAN from his appearance and you can tell a judicious man from his face."

The words of the biblical saying came to mind as Jessie stared at the man on trial for murder. If ever there was anyone who didn't look like a criminal, it was Tom McCullough. He looked like a well-respected, benevolent businessman—a philanthropist—which was how several character witnesses had described him. He appeared to be the kind of man who had always known his destination, and it wasn't meant to be sitting in the defendant's chair at a murder trial.

She had watched Tom McCullough's reaction to the medical examiner's testimony. He had looked as horrified by what had been said as she was. As the incriminating evidence had mounted, she had watched the play of emotions on his face, waiting for him to give some indication that he was guilty. There had been nothing to convince her.

As a juror, she had been instructed not to let emotions get in the way of good judgment, yet from the moment she had set eyes on him, something inside her had wanted to believe that this man couldn't have murdered anyone. As he was sworn in on the witness stand, Jessie hoped that his testimony would substantiate her belief in his innocence.

"Will you please tell us where you were and what you did the night Kathleen Daniels died?" Will Lepley instructed him when he was seated in the witness chair.

Tom McCullough cleared his throat, then began to tell his story. "I worked late that night at the office, until around seven-thirty, then I went over to Kathleen's apartment. She had called me earlier in the day asking me to stop by and collect my things."

"By things do you mean clothing and personal items?"

He nodded. "We had already agreed to end our relationship, and she wanted me to remove the few things I had left at her apartment."

"So you were not having an intimate relationship with Ms. Daniels at the time of her death?"

"No. We had broken up several weeks before."

"Tell us what happened when you went to get your belongings," Will Lepley ordered.

"When I got to her place she had made dinner. It was obvious that she had planned on me joining her."

"Did you have dinner with her?"

"Yes. I didn't want to, but I could see she was upset about something and I wanted to avoid arguing with her. We had done enough of that in the past."

"You say you had argued frequently. What about?"

"Ending our relationship."

"Were you the one who wanted to break things off?"

"Yes. I knew it had been a mistake on my part to become involved with her."

"Why was that? Because you were married?"

He looked past the defense attorney to the front row of spectator seats. "Because I love my wife."

"Yet you had an affair."

"It was a foolish thing for a man my age to do, but it happened...unfortunately." There was remorse in his voice as well as in his expression.

"So you had dinner with Kathleen Daniels. Then what happened?" the defense attorney continued.

"She kept talking about things in the past. When she asked me to spend the night, I told her that if she was hoping there was any future for us, she wasn't being realistic. When she wouldn't take no for an answer, I decided to leave. She followed me out of the apartment carrying a suitcase filled with the things she wanted to return to me."

"Do you remember what was said?"

He shook his head. "I kept telling her it was over, but she refused to listen to me."

"Did you force her into your car?"

"Yes, but only because she was creating a scene and she appeared to be out of control. I thought if I could get her into the car and drive around for a while, I could calm her down."

"What happened next?"

"We drove around for a while. She was crying, begging me to give our relationship one more chance. When I told her it simply wasn't going to happen, she reached back to get the suitcase—the one that contained my things. She pulled out a black dress—one I had bought for her—and began changing her clothes in the car."

"Which was why her red leather skirt and white blouse were found under the front seat of your car."

"Yes. She stuffed them under the seat, then ordered me to pull over to the curb. When I did, she jumped out and started running away."

"What did you do?"

"I got out of the car and shouted at her to come back. She didn't have a coat on and I was worried about her."

"But she didn't do as you asked?"

He shook his head. "No. She told me she had friends who would take care of her, then she disappeared around the corner."

"Then what did you do?"

"I tried to find her, but she was gone."

"How long did you look for her?"

"Maybe forty-five minutes, an hour."

"Then you went home?"

"Not right away. There's a place down by the river where I often go to do some thinking. That's where I went that night."

The defense attorney leaned up against the witness box and looked directly at the defendant. "Did you kill Kathleen Daniels?"

Without moving, Tom McCullough said clearly, "No. I could never harm her. I should have never become involved with her, and it's something I'll always regret, but I didn't want her dead and I certainly didn't kill her."

There was a quality in that square face with its wide forehead and sturdy bone structure that pleaded with Jessie to see an honest man with human weaknesses, not a merciless killer. And she wanted to believe what he said was true...until the district attorney rose and began cross-examining him.

"Did your wife know about your relationship with Ms. Daniels, Mr. McCullough?"

"No," he said quietly.

"Weren't you worried that Ms. Daniels would go to your wife and tell her about your affair?"

Looking toward the front row of spectator seats where Mrs. McCullough was seated, he said, "I hoped that she wouldn't say anything. I love my wife and I didn't want her to be hurt."

"And just how far would you go to keep your wife from being hurt, Mr. McCullough?" he drawled, his voice full of implications.

"I wouldn't commit murder, if that's what you're thinking!" he protested vigorously.

"Wasn't Kathleen Daniels threatening to go to your wife and tell her about your affair? Wasn't that the real reason why you went to see her that night? Because she was going to blow the whistle on you?" he accused, not giving him any time between questions to respond to his accusations.

"No!" he denied vehemently. "I told you the reason we quarreled. She wanted me to spend the night."

The district attorney continued to question him despite several objections from the defense. When it was over, Jessie's uneasiness had returned. Just whom was she supposed to believe?

She wanted the trial to be over. She hadn't wanted to sit in judgment of another human being, and now she felt even less comfortable with having to reach a verdict in the case.

She had thought that with the presentation of the evidence she would know—at least in her own mind—whether Tom McCullough was guilty. However, as the trial progressed, she found herself becoming more uncertain.

It didn't help that Aidan McCullough had been sitting in the front row since day one of the trial. Although she had purposely avoided looking at him, she knew that his gaze was often fixed on her. He looked at her in an almost challenging way. But challenging her to what? To find his father not guilty?

At one point he had even nodded his head when their eyes had met, and she wondered if it hadn't been a deliberate ploy to unsettle her. He had come close. In fact, he had caused her to break one of the jury rules—she had read a newspaper article about the trial. She hadn't exactly read it, just skimmed to the places where Aidan's name had been mentioned. Immediately after, she had felt guilty and had promised herself she would forget everything she had read.

Unfortunately, she couldn't. Every time she caught a glimpse of him she found her curiosity aroused. She wondered why he wasn't a part of McCullough Enterprises. The paper had hinted that he had been estranged from his family and had only returned to lend his support at the trial. He lived in California, which explained the golden color of his skin. Despite several photos of him at his mother's side, there had been only one quote in the newspaper. "My father is innocent, and I'm confident the jury will acquit him."

Of course he would think his father was innocent. What son wouldn't? She shoved that thought aside. It didn't matter what Aidan McCullough thought. She needed to focus on the evidence and forget about the distractingly attractive man in the front row.

She'd seen her share of good-looking men in the modeling profession. Men from all parts of the country. Pretty men. Smooth men. Muscular men. Aidan McCullough did not look pretty or smooth or muscular. He looked sensuous, which was why Jessie was having trouble ignoring his presence.

She would have liked to put in a request that he be moved out of sight. But there was no law against anyone looking at the jurors, only trying to speak to them. And just because she found his presence unsettling, it didn't mean anyone else did.

BY THE TIME THE WEEKEND arrived, Jessie was more than ready for a break from the past two weeks of courtroom proceedings. She was determined to get caught up on her sleep and spend much of the weekend reading. But sleep was difficult to come by, and there was little pleasure to be found lying in bed. Ever since the beginning of the trial, images of the beautiful Kathleen Daniels had haunted her, and now insomnia was becoming a regular occurrence. As it turned out, she was up early enough on Saturday morning to join her grandmother for breakfast.

"I thought you were going to sleep in this morning," her grandmother commented when she entered the kitchen.

Jessie shrugged. "Guess I'm too much of a morning person."

Her grandmother shot her a suspicious look. "You don't look like a morning person today. Another restless night?"

Jessie kneaded the muscles at the back of her neck. "I could have slept better," she admitted.

"It's not getting any easier, is it?"

"What isn't?" Jessie forced a cheerful smile to her face. She poured herself a cup of coffee, then added cream and a generous spoonful of sugar.

"That trial you're involved in. Ever since you were picked to be on that jury you haven't been sleeping well," her grandmother noted.

"I'm sorry if I disturbed you."

"You didn't disturb me, but it's not like you to be getting up during the night. Tonight I'll make you some chamomile tea before you go to bed."

"I've tried the chamomile, Gran, and it doesn't help." She leaned against the counter and gently rubbed her temples.

"You have a headache." Gran correctly interpreted the gesture. "You need one of my remedies," she said, reaching into a cupboard for a bottle of honey.

"You don't need to mix me up anything, Gran. I already took some aspirin," Jessie said, eyeing the garlic press being lifted from a drawer.

"I know you don't like the taste of this, but it will work better than aspirin. Your headache will be gone in no time."

And my stomach will feel miserable, Jessie thought to herself. Of all of her grandmother's home remedies, honey and garlic juice was the one she dreaded the most. She couldn't take it, not even to appease her lovely grandmother.

"No, really, Gran," Jessie insisted, placing a hand on her grandmother's busy hands. "The way my stomach feels this morning I don't think I should try anything but toast and tea."

"Then we'll try the lemon rinds," she suggested, moving toward the refrigerator.

Jessie wanted to refuse, especially since cutting up lemons and pressing the skins against her forehead hadn't ever alleviated her headache pain in the past. But thoughts of the other home remedy her grandmother often prescribed had her agreeing. Lemon rinds were preferable to a pack of

THE MODEL BRIDE 53

shredded raw onions wrapped in gauze on the back of her neck.

"What are your plans for today?" Jessie asked as her grandmother sliced a lemon on the cutting board.

"I'm going to make some cookies. The Women's Guild is selling baked goods at the Christmas bazaar tomorrow afternoon."

"Why don't you just take some of those you have stored in the pantry?" Jessie asked, popping a slice of bread into the toaster.

"Those are gone," Gran answered with a look of contentment.

"What do you mean, they're gone?" Jessie marched over to the wooden cupboard and opened the doors. The tins of cookies and pastries that had filled the pantry only a few days ago had vanished. Sitting alone on the middle shelf was a plastic container half-filled with butter cookies.

"I don't believe it! We couldn't have eaten everything!" Jessie exclaimed, facing her grandmother.

"I told you Melissa has a hearty appetite," she answered, reaching for the canister of flour.

"You must have sent some boxes home with her."

Gran only chuckled. "There wasn't much to send."

"Missy couldn't have eaten all those cookies," she said on a note of disbelief.

"She's a teenager. Haven't met one yet who couldn't eat you out of house and home."

Jessie shook her head. "But the whole time she was here all she did was worry about her weight."

"Talk. That's all it was." She glanced in Jessie's direction. "I don't know why it is that every young woman in this country thinks she needs to diet." She watched Jessie spread peanut butter on a slice of toast. "You didn't set a very good example, Jessie. You with your toast."

"I never eat a big breakfast, Gran, and it's not because I'm dieting. You know that."

"And you didn't eat a very big dinner last night, either. It's not like you to lose your appetite. Are you sure you're going to be all right?" The tender concern in Gran's wrinkled face made Jessie feel all warm inside.

"I'm fine, Gran. Really."

Gran made a sound of disbelief, then said, "You know, you haven't been yourself ever since that trial began. It's not good for a young girl to have to listen to such horrible things." She clicked her tongue in disapproval. "A trial like that one is not for the tenderhearted."

Jessie smiled to herself. "I'm not tenderhearted, Gran."

"*Ja,* you are. Oh, I know. You like to pretend that you're strong hearted and not easily swayed by your emotions, but the truth is you are affected deeply by what goes on around you. You just never let anyone know it."

Jessie knew her grandmother was right, which was one of the reasons she had moved in with the elderly woman after her divorce. Of all the people in her family, her grandmother was the only one who truly understood her. With her she didn't have to be the strong, independent woman in control of her emotions. Nor did she have to be the one always giving advice.

"It isn't easy sitting on a jury of a murder trial," Jessie admitted, safe in the knowledge that her grandmother would understand the emotional turmoil she had been experiencing lately.

"I know. I read the newspaper and listen to the TV news. What they are saying at the trial is bad for anyone to hear."

Jessie pushed her bangs back from her forehead. "It's just so confusing. The prosecution says one thing, the defense says another. It's hard to know who to believe."

"You know what my mother used to say? *I mørke er alle katter grå.*"

Jessie smiled to herself. Whenever her grandmother spoke of her relatives, she slipped into Norwegian.

"All cats are gray in the dark," Jessie translated the proverb.

"You need to make your own light, Jessie," she advised.

"And do you have any secret Norwegian recipes for that?" Jessie asked with a hint of amusement.

"Trust your instincts. They won't lead you astray," she said, pointing her finger for emphasis. "This is a wonderful country, Jessie," her grandmother continued. "But criminals here are shown too much mercy. Look how many people they hurt with their animallike behavior. Now a woman is dead, and you, an innocent girl, are having trouble eating and sleeping because..."

Noticing that her grandmother was getting worked up, Jessie said soothingly, "I'll be all right, Gran. In a few days it'll be over and I'll be able to forget all about Tom McCullough and Kathleen Daniels."

Gran sat beside her. "Of course you will, dear. And you mustn't worry about your decision." She patted her hand, saying, "You'll do the right thing. You've always been a fair and just person."

Jessie could only nod in agreement.

"Once this trial is over you'll go back to your work in the department-store window and everyone will look at you and think about happy things like Christmas and Santa Claus and elves. It's going to be a wonderful holiday this year."

Jessie smiled, touched by her grandmother's enthusiasm. Christmas was always a special time for the entire Paulson family, and this year would be no exception. She would put all thoughts of the trial behind her and forget the unpleasantness of the past two weeks.

The state versus Thomas McCullough would soon be history. No more courtroom scenes. No more furtive looks from Aidan McCullough. In fact, no more Aidan McCullough, period.

WHEN JESSIE HEARD Will Lepley say, "The defense rests," a chill had traveled up and down her spine, for she knew that soon it would be up to her and the rest of the jurors to decide Tom McCullough's fate.

Now that day had arrived. As she parked her car she thought of how little evidence there had been on either side. Yet the jury was going to be asked to make an enormous decision about a man's life based on that little bit of evidence.

Having left home without any breakfast, Jessie decided to stop at a small café near the courthouse for a cup of coffee and a pastry. Taking one of the vacant corner tables, she quickly gobbled down a powdered sugar doughnut, trying not to think of the day ahead of her.

Suddenly she was aware of voices coming from behind one of the glass partitions separating the smoking area from the nonsmoking section. Except for the back of his gray suit, Jessie could see little of the man closest to her. Without any effort her ears tuned in the conversation, which was actually an argument.

"Your judgment is clouded," one voice said in accusation.

"Just because I don't buy all this hearts-and-flowers sentiment he's been dishing out doesn't mean I want him to rot in prison," a deeper, more melodious voice denied.

"Then why didn't you testify for him?"

"Lepley didn't want me taking the stand."

"That's because he was worried you'd nail Dad's coffin shut."

Dad. Lepley. Suddenly Jessie realized that the voices could belong to only two men. The McCullough brothers.

"You think he's guilty, don't you?" the higher-pitched voice said accusingly.

Jessie's hands flew to her ears. She didn't want to hear what either of the men were saying. She wasn't supposed to hear what they were saying. She quickly looked around the restaurant, searching for a way to leave without being seen by the McCulloughs. But because she had chosen a table in the corner, there was no way she could reach the exit without passing the two of them.

With trembling hands she reached for her coat. In the process, she brushed up against the plate, sending a spray of powdered sugar crumbs onto her black skirt. Leaving a full cup of coffee on the table, she made her escape through the door marked Ladies.

As she stood in front of the large mirror, gazing at her reflection, she breathed in deeply. Then she wet a paper towel and dabbed at the powdered sugar on her skirt, trying not to think about the conversation she had overheard.

Whatever had been said, she needed to forget it completely. She would put it out of her mind, forget that she had heard either of the men speaking.

She stayed in the rest room as long as time would allow. When she walked out into the café, neither of the Mc-

Cullough brothers was there. She heaved a sigh of relief and on shaky legs made her way to the courthouse.

When she walked into the courtroom a short while later she was determined not to look at anyone other than the judge and the attorneys. As she sat down, her eyes betrayed her. She glanced over to the front row of spectators. As she expected, Aidan McCullough was looking at her.

CHAPTER FOUR

THE DEFENSE ATTORNEY bounced the pages of notes in front of him into a neat pile. When he stood, he reached over to touch Tom McCullough's forearm in a reassuring gesture before taking several steps toward the jury box.

He planted his feet directly in front of the wooden rail not more than an arm's length from Jessie, then said in a confident tone of voice, "Kathleen Daniels was murdered. None of us here is disputing that fact. We've seen and heard evidence presented by the district attorney that proves she was murdered. What we have not seen or heard is evidence that my client was the one who committed that murder."

Jessie shifted uncomfortably in her chair. Having heard the prosecutor's final attempt to persuade the jury that Tom McCullough was guilty, she knew that Will Lepley would use every persuasive tactic he possessed to convince them of his innocence.

And he did. Jessie thought there were probably few people in the courtroom who weren't moved by his emotional summation. Repeatedly he emphasized the words *beyond a reasonable doubt*, challenging the jurors to deny the district attorney's assertions and accept his.

When he was finished, the courtroom was silent and the atmosphere grew somber as the judge gave the jury their final instructions. Unable to stop herself, Jessie glanced at the defendant and saw an anxious and frightened man, not the confident, self-assured businessman who had sat rigidly beside the defense attorneys at the start of the trial.

Like an unwanted guest, a feeling skittered inside Jessie. Never had she experienced such a jolt of perception, and it frightened her, for the message it was sending to her was that Tom McCullough was innocent.

Startled, she quickly looked away from the defendant. Squeezing her eyes shut, she fought the wave of uncertainty filtering through her. Just as quickly as it had come, the sensation disappeared, leaving Jessie trembling and reaching for the railing separating the jury box from the rest of the courtroom. Taking a deep breath, she managed to follow the jurors to the deliberation room.

Fluorescent lights glared from the ceiling as the members of the jury took their places in the windowless room. They gathered around two large rectangular tables that had been shoved together to form a square. Everyone seemed to talk all at once now that they were finally free to discuss the trial. Emotions ran high and voices were raised until one man stood to restore order.

Carl Oleson was a rather quiet man whose glasses kept sliding down his nose. The few strands of hair he combed across the top of his head failed to conceal his bald spot. An accounting clerk with a local utilities company, he hadn't struck Jessie as the type to take command of a group of squabbling jurors, yet that was exactly what he did, rising to the occasion with an authority that earned him the position of jury foreman.

Carl insisted they take a vote right away to see where everyone stood. From the initial comments Jessie had heard from her peers, she was expecting that not everyone would agree on the verdict. What she didn't expect was that she'd be in the minority opinion.

"We have nine guilty and three not guilty," Carl announced when the ballots had been counted.

"Three voted not guilty?" Disbelief was written all over the face of a man who ever since day one of the trial had reminded Jessie of a Doberman guarding his lunch.

She looked at the hostile face and felt her annoyance flare. Not a day had gone by that this particular man hadn't made an arrogant statement. Now he was acting as though guilty were the only possible verdict they could return in the case and anyone who didn't agree with him was wrong.

"I'm not sure Mr. McCullough is guilty," Jessie stated clearly, refusing to be intimidated.

"Neither am I," said a gray-haired woman Jessie had become friendly with during the course of the trial. She was a schoolteacher of Norwegian descent whom Jessie had sat next to during lunch. They often talked about their Scandinavian heritage and their mutual desire to visit Norway.

"I voted not guilty also." The third and final dissenter came forward. He was a postal worker with deep lines creasing his weathered cheeks and a headful of auburn hair.

"He had the motive. His girlfriend was threatening to expose their affair," the man who looked like a Doberman said smugly.

"That doesn't prove he killed her," Jessie contended.

"What about the neighbor who heard him say he was going to get her out of his life, one way or another?" the Doberman argued.

"People say lots of things when they're angry," Jessie countered.

"Well, I don't buy that bit about her getting out of his car and walking off without him," another voice contributed.

"What if that's the way it did happen?" Jessie posed the question. "Maybe Kathleen Daniels did get out of his car and was hitchhiking home when the real murderer came by."

"I say we have the real murderer. He's Tom McCullough," the Doberman insisted.

"I'm with you," a bearded construction worker piped up. "If the old guy had an alibi, I might have believed him. But you have to admit, his excuse is rather flimsy. I mean, to say he was driving around and stopped to think . . ." He trailed off with a lift of his shoulders.

"Yeah, and don't forget about the eyewitness who heard him say 'I won't let you do it.'" This time it was a different woman who spoke, a housewife who always wore a pious expression.

"What about the fibers under her fingernails?" another juror tossed out.

"You heard what the defense attorney said. Those could have been from when she clutched his arms in an embrace." The man who had voted not guilty joined in the debate. Jessie quickly interjected her thoughts. "We're supposed to believe him to be guilty beyond a reasonable doubt. I didn't vote guilty because I have reasonable doubts," she admitted.

"The reason you have those doubts is because that fast-talking, million-dollar lawyer wants you to have them." The man who looked like a Doberman spoke again. "If you ask me, he deliberately used doublespeak to confuse the issue."

"The district attorney wasn't without fault, either," the schoolteacher added. "Don't forget, he was rebuked by the judge on several occasions." Jessie wanted to smile gratefully at the older woman, but stifled the urge.

"Did you see his poor wife? She looked completely humiliated by the entire process." The housewife's lip curled as she spoke.

"She did testify on his behalf, though," Jessie reminded everyone.

"Maybe he forced her to. . . just like he forced that little girl into the car," another juror said.

"If you ask me, his wife must be a saint. He was cheating on her with a woman young enough to be his daughter, yet she gets on the stand and testifies on his behalf." A different woman spoke this time.

"Look, the man's on trial for murder, not adultery," Jessie pointed out. "If he's going to be convicted, it should be because of evidence regarding that crime. . . not because he was unfaithful to his wife."

Carl Oleson took charge once again. "The way I see it, we need to go over the evidence." Everyone murmured in agreement, and the exhibits and transcripts were brought in for review.

There was an outpouring of opinions and emotions as the jurors struggled to resolve their differences. After only a couple of hours of heated discussion, Jessie knew that the man and the woman who had been arguing for acquittal had changed their position. That left only one dissenting vote. Hers.

Having examined the evidence, Jessie could see why everyone had voted guilty. All that was keeping her from agreeing with them was her intuition. It was the evidence versus her feelings.

One was concrete; one was not. If she ignored the instinct that told her Tom McCullough was innocent, she could agree with the others.

When the foreman announced they were going to take another vote, she knew the time had come for her to decide.

Just before Carl passed out the ballots, he stood in front of the group and said, "None of us wants to convict a man and send him off to prison, but when we were sworn in as jurors we took an oath to see that justice is done. It's a tremendous responsibility and it isn't easy finding anyone guilty of such a horrendous crime, but are we any better human beings if we let a murderer walk away without being punished?''

As soon as the words were out of his mouth, Jessie realized that part of her hesitancy to convict Tom McCullough was because she didn't want the responsibility of sending a man to prison. What if she was wrong in her decision? What if the feeling she had experienced as she left the courtroom had been accurate? What if Tom McCullough had been telling the truth?

She pressed her fingers to her temples and closed her eyes. There was no easy answer. From the evidence presented, no one would accuse her of making a wrong decision. Hadn't the judge instructed them *not* to allow emotions to enter their decisions?

When she received her piece of paper she wrote with unsteady fingers the only choice she had. Guilty.

As Carl Oleson counted the ballots, relief slowly settled like a comforting cloak around Jessie's stiff shoulders as each guilty verdict was read. It was finally over. Soon she would be free of the tangled emotions, free to go home, free to forget.

When the court reconvened, Jessie avoided looking at the defendant or his family sitting behind him. She kept her eyes fixed on the symbol of justice hanging on the wall behind the bench.

''Members of the jury, have you reached a verdict?'' The judge's words drew Jessie's attention to the foreman.

''Yes, we have, Your Honor,'' Carl Oleson replied, passing a piece of paper to the bailiff, who in turn gave it to the judge. When he had taken a look at the paper he folded it and gave it back to the bailiff, who returned it to the foreman.

"How do you find?" the judge asked the foreman.

"We find the defendant guilty," the foreman answered on behalf of the jury.

A distraught voice cried out, "No! He didn't do it!" All eyes were on the first row of spectator seats where Mrs. McCullough had struggled to her feet, a look of horror on her face. Aidan McCullough reached for his mother's agitated form. Jessie felt a prickly sensation at the back of her throat as the woman fell helplessly against him.

There was a brief period of pandemonium as Tom McCullough tried to get to his wife. The judge pounded his gavel and called for order while the two defense attorneys wrestled with the defendant. Jessie tried to look away from the scene, but her eyes were riveted to Aidan McCullough.

"We'd like the jury polled, Your Honor," Will Lepley requested when order had finally been restored.

One by one the jury confirmed the decision the foreman had read. When it came time for Jessie to speak, her throat muscles tightened as she uttered a soft "guilty." Unable to resist, she looked at Aidan McCullough and saw an implacable hardness on his face. Immediately she pulled her eyes away from his.

Mrs. McCullough continued to sob until the proceedings were over and the judge had pronounced, "Court is adjourned."

Although the other jurors willingly submitted to interviews from the media as they exited the courthouse, Jessie avoided talking to anyone. All she wanted was to go home and put the entire experience behind her. However, she couldn't get out of the building without saying goodbye to several of the jurors.

"We did the right thing," the Norwegian schoolteacher said softly in her ear as she gave Jessie a hug.

Jessie didn't comment on the verdict, but said, "It was nice meeting you, Mrs. Abbott. I hope you get to Norway someday soon."

"Maybe we'll see each other there. You and your grandmother...me and my grandson."

Jessie forced a smile, then quickly left before any of the others could detain her. She kept telling herself she had done the right thing, that the jury had done what the judge had instructed them to do. They had carried out justice.

But as she walked past the defense attorneys she deliberately looked away, not wanting to see the expressions on their faces. She kept hearing words from Will Lepley's final summation. *Tom McCullough is a man with human weaknesses, but he is no murderer.*

Rather than wait for someone to escort her to her car, she chose to leave by the side door, hoping to avoid the onslaught of reporters who were thrusting microphones into faces, hoping to get juror comments. It was dark as she stepped out onto the streets of Buffalo. In the cold, crisp December air, the sounds of her footsteps were amplified, but Jessie didn't notice. The only noise she heard was the echo of Mrs. McCullough's plaintive cry.

He didn't do it. He didn't do it.

Briefly she closed her eyes, wanting to blot out the look of absolute panic that had been on Tom McCullough's face when he had heard the verdict. The wintry air stung her cheeks, but it felt good. Invigorating. Refreshing.

Because the trial had attracted so many onlookers, she had been forced to park her car several blocks from the courthouse. As she hurried across sidewalks covered with a light dusting of snow, she became aware of the sound of footsteps behind her.

After years of living in the city, Jessie automatically felt a moment of anxiety. She was tempted to glance over her shoulder, but decided to keep moving as if no one threatened her safety. She reached the corner and was forced to wait for several cars to pass before proceeding across the street. When a person stepped alongside her, she decided to confront whoever it was following her. She turned to see if it was a man or a woman and nearly gasped as she came face-to-face with Aidan McCullough.

"It's a small world, isn't it." It wasn't a question but more of a statement, and Jessie knew he wasn't simply referring to them both standing on the same street corner. Jessie shifted uncomfortably, wondering how much farther he was going to follow her.

He continued to stare at her and Jessie could feel her nerves coming apart. What she didn't need after the emotional day she'd had was to have this guy looking at her as though she were some bug under a glass.

"Must you stare at me? You've often stared at me during the trial, and quite frankly, I don't like it." There was little emotion in her voice, for she had none left to give.

"That's a rather peculiar attitude coming from someone who makes her living trying to attract people's attention," he taunted her.

Jessie knew he was right, but she wouldn't admit to him that other people's attention didn't disturb her. Just his. She simply looked away as if bored, mumbling, "Suit yourself."

When the street was clear of traffic and she made no attempt to step off the curb, he asked, "Aren't you going to cross the street?"

"I'm waiting for someone," she lied.

He stepped closer to her. "You can cross the street. I'm not going to jump on you," he said, his voice laced with anger.

"I told you, I'm waiting for someone," she said coolly.

He wasn't deterred. "Look, you know who I am and I know who you are." When she didn't make any effort to move, he simply shrugged and said, "It's too cold to argue."

She bit down on her upper lip and stepped into the street. When she reached the opposite side she continued straight ahead down a street that had few street lamps and seemed unusually dark to Jessie. Fortunately her car wasn't far away. Without looking to see which direction Aidan was going, she made a beeline for her red compact. Much to her dismay, he followed her.

"I'd like to talk to you."

His words caught her totally off guard, so much so that she dropped her keys. "I don't think that's such a good idea." She bent to pick up her keys. When she stood, he had moved closer to her and his eyes were fixed upon her thoughtfully, holding her still.

For the first time since the day he had chased away the teenagers she looked him squarely in the face. What she saw nearly took her breath away. Every emotion he was feeling was there for her to see—anger, sadness, helplessness. Desire.

It was the last one that kept her motionless. This wasn't about the trial or the fact that she had been on the jury. This was about her being a woman and his being a man.

"No, it's not a good idea," she repeated, so quietly it was as though she were talking to herself.

His eyes had a determined look in them, but to her surprise he took a step backward and said, "Maybe you're right."

She would have liked to have jumped into her car and driven off without looking back, but after sitting all day, the tiny compact was cold. She knew from experience that if she didn't warm it up before she shifted into gear, it would stall. So instead of driving away she sat in a cold car, her teeth chattering as she watched Aidan through her rearview mirror. He walked down the street about a hundred feet and stopped at a white Lincoln town car. It was only a matter of seconds before his car went swooshing by.

Jessie, who had been sitting stiffly, let her body slump back against the seat. After only a few minutes she shifted the car into Reverse and backed out of the parking space. She needed to get to familiar surroundings. To the warmth of her grandmother's kitchen with its wonderful aromas of freshly baked bread and cinnamon rolls.

As she drove she thought of what she would do as soon as she reached home. She'd take a nice long soak in a hot bathtub filled with the scented oil her grandmother had given her for her birthday—an exotic blend of Hawaiian herbs and flowers that made her feel as if she were on some tropical island without a care in the world.

Then she'd slip into a cotton flannel nightgown, and after a brief meditation she'd snuggle down into the warm covers and fall asleep. It would be a deep, peaceful sleep, for there was no longer the uncertainty of the trial hanging over her head. No more gruesome pictures to view, no more testimony to hear, no decisions to make regarding a man's life.

She had done her civic duty.

Service will bring you pride and satisfaction in your government and in yourself. That was the message she had been given when she had watched the required instructional film the first day she had arrived at the courthouse.

Pride and satisfaction. Jessie felt neither at the moment. Only an empty, sick feeling that made her wish she could forget the past two weeks had ever happened.

She would forget. And she wouldn't question the decision she had made. If there was one thing she had learned from her father it was never to second-guess herself.

Jessie, dwelling on the past does a person no good. She could hear his words as if he were riding right beside her in the car. *Too many people torture themselves wondering if they should have done things differently. But everybody makes mistakes, Jessie. What's important is that when you do, you go on and you don't do it again.*

But she hadn't made a mistake. Or had she?

"Don't do this to yourself," she scolded herself. "It's over and done with."

But no amount of self-recrimination could erase the doubts that had etched themselves in her mind like cold frost on warm windowpanes.

For the first time in a long time she wished she was back on the farm, where locks weren't needed to keep people safe and the only light at night came from the moon and the stars. She had a crazy notion to drive to Harding tonight. But that was all it was—a crazy notion. She wasn't the type to act impulsively, and she had learned long ago it was best to think through a plan of action before proceeding.

What she needed was sleep. Then she would go back to the city with its two and a half million people hustling through the streets and shopping malls in a holiday frenzy. Back to the buses and taxis and impatient drivers stuck in traffic jams. Work and a regular routine would help her forget, make her life normal again.

She hoped.

CHAPTER FIVE

JESSIE SPENT THE NEXT TWO DAYS at a suburban mall spraying samples of men's cologne on holiday shoppers, since she wasn't scheduled to return to Braxton's until the following Monday. While standing in the center aisle of the busy department store during the holiday rush, Jessie was jostled and bumped by holiday shoppers and their over-loaded shopping bags.

It was with a strange mixture of relief and anxiety that she returned to Braxton's window on Monday. After the cologne promotion, it would be a relief to stand statue-still in a plate-glass display window. She was much more comfortable with the idea of shoppers being on the outside looking in, where they couldn't touch her or talk to her.

If she had any anxiety, it was due to the fact that she didn't know whether Aidan McCullough would show up outside the window. She hoped that by now he had returned to California and that she would never see him again.

When she arrived at Braxton's she discovered that during her absence changes had been made in the Christmas window. Not only was there a different man dressed up as Santa, a telephone had been installed that connected the models to the outside world. During the five minutes they were allowed to move around, children could pick up a red phone on the outside and ask for Santa Claus on the inside.

It was obvious by the size of the crowd that the addition of the telephone had increased the popularity of the window. Before the phone had been added, the crowd usually thinned after the brief interlude when the mannequins came to life. But now a steady stream of children wound its way around the corner of the building as they waited patiently for a turn to speak to Santa.

By the end of the day Jessie was stiff and tired, but it was a happy tired. She was surprised at how quickly time had passed, and chided herself for wasting energy worrying that Aidan McCullough might show up at the window.

As the fairy dust fell for the final time, Jessie relaxed and gave her undivided attention to the children on the other side of the glass. Leaving Devony to handle the phone, she blew a kiss to a tiny tot who had been trying diligently to get her attention.

After only a few minutes she heard Devony call to her, "Jess, the phone's for you."

Automatically Jessie's eyes moved to the corner of the window where the line of people waiting to speak to Santa Claus began. Expecting to see a small child, she was startled to see Sean McCullough close to the glass.

He was wearing a dark wool overcoat with a white shirt and a red tie poking out the V-shaped neckline. There was neither a child at his side nor a toddler in his arms.

Reluctant to speak to him, Jessie said to Devony, "I thought the phone was for kids to talk to Santa."

Devony shrugged. "Last week some guy asked to speak to Vicki, too. Apparently Braxton's wants us to do whatever will make the customer happy," she answered, motioning for her to take the phone. "He probably just wants to flirt with you."

Unwillingly Jessie crossed the display case. "This doesn't seem right. This should be for the kids," she said in a near

hisper even though no one on the outside could hear
lem.

"Just say hello and Merry Christmas," Devony in-
tructed, handing her the red receiver.

There were lots of eyes on Jessie as she put the receiver
) her ear, but she was conscious only of one dark, pene-
:ating pair. Framed by heavy brows, they conveyed a
lessage Jessie didn't want to see—that Sean McCullough
new exactly who she was.

She deliberately focused her attention on his cashmere
oat. "Hello. Merry Christmas," she said cheerfully, try-
ig to control the shiver of apprehension that was sending
oose bumps up and down her arms.

When he didn't respond to her greeting, instinct had
essie lifting her eyes to his. The shiver of apprehension
ecame a tremor of fear. There was anger simmering in his
eep-set eyes, eyes that reminded Jessie of another man
/ho had stared at her with a similar hostility.

When he finally spoke, the words crackled through the
elephone wire with a sharpness that had Jessie's fingers
ightening around the red receiver. "Why did you convict
n innocent man?"

She took a deep breath, struggling to maintain her com-
osure. She tried to speak, but it was as though all of the
ir had been sucked out of her lungs. "I'm sorry," she fi-
ally managed to answer, but by then Sean McCullough
ad hung up the phone and was pushing his way through
he crowd. He looked as though he couldn't get away fast
nough, and Jessie stood watching in a sort of stunned
orror.

A tiny voice jerked her back to reality. "Can I pweeze
alk to Santa Claus?"

Jessie looked down at the little girl who was now hold-
ng the red Santa phone between two purple mittens. "Of

course,'' she answered, forcing a smile to her face. Then she handed the phone to Nick Taggert, the male model in the Santa Claus suit.

"Jess, who was that guy?" Devony asked quietly.

"He didn't give me his name," she said flatly.

"Why were you apologizing to him?"

"I was expressing sympathy. He said something sad,'' she answered, trying to behave as though nothing out of the ordinary had happened.

Devony wanted to press her on the subject, but a soft alarm sounded, indicating the metallic snowflakes were about to cease.

Normally the three models would have returned to their statuelike poses, but since it was closing time they faced the crowd and waved goodbye. A burgundy velvet curtain slowly descended from the ceiling, effectively shutting out the outside world.

As soon as the curtain hit the floor Jessie stepped down from the platform. She looked at the man who was pulling the snow-white beard away from his chin in order to scratch his jaw.

"Nice job, Nick. You were great with the kids."

"Thanks," he acknowledged with a half bow. "It's not a bad way to spend a day, but I think I'm ready for a little adult conversation. Anyone interested in stopping at the Cabooze for a couple of drinks?" He looked inquisitively from Jessie to Devony.

Devony's face lit up at the suggestion. "Sounds like fun. I'm for it."

The Cabooze was a nightclub not far from Braxton's that had live entertainment and a reputation as a good meeting place for singles. Jessie had been there on several occasions and had enjoyed herself, but tonight she wanted no part of it. "I think I'll pass."

"Aw, come on, Jess!" Devony pleaded.

"I'm just not up to it tonight, Dev," Jessie answered. "Sorry."

"Are you still coming, Devony?" Nick looked at the brunette with obvious interest.

"I'm afraid I'm without wheels. Jessie's giving me a ride home."

"I can take you home," Nick offered, taking off the red cap that was attached to a wig of white hair. Suddenly Jessie could see the reason Devony was eager to go to the Cabooze. Nick was one good-looking man, and from the way he was looking at Devony it was obvious that a chemistry was working between the two of them.

"It's all right with me," Jessie said when Devony looked at her to see if she minded.

"Should I meet you at the employee entrance in about twenty minutes?" Devony asked Nick, her eyes sparkling with enthusiasm.

"Twenty minutes it is," he said with a wink, then reached for the door that was camouflaged in the snowy scene painted on the backdrop. Devony and Jessie followed him as he slid through the narrow exit.

"It feels good to get out of that place," Jessie commented as the door swung shut behind them. "Was it my imagination, or was it warmer than usual in there?"

"Hot would be a better word," Devony replied with disgust. "That's because Miss Vicki had them raise the temperature while you were gone. She said there was a draft coming through the glass."

"A draft?" Jessie repeated in disbelief.

"I swear, the woman's impossible to work with. All she did was complain about one thing or another. She couldn't stand in the front of the window because it was too cold. But if she stood on Nick's right side there wasn't enough room for her to pose. And if she stood behind him her perfect profile wasn't in a favorable light." She made a sound of exasperation. "I am so glad you're back, Jessie. Promise me you'll be here until Christmas or I swear I'll do something totally insane."

"After nearly getting mangled trying to spray cologne at the mall, this job is a piece of cake...at least, it will be once I get used to posing again." She rolled her shoulder muscles in an attempt to ease the stiffness.

"So what do you think of the changes they've made since you left?" Devony asked as they walked back to the dressing room.

"Nick I like. Have you been out with him before?"

"No, this is my first time. I thought maybe he was only asking me because he wanted to ask you."

"Are you kidding? Didn't you see the way he was looking at you?"

Devony beamed smugly. "Isn't the phone a neat idea? Nick was the one who suggested it."

"It's great. I just wish they'd limit its use to little kids."

"Why? What did that guy say to you?"

"Nothing important," Jessie answered, trying not to reveal just how unsettling his words had been.

"Are you sure? Now that I think about it, you had a pretty weird look on your face when you were finished."

"That was probably because I just spent the past two days inhaling men's cologne and my sinuses still haven't cleared," she retorted dryly.

Devony chuckled. "Well, it's good to have you back. You never did tell me how jury duty was," Devony reminded her, unaware that her words put her friend's insides into a turmoil.

"There's really not much to tell," Jessie said soberly.

"I was going to call you during the trial, but I didn't think it would be right," Devony told her. When Jessie looked at her inquisitively, she added, "I think I met Kathleen Daniels at a party a couple of years ago."

"You knew her?"

"We were introduced—that's not exactly the same thing. But I thought if you thought that I knew her it would put you in an awkward position as a juror." She paused, glancing sideways at Jessie. "You know what I mean?"

Jessie didn't think that it would have mattered, but nodded, anyway. "Whose party was it?" she asked, curious to learn more about Kathleen Daniels.

"Gosh, I don't remember, Jess. It had to have been a couple of years ago. Maybe it had something to do with the dating service, I don't know." She shrugged. "It was just that when I saw her picture in the paper she looked familiar."

"You don't know anyone who dated her, do you?"

"No, why?"

"I'm just curious, that's all," Jessie answered, trying to sound nonchalant.

"Well, you probably know more about her than I do, especially after listening to all that stuff at the trial."

A dull ache was beginning to throb over Jessie's temple. "Look, Dev, if you don't mind, I'd rather not talk about the trial."

"Was it that bad?" Devony's voice softened in sympathy.

"I wish I could forget it ever happened," Jessie said with more candor than she had intended. "I can tell you it's nothing like what you see on TV, that's for sure." She shuddered and hugged her arms around her body.

She was relieved when Devony changed the subject. Even though they were close friends, Jessie didn't want to admit to her that the trial had left painful scars that still hadn't faded.

Jury duty had taken a toll on her emotional health. She hoped that with time she would forget all the unpleasantness associated with the trial. But it wasn't only the memories of what Kathleen Daniels's body had looked like in the morgue that haunted her. It was guilt.

No matter how hard she tried, she couldn't stop wondering if she hadn't made a mistake in changing her vote to guilty. She was plagued by doubts, thinking she might have sent an innocent man to jail.

That was why when Sean McCullough had spoken to her on the Santa phone, she *had* looked weird. Because deep in her soul she worried that she had made a mistake. What if her instincts had been right and Tom McCullough was innocent?

It was such thoughts that kept her tossing and turning long after she went to bed that night. Despite the cup of chamomile tea her grandmother had made for her to help her sleep, she was still awake long after she had climbed into the big four-poster bed.

Jessie attributed part of her restlessness to the fact that her muscles were sore. Thinking a heating pad would ease the tension in her neck and shoulders, she climbed out of bed and went to look for the one her grandmother kept in the linen closet. Only it wasn't in its usual spot.

Remembering that Melissa had used it after they had been skiing, Jessie carefully made her way through the dark house to the guest bedroom. After searching through the chest of drawers and the closet and coming up empty-handed, she wondered if her niece might have shoved it under the bed.

Bending down on all fours, Jessie groped beneath the dust ruffle and discovered not only an electrical cord but an assortment of debris. With a sweeping motion of her arm, she managed to scoop everything out from under the bed.

Besides the heating pad, a pair of socks and a teen magazine, there were all sorts of candy wrappers. But it was two square packages that held Jessie's attention. One was an empty cigarette wrapper, the other was a box of laxatives, only partially empty.

Having noticed the smell of cigarette smoke on Melissa's clothing, Jessie wasn't surprised to find the empty cigarette package. The laxatives were another story.

As Jessie quietly made her way back to her room, she kept thinking about all the times Melissa had turned down food when she had been staying with them. She also remembered how frequently she complained about her weight.

Having been in the modeling profession for several years, Jessie was no stranger to the methods some women used to keep from gaining weight. The question was, had her niece purchased the laxatives for the same reason? Was she hoping to rid herself of excess pounds?

Jessie knew that she was going to have to call Harding tomorrow. Only she wasn't quite sure if she should talk to Missy or Carla.

The decision was made for her the following morning. Before she was even out of bed, her sister telephoned.

"I'm sorry if I woke you, Jess, but I wanted to catch you before you went to work," she said unevenly.

"It's all right. I was about to get up, anyway," Jessie fibbed, suppressing the groan of disappointment that nearly escaped when she noticed it was only seven o'clock.

"How's everything?"

"Everything's all right. What about you?" she asked sleepily.

"Oh, everything's okay here, too," Carla answered a little too brightly to convince Jessie she was being honest.

"Carla, is something wrong?"

"No, I just wanted to talk to you about Christmas. When are you coming home?"

"Probably not till Christmas Eve." Jessie stretched like a cat. "Gran wants to come earlier, but I have to work until two."

"Hopefully traffic won't be too bad."

Again there was something in her sister's voice that alerted Jessie that all was not right. "Are you sure nothing's wrong? You sound a little uneasy."

"I'm just tired. Missy's been giving me grief lately."

"Over what?"

There was a humorless chuckle. "Just about everything a mother and daughter can disagree on."

Jessie raised herself up on one elbow. "Has she been in more trouble at school?"

"No, it's not that."

"Then what is it?" Jessie asked cautiously.

"She's changed, Jess."

"In what way?"

"In the way she dresses, for one thing. You wouldn't believe the weird clothes she's started to wear. I hate to say anything because she always jumps on my case and says I'm picking on her."

"Clothes are a way for teenagers to express themselves," Jessie said calmly.

"She's doing other strange things, too."

"Such as?"

"She sleeps with the window open."

"In the middle of winter? Why would she want to do that?"

"Because she thinks she's fat. She heard that her body will burn more calories if it's trying to keep warm," Carla explained.

Jessie ran her fingers through her tangled hair. "You told her it wasn't true, didn't you?"

"Sure, but she didn't believe me. Now she's given up wearing a jacket and you know how cold it's been. She doesn't listen to me, Jess."

"What about her father? Has Gene tried talking to her?" Jessie asked.

"He's feeling just as frustrated as I am. It's this weight business. It's all Missy ever talks about. She's convinced that she's fat."

"I noticed it, too, when she was here with me and Gran," Jessie observed pensively.

"She skips meals, and when she does eat she eats junk food. Sooner or later she's going to get sick."

Jessie sighed, wondering how she should approach the subject. "Maybe she already is."

"What do you mean?"

"Is there any reason why Missy should be using laxatives?"

"No, of course not. Why do you ask?"

"Because I found some in the guest bedroom she used while she was staying with us."

"They're probably Gran's."

"Carla, they were hidden under the bed along with some candy wrappers, a teen magazine and a bunch of junk I recognized as Missy's," Jessie said solemnly.

"But why would she have laxatives? We never use them here."

Jessie paused, looking for the right choice of words. "Maybe she's using them for weight control. Does she spend a lot of time in the bathroom after dinner?"

"What are you getting at, Jess?" Carla demanded uneasily.

Jessie knew there was no easy way to voice her suspicions. "I'm wondering if Missy isn't purging as a way of trying to stay thin."

"Purging! My God, Jess, Missy would never do anything so disgusting!" Her voice rose an octave.

"Are you sure?"

"Of course I'm sure," she snapped irritably, and Jessie knew she needed to back off a bit. "She's my daughter. I live with her. Don't you think I would know if she was doing such a thing?"

"Look, I'm sorry. I didn't mean to upset you, but I had to ask. Maybe she's taken the laxatives only occasionally."

"You don't even know if they were her laxatives," Carla reminded her stiffly.

"You're right, I don't. But you yourself have admitted that something isn't right with Missy. Probably the best thing you can do is to sit down with her and find out just what it is she is doing to diet," Jessie suggested calmly.

"I can tell you she's not purging. She might have tried laxatives because she's heard other girls use them, but she wouldn't do anything so gross," she said emphatically.

"All right, all right," Jessie said soothingly. "When's the last time she had a physical?"

"She had one when she started high school. Why?"

"Maybe it would be a good idea to have a doctor give her a thorough exam. He could reassure her that she's not overweight."

"I don't see what Dr. Conroy can say that will make any difference to her way of thinking. A million people could tell her she's thin and she wouldn't believe them because she's got it in her head that she's fat."

"I'm not talking about Dr. Conroy. Maybe you should try one of the doctors in Minneapolis, someone who specializes in eating disorders."

"She doesn't have an eating disorder, Jessie," Carla objected emotionally.

"I didn't say she did, but doesn't it make sense to send her to someone who recognizes the symptoms of eating disorders rather than someone who's unfamiliar with them? This way you'll be able to rule out bulimia and anorexia as well as get some good advice on dieting," she rationalized.

There was a brief pause before Carla finally agreed. "I suppose you're right. I'm not sure I can convince Missy that it's a good idea, though."

"Sell it to her as a chance to go shopping," Jessie suggested. "She loves going to the Mall of America."

"I suppose I could do that," Carla said hesitantly. "But I don't even know where to call for an appointment."

"Would you like me to arrange it for you?"

"Could you?"

Jessie heard the anxiety in her sister's voice and reassured her that she'd take care of all the details. "Try not to worry" were her last words as she said goodbye.

"Some advice," Jessie mumbled to herself when she caught sight of her reflection in the mirror. Her puffy eyes proclaimed she hadn't slept well last night. After taking her shower, she dipped two cotton balls in cider vinegar and pressed them against the sagging skin.

"Thank goodness for stage makeup," she murmured when she removed the cotton pads and the swelling hadn't disappeared.

Before leaving for work she called the eating disorder clinic recommended by a local doctor and made an appointment for Missy. With her mind on her niece's troubles she hadn't had any time to worry about whether Sean McCullough would return to Braxton's window.

It wasn't Sean McCullough, however, who turned up the following day, but his brother, Aidan. When Jessie saw him her heart began to beat to a foreign rhythm. As he stepped out of her line of vision she nearly broke her pose, wanting to follow his movements, but she managed to stand perfectly still, giving no indication that she had recognized him in the crowd.

It wasn't until the fairy dust fell that she moved, her eyes scanning the crowd gathered outside the window in search of his handsome face. He was on the opposite side of the corner window, but he was not waiting in line to use the Santa phone.

He was watching her, however, with a penetrating gaze. There was a puzzled, almost suspicious expression on his face as he stood with his hands behind his back. As much as Sean's appearance had disturbed her yesterday, Jessie found Aidan's presence much more unnerving, for there was some other emotion in his eyes besides animosity.

Just when she was about to look away from his potent gaze, he pulled a hand from behind his back and waved. An unfamiliar heat seeped through Jessie's body.

With a supreme effort she dragged her eyes away from his and turned to the many children who were vying for her attention. But no matter how many happy faces she gazed into, she couldn't manage to block Aidan McCullough from her peripheral vision. He was watching her, only this time there was no mistaking the look in his eye. He was looking at her the way a man looks at a woman he desires, and the thought was enough to send her emotions into a tailspin.

As the five-minute break came to an end, she took several deep breaths and resumed her mannequin pose. Although she was acutely aware of Aidan's nearness, she managed to block out everything on the outside of the window, including his distracting presence.

She assumed that he had given up waiting for her to respond to him, for when the fairy dust fell again, he was gone. But not so easily forgotten.

Later that evening, as she left the department store, she hoped Aidan McCullough hadn't returned. She welcomed Fred's offer to walk her to her car, but she didn't relax until she had exited the parking ramp and a glance in her rearview mirror told her no one was following her.

As she prepared for bed that night, she couldn't stop thinking about Aidan McCullough. There was a smoldering sexiness about him that was intriguing. As much as she hated to admit it, for the first time in a long time she was attracted to a man, and not just any man. The man whose father she had sent to jail.

She would give him no encouragement, she decided in the wee hours of the morning as she lay awake. She was certain that Aidan was waiting for her composure to slip. What he didn't know was that she was a pro when it came to self-control. He was in for a disappointment if he thought any differently.

With such resolve, Jessie finally fell asleep. When she went to work the next day she was mentally prepared for Aidan McCullough to turn up.

He did. Twice.

But again, he made no attempt to speak to her. He simply stood outside the window for a few minutes.

What Jessie didn't know was that Aidan didn't want to be outside the window. He had thought that after the trial was over he would forget about Jessina Paulson, but like the Christmas carols blasting over the outdoor speaker system, thoughts of her kept playing over and over in his mind.

That was why he had made it a point to walk past Braxton's on his way to and from his father's office. He had told himself it was because of Kate—that he needed to exorcise her ghost from his mind. Now he knew he was only fooling himself.

It wasn't Kate who was occupying his thoughts, but a blond elf. He was mesmerized by the sight of her long legs and her perfectly shaped body. When she fixed her compelling blue eyes on him, every molecule in his body seemed to forget its place.

It was a good thing he would be going back to California soon. He didn't need this kind of distraction. He didn't need Minnesota. He was tired of picking his way around pools of half-melted snow and stepping on puddles glazed over with thin sheets of ice that didn't hold his weight.

He hunched his shoulders deeper into the turned-up collar. No, he definitely didn't need the distraction an attractive woman could cause in his life right now. Tomorrow he would park on the opposite end of town so he wouldn't have any reason to walk past Braxton's.

WHEN JESSIE'S SHIFT ENDED the following evening without any sign of Aidan McCullough outside the window, she couldn't help but breathe a sigh of relief. Unfortunately she also felt a pang of disappointment, but she didn't want to examine the reason for that feeling. She wondered if maybe the Californian had finally returned to L.A.

By the time she arrived home she had convinced herself that was exactly what Aidan McCullough had done. He had gone back to the West Coast and she would probably never see him again.

But while listening to the nightly news just before bed, Jessie discovered his absence was due to entirely different circumstances. Tom McCullough had suffered a heart attack and, according to the news anchor, had been transferred to a hospital in downtown Minneapolis where he was listed as being in critical condition.

Guilt washed over Jessie, making her feel as though someone was slowly draining the blood from her body. Did his collapse have anything to do with his incarceration? Would he have suffered the heart attack had he not been found guilty? And the worst question of all—what if he was innocent? What if she had sent an innocent man to prison and as a result he had suffered a fatal heart attack?

They were questions that tormented her as she tried to sleep that night. Along with such thoughts came memories of the trial. She kept hearing Tom McCullough's plea of innocence and seeing his wife, Helen, collapse when the verdict was announced.

The next day, after careful consideration, Jessie decided something had to be done if she was ever going to be at peace with herself again. There was only one thing she could do. She called a lawyer.

Brian Haugen had been a friend of Jessie's ever since the first grade when he had carried her books at school. Many in the small town of Harding had expected the two of them to marry, but what the people of Harding didn't know was that their relationship was more like that of a brother and sister, rather than a boyfriend and girlfriend.

Even though they lost contact with each other after graduating from high school, when Jessie's marriage ended it was Brian who represented her in the divorce proceedings. Ever since that traumatic period in her life she had known that if she ever needed a friend or legal advice, Brian would be there for her. Right now she felt she needed both.

"Brian, is there any way a jury's verdict can be changed?" Jessie got straight to the point as soon as he answered the phone.

"Jessie, you're not in any kind of trouble, are you?"

"No, it's not that," she answered, then took a deep breath and told him her story.

When she was finished, Brian asked, "Have you talked to anyone else about this?"

"Of course not."

"Of course not," he repeated to himself, as though suddenly remembering that Jessie had never been one to confide in others. "Maybe you should. It sounds to me like you're experiencing posttrial stress. I could give you the name of a psychologist who's done quite a bit of work with jurors suffering emotional problems after serving on a murder trial."

"Brian, I don't need a psychologist. Don't you understand? I made a mistake," she stated unequivocally. "Is there any way the verdict can be overturned?"

"I'm afraid not."

"Can't it be declared a mistrial or something?"

"It isn't that simple. First of all, a juror may not testify to anything that took place in the jury room for the purpose of showing that the verdict was arrived at through a mistake," he recited in his legal manner.

"I don't want to point the finger at anyone else. I simply want to testify that I made a mistake."

"You do that and you'll risk being brought up on charges of misconduct," he warned. "You'd better think carefully about this, Jess."

She was silent for a moment, then said, "Wouldn't it be better for me to be charged with misconduct than for an innocent man to go to prison?"

"Jess, you don't know that he *is* innocent," he argued. "Are you sure you're not simply feeling guilty because of the difficulty you had to face in making that decision?"

"No." She didn't want to tell him of the strange feeling she had experienced just before jury deliberations had begun, but it was the only way she'd be able to convince him to take her seriously. "Bri, I know this is going to sound a little off the wall, but it's almost as if I had a psychic experience. Just before I went to the deliberations room, I looked at Tom McCullough and had the strangest feeling. It was as if I *knew* he was innocent."

Jessie heard a sigh of frustration and she could imagine the heavyset Brian stretching back in his chair and scratching the thick, wiry beard he had grown to hide his double chin.

"Wait a minute. You're telling me that the reason you think this guy should be released is because you had a psychic experience?" Disbelief raised the pitch of his voice.

"That's the only way I can explain it," she said weakly. "I've tried to ignore it, but I can't stop thinking that he's innocent."

There was another sigh. "I followed that trial, and I have to tell you I agree with the jury. You didn't make a mistake, Jess," he said with strong conviction.

"So you don't think I should do anything?"

"There's not much you can do. Even if charges of misconduct were brought against you as a juror, Tom McCullough's verdict would not be affected."

"Why is that?"

"Because you can't impeach a verdict. The only way he's going to get a new trial is if his lawyers file an appeal, which, by the way, I'm sure they've already done."

"Then I should contact his attorneys," Jessie concluded.

"No," he replied quickly. "As your attorney, I'd advise you not to do that. Jess, you're only going to get yourself into trouble."

"Brian, I'm in trouble now." She didn't want to admit to him just how heavy the emotional baggage was that she was carrying around as a result of the trial.

"Let me give you the name of someone who'll help you work through this," he suggested. "I know a psychologist who's had a lot of experience in this area."

She appreciated the tenderness in his voice, but she shrugged off his offer. "No, it's all right. I'll handle it, Bri."

"Promise me you won't take any action without my advice," he ordered.

This time it was Jessie who sighed. "I won't. I just wish I didn't have this feeling that Tom McCullough's innocent."

"Jess, listen to me. Eleven other people came to the same conclusion you did. You did the right thing," he said firmly.

"I sure hope you're right," she answered, but in her heart she was afraid he wasn't.

THERE WAS LITTLE information about Tom McCullough's condition on any of the television news reports or in the newspapers the following day. Jessie assumed that he was still alive or else there would have been news of his death.

As it turned out, she was soon able to find out firsthand what condition he was in. One of her grandmother's friends had fallen on the ice and had been taken to the same hospital where Tom McCullough was staying. Jessie figured it had to be fate that her grandmother would ask her to drive her into the city to visit her convalescing friend.

Agreeing to wait for her grandmother in the coffee shop, she found it difficult to focus on her embroidery when a man she had convicted of murder was somewhere in the same building. *A man with human weaknesses, but not a murderer.* The words of the defense attorney played in her mind, taunting her with memories of the trial.

As hard as she tried to forget, Jessie couldn't seem to put Tom McCullough out of her mind. If only she knew what his condition was. Did she dare sneak up to the critical care unit and see how he was doing?

She sat for several minutes, contemplating the idea, weighing its pros and cons, before finally shoving her needlework back into her bag. After disposing of her cup and saucer she headed for the information desk, where she received instructions on how to reach the cardiac care unit. Then she got on the elevator, rehearsing in her mind what she would say when she arrived.

"My uncle, Tom McCullough, is a patient here...."

No, she couldn't lie about being related to him, not after what she had done.

"A friend of mine's father is a patient here. I was wondering if I could find out how he's doing?"

No, she couldn't pretend to be either Aidan or Sean McCullough's friend.

Maybe it wasn't such a good idea after all, she thought as the lights blinked off the numbers of the floors. She was a miserable liar. It would be much easier to call the nursing station and inquire as to his condition.

As the elevator came to a stop at the fifth floor, the doors slid open. Rather than ride to the top and then back down again, Jessie stepped out into the corridor. She headed straight for the elevator call buttons on the wall. She was about to press the Down button when she saw that it was already lit.

Automatically she glanced around to see who was waiting for an elevator car. As she expected, she was not alone. Standing in the corridor with his hands in his pockets was Aidan McCullough.

CHAPTER SIX

"SMALL WORLD, ISN'T IT?" His voice was deep and held a hint of sarcasm.

Jessie didn't like what it was doing to her nerve endings. She acknowledged his greeting with a half smile, the one she often used in situations demanding professional courtesy. Then she focused her attention on the bank of elevators, dismissing his presence with a tilt of her blond head.

Aidan, however, was not about to be dismissed. "Did you get off on the wrong floor?"

"Yes." Again she forced the half smile to her face, intending to give him a quick, polite glance. When her eyes met his, however, she found herself giving an explanation. "I meant to press four instead of five."

"Four?"

"Four," she repeated.

He simply nodded, and Jessie was grateful when a soft *ping* announced the arrival of an elevator car. To her dismay Aidan followed her as she stepped inside the empty compartment. When her finger reached for the button with the number four, it stopped in midair. There was a piece of tape over that particular knob with a small notice beside it indicating the fourth floor was closed due to remodeling. How could she not have noticed it on the way up?

Automatically Jessie's eyes moved to Aidan. He was looking rather smug.

"Are you sure you didn't want five?"

Jessie didn't answer, but punched the button labeled Lobby, her face coloring slightly as she stepped back to allow him access to the control panel. When he didn't reach for any of the buttons she knew he was riding down to the main floor with her.

There was an uncomfortable silence as the car slowly descended. Jessie tried not to squirm under his scrutiny, but other than looking at the blinking lights over the door that indicated which floor they were passing, there was nowhere else to look. She wished the elevator would stop and someone—anyone—would get on.

No one did. When the doors finally slid open, they were on the main floor. Jessie thought she was going to be able to get away without saying another word to him, but before she had taken a couple of steps she heard his voice over her shoulder.

"He's in critical condition, in case you're wondering."

That stopped Jessie's feet from moving any farther. Slowly she turned to face him. Noticing the tiny lines of stress around his eyes, she felt a wave of sympathy. She took a deep breath to steady her nerves and swallowed nervously before asking, "Is he going to be all right?"

He shrugged. "It's too early to tell, but the doctors are optimistic."

"I'm glad to hear that," she said evenly.

"Are you?"

Any sympathy she had for him disappeared as antagonism flared between them. "Yes, I am." She stiffened her shoulders. "Just because I sat on a jury doesn't mean I'm without compassion. If you'll excuse me," she said coolly, then turned and started walking again. He followed her.

"Why did you come to the hospital?" he asked, catching up with her.

She didn't break her stride but kept on walking, trying to ignore the fact that he was at her elbow. "I don't think that's any of your business," she said, deliberately keeping her voice brusque.

"You want to know what I think?"

"Not really."

He ignored her response. "I think you wanted to find out how bad off my father is."

She stopped moving and turned to face him, taking another calming breath before she spoke. "Just to set the record straight, I didn't come to see your father. I'm here with my grandmother, who is visiting a friend."

"Where? On the fourth floor?" he asked in a taunting tone, but Jessie refused to meet his eyes, even though she knew there'd be more than a hint of satisfaction in them.

They had come to the end of the corridor and she was faced with two choices—either take a right to the information desk or a left to the cafeteria. Jessie followed the arrow that pointed left. So did Aidan.

"Why are you following me?" she asked as he continued to match her stride.

"I thought you wanted to hear about my father," he said in an infuriatingly smooth voice.

Although she felt insecure with this man, she was determined not to give in to her emotions. "I really don't think we should be discussing this."

"Then you don't want to hear what caused his heart attack?"

"Yes…no…." she stammered. He was getting closer to that place in her heart she kept neatly fenced. Whether or not he thought she was responsible for his father's heart attack didn't matter. *She* felt guilty, and too many nights of tossing and turning had taken its toll. In a rare display of emotions, she allowed the anxiety of the past three weeks to come pouring out in her response.

"I'm sorry that your father's had a heart attack, but it's not my fault, and for you to imply that it is is simply not fair. There were twelve jurors on that jury, Mr. Mc-Cullough, and every one of them agreed on the verdict," she said, her voice rising with each successive word. "You have no right to accuse me of anything. I wasn't the one on trial, your father was. I don't know what it is you want from me, but if you and your brother don't stop harassing me, I'm going to call the police."

It was only when she ran out of breath that she realized how upset she was. Suddenly aware of the curious looks they were drawing standing in the middle of the corridor, she made a dash for the rest room before he had a chance to reply.

Surprised by her outburst, Aidan watched her tall, willowy figure disappear. Not once since he'd been watching her through Braxton's window had she allowed her composure to slip. Could it be that Jessina Paulson wasn't as indifferent as she wanted him to believe she was?

He knew that if he had a lick of sense he'd leave well enough alone and not try to find out. His life was complicated enough without getting tangled up with a woman who had sat on the jury that had found his father guilty of murder. He should get the coffee he had come down for, go back upstairs and forget that he had even seen her.

Only she wasn't the type of woman one easily forgot. The past few weeks had proved that. During the entire trial he had watched her day after day, sitting regally in the jury box as though she were watching a polo match. She had given him no indication that she found him attractive, yet her mere presence could send something warm tingling through him.

Now that the trial was over he hadn't been able to resist walking past the store window. On more than one occasion he had been tempted to pick up the phone at Braxton's and speak to her, but he hadn't been able to think of anything to say that would sound normal.

Well, he definitely hadn't sounded normal this afternoon, he reflected, running a hand through his hair. What had possessed him to insult her the way he had? In his heart he knew she wasn't responsible for his father's health any more than he was.

He glanced at his watch. She wasn't going to want to speak to him when she came out, yet he couldn't leave without setting the record straight. So he propped himself up against the wall and waited patiently for her to reappear.

When she finally stepped out into the corridor she looked as cool and collected as she had each day of the trial. Except for a quick, apprehensive survey of the hall, there was no indication that she had been upset only minutes ago. When she saw him there was a brief flicker of annoyance in her eyes, then she looked right through him as though he didn't exist. *That* annoyed him.

He deliberately stepped in front of her so that she had no option but to listen to him. "I'm not going to bother you. I simply want to apologize. You're not responsible for my father's heart attack and I had no right to imply that you were. I'm sorry."

She eyed him suspiciously for several moments before saying, "Apology accepted." She was about to walk away when he put a hand on her arm. A startled look crossed her face and he immediately lifted his fingers.

"Sorry." Almost immediately her composure was back and Aidan could see that she was not about to lose control again. "Have a nice day," he called out as she hurried past him.

Watching her gracefully disappear down the hallway, he was filled with mixed emotions. He couldn't explain this ambiguous feeling he had for her—wanting to be with her, yet wanting to get away from her. Maybe it was an instinct of self-preservation.

Had it merely been a coincidence that she had shown up at the hospital? He rather doubted it. Judging from her emotional outburst he'd guess that she *was* feeling guilty despite her protests to the contrary. Maybe there was a warm, compassionate heart beating inside that lovely body, after all.

Not that he'd ever find out. As soon as his father was out of danger and the holidays were over, he'd be far away from the frosty climate of Minnesota. No more slushy streets and icy sidewalks. No more windchill factors.

Just thinking about the cold weather caused him to shiver, and he remembered the reason he had come downstairs. He needed a cup of hot, black coffee.

It was the reason he had run into Jessina in the first place. The staff on the critical care unit provided fresh coffee for its visitors, but after sitting with his mother since early morning he was in need of some time away from the hospital room. As he entered the cafeteria, the tempting aroma of food reminded him that he hadn't eaten since morning, either. With tray in hand he joined the serving line, selecting the wild rice soup and a turkey sandwich.

He stopped at the condiments bar for napkins and a plastic soup spoon, then scanned the pristine white tables for a place to sit. The small cafeteria was crowded, with only one table vacant—near the large plate-glass window, a window laced with frost. It wasn't exactly an ideal spot for someone who was already chilled.

As Aidan walked toward it he saw that the location wasn't the table's only disadvantage. Seated not more than a foot away was Jessina Paulson. She had a piece of cloth in one hand, a needle and thread in the other.

Aidan paused briefly, then strode forward, depositing his plastic tray on the tabletop. "Can I sit here or will that be classified as harassment?" he asked as she glanced up at him. He knew he sounded petty, but he couldn't help himself. It still annoyed him the way she could so easily dismiss him. "This is the only vacant spot, otherwise I wouldn't be here," he added when she gave him a patronizing glare.

"It doesn't matter," she answered, her eyes returning to the embroidery in her hands.

Again she had easily dismissed him and Aidan had to dig deep for the self-control that kept him from making a caustic remark. Her beautifully manicured fingers moved with a delicate rhythm in an almost effortless fashion as she concentrated on her needlework. None of the women he knew embroidered, with the exception of a couple of elderly aunts, and Aidan found her actions fascinating.

Although they were seated at separate tables, there was very little room between them, making it difficult not to hear the sounds each other made. Even when he wasn't looking at her, Aidan knew just when she picked up her coffee cup and when she placed it back down on the saucer.

At the sound of a tiny gasp he automatically glanced at her. She had pricked her finger and was sucking on it to stop the bleeding. He leaned over to pass her several paper napkins.

"Thank you." Her words were softly spoken.

"You're welcome," he answered politely, watching as she dipped the end of the napkin into her glass of ice water, then dabbed at her forefinger. Holding the napkin in place with her thumb, she used her other hand to scoop up the fabric and shove it back into her tote bag.

Aidan returned his attention to his soup. Despite his effort to ignore her, he could see her movements out of the corner of his eye. The harder he tried not to look at her, the more he wanted to see the expression on her face.

Unable to resist, he stole another glance at her. Much to his annoyance, she was staring blankly out the window, as though she didn't give two hoots whether he was sitting there or not. Then she stood, and he thought that she was going to leave. His eyes followed her slender figure as it made its way across the cafeteria...not to the exit but to the serving line.

She was wearing a fuzzy peach sweater and black stretch pants that hugged her curves comfortably. Aidan liked to watch her graceful movements, but it was her hair that captivated him. It looked shiny and clean, and made him wonder if it smelled of wildflowers.

When she sat back down, she gave him a cursory glance, her face revealing no emotion whatsoever. He watched her tear back the foil top of a container of cream and empty it into her cup. Then she ripped open a packet of sugar and measured out a small portion onto her spoon. He didn't realize that he was gawking at her until her eyes caught his.

"Coffee's not bad, is it?" He tried to give her the same blank look she was giving him, but he knew he had failed.

She gave him a rather uninterested sound of agreement, then turned her attention to the spoon she was swirling in her cup.

When she glanced at her watch, Aidan asked, "Waiting for someone?"

This time she did meet his gaze and the effect on his insides was dramatic. "Yes, my grandmother." She began to fidget with the empty cream package, giving him a hint that she might not be as composed as she wanted him to think.

Aidan took a bite of his sandwich, which by now tasted like cardboard, then asked, "Am I making you uncomfortable?"

"You need to ask?" Her blue eyes stared at him with a frankness he found rather disarming.

"I don't want you to feel uncomfortable with me."

One perfectly shaped eyebrow lifted. "You don't?"

"No, I don't," he said, realizing for the first time just how true his words were.

"I don't see that it can be any other way. I was on the jury," she said rather solemnly.

"Yes, which is why you know who I am and I know who you are. Our lives have come together by a rather strange twist of fate."

"It has been strange," she murmured in agreement.

"Maybe we should start over," he suggested. "If the trial hadn't happened, I would have come in, seen you sitting here and said something like, 'Aren't you that model in Braxton's window?' We could have introduced ourselves, had a cup of coffee together...."

She shook her head, her lips curving ever so slightly before she said, "I'm not in the habit of having coffee with strangers."

His eyes pierced hers. "We're hardly strangers... Jessina."

Her teeth tugged on her lower lip briefly, then she said, "It's Jessie. Only my grandmother calls me Jessina."

"I don't think I've ever heard that name before," he told her, thinking it was a beautiful name, and so fitting for the lovely woman seated across from him.

"It's an old Norwegian name and not very common. In fact, I've never come across anyone else who uses it."

"You're Scandinavian?" he asked, understanding now why she was tall, blond and fair skinned.

"Mmm-hmm." She gave him a polite smile and once more there was silence.

"I'm Irish—which is why, as my grandmother would say, I often let my emotions instead of my head guide my tongue. That's what happened when I ran into you on the elevator. Were you coming to see how my father is, Jessie? Is that why you were on the fifth floor?" he asked.

"I told you. My grandmother's here visiting a friend and I..."

"Got off on the wrong floor," he finished for her.

She took a sip of her coffee, then looked at him and said, "Yes. It was the wrong floor. I did want to see how your father was, but after I got to the fifth floor I realized I shouldn't be there." She lowered her eyes.

He sighed and admitted, "No, I guess you shouldn't." There was another stretch of silence, then he asked, "What did you mean when you said my brother had been harassing you?"

She took another sip of coffee, then folded her arms across her chest. "He came by Braxton's after the trial was over and picked up the telephone children use to speak to Santa."

"I take it he didn't want to speak to Santa."

"No, he asked for me."

"And?"

"I believe his words were, 'Why did you convict an innocent man?'"

Aidan shoved his plate with his half-eaten sandwich away from him. "I'm sorry. He had no right to do that. In his defense I guess all I can say is that he's looking for someone he can blame for what's happened to our father."

"And what about you?" she asked, but before he could answer she added, "This is crazy." She looked around the cafeteria in disbelief. "I can't believe I'm sitting here discussing this with you."

"The trial's over, Jessie. It's not illegal for us to talk to each other."

"It might not be illegal, but it's... it's..."

He could see that she was having trouble describing the way she was feeling. "It doesn't seem right. Is that what you're thinking?"

"I don't know what it is you want from me," she said, revealing a vulnerability that had Aidan wanting to tell her exactly what he was feeling.

He could just imagine what she'd say if he told her that ever since he had seen her modeling in Braxton's store window he hadn't been able to stop wondering what it would be like to lie beside her in a warm bed.

"I don't know, either," he answered, which was partially true. Besides the fact that the mere sight of her was enough to cause aches in places he didn't even know existed, he wasn't sure what it was he wanted from her. "You just keep turning up in my life and I don't understand why."

Jessie didn't understand why, either. From the way he was watching her she had the crazy sensation that he was reaching out and touching her. She didn't want to have any feelings for him and unconsciously leaned away from him.

"It's probably just a coincidence," she said with a hint of uncertainty.

He shook his head. "I don't think so."

"No, I guess it's not," she agreed, recalling his visits to the window. "Why have you been coming to Braxton's?" she asked bluntly, meeting his gaze.

"I've been doing some work at my father's office and it just so happens that I pass by the department store on my way there every day," he explained.

"Oh, really," she said skeptically.

"Yes, really," he insisted. "It hasn't been because I've wanted to harass you—which is what I know you're thinking."

"That's a comfort," she said in a mockingly sweet voice.

"Actually, you remind me of someone I used to know," he said pensively, all traces of antagonism gone.

"People tell me that quite often," she replied evenly. "It's probably because you've seen my face on a billboard."

He looked at her over his coffee cup, his eyes thoughtful. "I don't live around here, so I haven't seen many billboards." He raised a thick, dark eyebrow. "Maybe I just like looking at you."

Jessie nearly choked on her coffee. She hadn't expected him to be so direct. She decided to ignore him from that point on but he wasn't about to be ignored.

"You don't believe me, do you?" he asked.

"Is it important that I do?"

He shrugged, his dark eyebrows lifting slightly. "Tell me, how do you manage to keep so still in that window?"

"It isn't that hard with a little practice. I usually block out the world outside...try to imagine I'm somewhere else."

"Then you don't always notice what's going on outside?"

"Not always, but then there are some things one can't help but notice." She was referring to his presence, but he misunderstood.

"You're talking about the teenagers I chased away."

"That, too," she answered, and saw a slight grin curve his mustache at the realization. "I should have thanked you for chasing them away."

He shrugged effortlessly. "Do you get many people trying to harass you?" he asked. "I mean, besides me and my brother."

This time when he smiled a tiny dimple puckered his left cheek and Jessie felt the pull of his charismatic personality. "No. Mostly they want to see if they can get me to move."

"I bet they don't have much luck. You're very good at what you do."

Jessie nearly blushed at the compliment, but managed to resist his charm. What was it about this man that stirred such commotion inside her? She didn't think it would be wise to learn the answer, and decided his antagonism was much safer than his charm.

Fortunately her grandmother chose that moment to make her appearance. Seeing her anxiously scanning the occupants of the cafeteria, Jessie jumped up and went to get her.

"I'm over by the window, Gran," she explained as she gave her an arm to cling to.

"Do we have time for a cup of coffee, dear?" she asked as Jessie led her across the cafeteria.

Jessie stifled a groan and smiled pleasantly. "Sure. Why don't you sit down and I'll get you some."

Aidan said nothing as Jessie eased her grandmother down onto the chair beside him. He simply watched with an amused grin as Jessie fussed over her.

The last thing Jessie wanted was for Aidan McCullough to eavesdrop on her conversation with her grandmother. But to her surprise, by the time she returned with the coffee he was gone.

When her grandmother saw her eyes searching the caf
teria, she said, "If you're looking for that gentleman wh
was sitting next to you, he's gone. He said to tell you he'
see you soon."

"He spoke to you?"

"*Ja.* Who was he, dear?" she asked brightly.

"Just someone I bumped into on the elevator."

"Oh." Her face fell in disappointment. "I thought yc
knew him. He's very handsome, isn't he?" she said, he
eyes dancing behind the thick lenses of her glasses.

"Yes, Gran. He's very handsome," Jessie answered, n
bothering to deny the truth.

JUST AS JESSIE EXPECTED, Aidan showed up at Braxton
on Monday. He stood watching her, arms folded across h
chest, a smug look on his face. There was no attempt on h
part to get her attention, no waving, no winking, no funn
faces.

Despite the unsettled feeling his presence created in he
stomach, Jessie managed to hold her pose. She tried to pt
him out of her mind, but she kept hearing his voice saying
"I like looking at you."

Judging by the expression on his face, he did like look
ing at her and Jessie wondered what she would do when th
fairy dust fell and she had no reason not to acknowledge h
presence.

As it turned out, Aidan was gone by the time the meta
lic snowflakes fell. Jessie's eyes scanned the crowd lookin
for him, but he was not on the street. For the remainder c
her shift she kept an eye out for him, but he didn't return

Someone who did nearly cause Jessie to break her pos
was her niece Melissa. Although Jessie knew that Carla an
Missy were coming to the city for her niece's doctor's ap
pointment, she was surprised to see them outside Brax

on's. However, it wasn't Carla's enthusiastic wave that early broke Jessie's concentration, but her niece's appearance.

Melissa was dressed in black, from the leather jacket studded with metal to the men's shoes on her feet. Even more disturbing was what she had done with her hair. What once had been blond layers of curls was now a black bowl cut with the lower half of her head completely shaved. Even her fingernails were painted black, and the only makeup she wore was heavy black eyeliner. Unlike her mother, who was fascinated with the holiday window, she looked sullen and uninterested in her whereabouts.

It was only because of her strict self-discipline that Jessie was able to finish out her stint in the window. By the time the curtain closed for the evening she was anxious to speak to both of them.

"Well, isn't this something!" Carla exclaimed as Jessie and Devony stepped out from the display window. "When you told me you were modeling in a window, I didn't think it'd be such a fancy setup."

Jessie hugged her sister and introduced her to Devony, who judging by her expression was as shocked by Missy's appearance as Jessie was.

"It must be fun having all those people watching you," Carla said enviously, eyeing the two slender elves.

"It's just a job, Carla," Jessie answered, noticing how Missy was hanging back from the others. "Hi, Missy. How are you?"

"Okay," was her reply.

Jessie gave her a hug, gently drawing her into their circle. "You remember meeting Devony, don't you?"

Missy simply nodded, the black curtain of hair falling across her face as she stared at the floor.

"So what brings you to the Cities? Have you come to d
some Christmas shopping?" Devony asked in her usua
perky manner.

"We have an appointment to see a doctor over at th
Riverdale Clinic tomorrow," Carla explained, eyeing he
daughter cautiously. "Then we're going over to the Mall c
America."

"I told you I'm not going to some doctor I don't even
know," Missy announced, folding her arms stubbornly
across her chest.

Carla and Jessie exchanged surreptitious glances.

"I'm starved. Is anyone interested in stopping for pizz
on the way home?" Jessie asked, attempting to ease th
tension.

"We could go to that new place on Seventh Street,"
Devony suggested. "They have Chicago-style deep-dish
pizza that is out of this world!"

"That sounds like fun," Carla said in a falsely enthusi
astic voice. "We haven't eaten since lunchtime."

"What do you think, Missy?" Jessie asked, still trou
bled by her niece's appearance.

"I'm not into pizza," Missy answered in a bored tone.

"What do you mean you're not into pizza. You can
practically eat a whole pepperoni by yourself." Carla's
voice had lost its gaiety and had an edge to it now.

Seeing the teenager wince at her mother's words, Jessie
quickly said, "They serve hamburgers and fries, too."

"It doesn't matter. I'm not hungry," Melissa informed
them with a shrug.

"Maybe we should make it another time," Devony said
apprehensively, her glance flitting between them.

"No, it's all right," Carla insisted. "She can come along
and sit and visit even if she doesn't want to eat."

Jessie could see the idea wasn't appealing to her niece. "Maybe it would be better if we went straight back to Gran's. If you've just arrived you probably want to get settled in."

"We've already stopped by Gran's," Carla answered.

"But if Missy's tired we can go for pizza another time," Jessie said, noticing her niece's pale features.

"Are you tired, Melissa?" Carla asked her daughter in a voice that warned her not to admit she was.

Again she shrugged. "Not really. I'll have a soda or something if everyone else wants to go."

"Then it's settled. We'll go," Carla said enthusiastically.

The place they finally decided on was a new sports bar that had been open only a few days and was in the process of celebrating its grand opening. The minute they stepped in the door Jessie was wishing she had insisted they go someplace quieter.

They had been seated only a few minutes when Missy excused herself to go to the bathroom. Jessie had an idea it was because of the magician who was moving from table to table performing magic tricks.

"See how moody she is?" Carla asked as soon as the teenager was gone.

"She's just a teenager, Carla." Jessie wasn't comfortable talking about her niece in front of Devony and quickly changed the subject. "How's everyone in Harding?"

To Jessie's relief Carla took the hint and for the next few minutes talk was about Jessie's family back in Harding. When the magician stopped at their table, he had Devony tear a newspaper into small strips, then with a bit of magic he put them back together again.

"He's really good, isn't he?" Carla commented, watching the tuxedoed man move to the next table. "We don't

have anything like this back in Harding. I'm glad we cam
to this place. Did you see the prizes they're giving away
Two trips to the Caribbean island of your choice,'' she sai
longingly.

"Too bad they aren't providing the men to go with
them," Devony said on a chuckle.

"Speaking of men, there's a guy sitting across from u
who keeps looking at you two. You know what I mean?'
Carla told them with a wriggle of her eyebrows.

"Is he alone?" Devony immediately asked.

"No, he's with another guy. They are cute with a capita
C," Carla answered.

"It's probably someone who's recognized us from th
window. Do we dare turn around or will that look too ob
vious?" Devony asked.

"I don't know how you do things down here in th
Cities," Carla said with a humorous grin. "If it were me
I'd look him smack-dab in the face and wink. What do yo
think, Jess?"

Jessie didn't need to turn in her chair to know who wa:
sitting behind her. Ever since she had sat down she had fel
something wasn't quite right. At first she had thought it wa:
because of Melissa. But now she had the feeling that if she
turned around she'd know the real reason.

Jessie slowly peeked over her shoulder. As she had sus
pected, Aidan McCullough was sitting not more than six
feet away from her with Will Lepley's partner—the attor
ney for Tom McCullough's defense.

CHAPTER SEVEN

"YOU KNOW HIM?" Carla squeaked as Jessie returned Aidan's nod with a limp wave of her fingers.

Devony glanced over her shoulder. "He looks familiar, Jess. Who is he?"

"Just someone I ran into on the elevator at the hospital yesterday," she said, reaching for a menu. "If you don't mind, I'd rather not talk about it."

"Why? Did he try to pick you up or something?" Carla asked.

"Or something," Jessie said dryly. "I wonder what the soup of the day is."

"What do you mean, 'or something?'" Carla persisted, not buying Jessie's diversionary tactic.

"Hey! Hasn't he been showing up at the window on a regular basis?" Devony asked, discreetly looking back over her shoulder.

"I'm not sure," she answered absently, pretending to be studying the menu. "I think the grilled chicken sandwich sounds good. What do you think?"

"I think you should put down that menu and tell us about this guy. What does he do? Flirt with you while you're in the window?" Carla wanted to know.

"The guy reeks of macho. I wish I had a *friend* like that," Devony drawled enviously.

"He's not exactly a friend and I really wish we coul‹ discuss the food instead of the scenery," Jessie said with pleading smile.

"Is he married? Is that why you don't want to talk t‹ him?" Carla asked, ignoring her sister's request.

"No, he's not married," Jessie replied, her eyes warnin‹ her sister she was on dangerous ground.

Carla took the hint, but Devony didn't. "What about th‹ other guy he's with?"

"I don't know about the other guy," Jessie snapped a bi‹ impatiently, wondering if the attorney had recognized he‹ as one of the trial jurors.

"He's not as good-looking as your admirer, but he's no‹ bad," Devony said pensively after another glance over he‹ shoulder.

Jessie set the menu aside. "Dev, do you have to kee‹ looking over there?" she asked, wishing more than eve‹ that she had gone home rather than stopped for a bite t‹ eat.

"I'm not just looking over *there,* Jess," Devony said, he‹ head slowly rotating as she glanced around. "I want to se‹ why everyone thinks this is such a good place to mee‹ guys."

"Is this a singles' bar?" Carla asked, her brow wrin‹ kling with concern.

"No, it's a sports bar," Jessie replied. "That's why ther‹ are so many television screens. People come here to watc‹ the sports events while they eat."

"Missy probably shouldn't be roaming around in thi‹ place alone. I wonder what's keeping her?" Carla crane‹ her neck in the direction of the women's rest room.

The thought of getting away from the probing eyes o‹ Aidan McCullough and his attorney was too tempting fo‹ Jessie to resist. "Why don't I go check?" she offered‹

reaching for her purse. "I should call Gran, anyway, and let her know we're going to be late."

"What if the waitress comes while you're gone? What do you want?" Carla asked.

"Order whatever you're having. I'll eat anything," Jessie announced as she stood up.

Carefully avoiding looking in Aidan's direction, she made her way through the crowded restaurant to the ladies' room. Inside, she found Missy sitting with a hip propped up on the vanity, her face close to the mirror as she outlined her eyes in black.

Jessie detected a hint of cigarette smoke in the rest room and wondered if it was Melissa's.

When Missy saw her aunt she immediately stiffened. "Did Mom send you in here to check up on me?"

Jessie swallowed back the lecture that was ready to spring forth from her lips. "No, we're ready to order and we weren't sure what you wanted."

"I told Mom I wasn't eating," she retorted, her concentration back on the fine line she was painting across her eyelid.

"We thought you might want something to drink. I hear they have pretty good milk shakes and floats."

Missy stuck the eyeliner wand back into its case. "I only want a diet Coke." She shoved the tube back into the pocket of her leather jacket, then slid off the vanity and faced her aunt. "I might as well go tell her myself or else she'll be on my case all night. Do you want me to wait for you?"

"No, that's all right. You go ahead. I need to call Gran." She motioned toward the pay phone on the wall.

"Whatever," Missy said in a bored tone and started toward the door.

Just as she was about to open it, Jessie called out to her. "Missy, wait."

The teenager paused, apprehension clouding her already-troubled face. She shifted her weight from her left foot to her right, thrusting one fist to her hip.

Indecision wavered in Jessie. Should she try to find out the reason for her niece's drastic change in appearance or simply ignore it? Deciding that the ladies' rest room at a sports bar was probably the last place Missy would want to have a heart-to-heart talk, she finally said, "Tell your mom to order me a diet Coke, too, okay?"

"Okay." It was accompanied by a shrug, but Jessie could see the relief in her face.

As soon as she was gone, Jessie noticed the scrunched up cigarette package beside the wastebasket. Curious, she unfolded the paper and discovered it was the same brand she had found beneath Missy's bed.

Jessie sighed, wondering what could have happened to the little girl who used to play with Barbie dolls and make miniature cakes in her easy-bake oven. Adolescence was supposed to be trying, but she was afraid Missy's problems weren't as easy to solve as mending a broken doll or frosting a lopsided cake.

Even more disturbing than the knowledge that her niece was having problems was knowing that Carla would expect Jessie to have all the answers. Jessie was the one person in her family everyone turned to in a crisis. She had always been the strong one, the reliable one, the one who never let her emotions get the better of her.

Jessie stared at her pale reflection and thought what a joke that was. Right now she felt as though someone had stuck a key in her back and wound her up. Her insides were churning and she wanted nothing better than to be like Melissa and hide away in the ladies' room. Her nerves were threatening to become unraveled, and for the first time in her life she wasn't sure how to prevent that from happening.

Part of the problem was sitting not six feet away from her niece and sister. Why did Aidan McCullough and his father's attorney have to show up at the sports bar? Was it another strange twist of fate?

Whatever it was, Jessie was not looking forward to going back out into the restaurant. Coping with Missy's difficult behavior was going to be enough of a challenge without having Aidan McCullough playing havoc with her emotions.

Except for a cursory glance as she took her place at the table, Jessie ignored his presence even though she knew that his eyes were drilling holes in the back of her shirt. Despite her attempts to push all thoughts of him from her mind, she couldn't help but wonder if he was discussing his father's appeal with the man seated across from him. Part of her wanted to know what was being said, and part of her wanted to forget the two of them were even there.

Thanks to Devony's vivacious chatter and Carla's insatiable curiosity about the city, no one seemed to notice that Jessie was a bit subdued while they ate. When it came time to leave, she finally glanced in Aidan's direction, only to discover that a young couple was now sitting at that table, their heads close together. Aidan had left without saying a word to her.

Jessie hadn't wanted him to stop and talk, yet now that he had gone she felt disappointed.

Only he hadn't left. When she and Devony walked past the entrance to the lounge she saw him sitting on a high stool at the end of the bar, his hand wrapped around a mug of beer.

Jessie pretended not to notice him, but not so Devony. "Check out the bar. That good-looking guy you didn't want me staring at is having a beer," she said, nudging Jessie as they waited for Carla and Missy in the small entry separating the lounge from the dining area. "He's looking this way."

"He can just keep on looking." Jessie deliberately turned her back to the patrons in the bar.

"I think he wants to talk to you. If you want to go in and say hi, I can watch for Carla and Missy," Devony offered.

"No, thank you," she said sarcastically. Seeing Devony's puzzled look she added, "It's not what you think, Dev. He's just an acquaintance."

"He's not looking at you like he's some insurance salesman, Jess."

Jessie shifted uncomfortably and glanced down the corridor leading to the women's rest room. "Maybe I should go see what's taking Missy and Carla so long."

"Uh-uh. Too late. He's coming this way," Devony said in a low voice.

Jessie's heart lodged somewhere between her throat and her lungs. The last thing she wanted was to talk to Aidan McCullough—or was it?

The minute he was directly behind her, her body started to tingle, just as it always did whenever she saw him. She turned around slowly and said, "Hello, Aidan."

"Jessie." He nodded as he spoke her name. "This is a surprise."

Jessie almost drawled sarcastically, "Uh-huh. Yeah, right," but resisted the urge. She introduced Devony, then looked around for the attorney who had been sitting with Aidan earlier, but he was still seated at the bar.

"Who's winning the game?" Devony asked when a roar from the crowd in the lounge indicated a big play had been made in the basketball game being telecast on several TV screens.

"The Wolves are down by ten," Aidan answered with a sympathetic grin.

"It figures," Devony said breezily, then proceeded to impress Aidan with NBA statistics.

Jessie could only look on in amazement. No matter where they went, Devony was never at a loss for words when it came to talking to men. It helped that she had grown up with three brothers, but Jessie was pretty certain that even had Devony been an orphan she would have known how to talk to the opposite sex.

In just a few minutes Jessie learned Aidan was a graduate of the University of Minnesota with an M.B.A. from the Carlson School of Management, he lived in Pasadena and his favorite sport was basketball. All this she discovered without opening her mouth.

Actually, she was content to have Devony do all the talking and was taken by surprise when her friend said, "Jess, why don't you wait here and I'll go see what's keeping Carla and Missy."

There were several moments of awkward silence, during which Jessie became familiar with the size of Aidan's hands, the size of his feet, the size of his elbows and just about anything else that would keep her eyes off his face.

"It really is a small world, isn't it?" Aidan drawled in a voice that reminded her that the owner of the elbows and hands and feet was one sexy man.

"You must be doing a lot of work at your father's office." She meant the words to sound sarcastic, but by the way he was smiling she could see that he was pleased she had noticed him.

"I'm keeping busy," he answered, his gaze unwavering.

Jessie had been around enough men to know that he wasn't looking at her because he wanted to make polite conversation. He was as aware of her as she was of him.

"And your father... has there been any change in his condition?" she asked, needing to dilute the strength of the sensuality humming around them.

"He's better."

"Good."

Again there were several awkward moments of silence, and Jessie thought she should have been happy that the flicker of desire had been driven from his eyes. But then he said, "Can I buy you a drink?"

"I don't think so. I'm with my sister and my niece," she answered politely.

"And you wouldn't even if you could, would you?"

She didn't see any point in lying. "Probably not."

"Does it bother you that I come by the window?"

She should have told him yes, but something in the way he was looking at her had her shrugging and saying, "As you said, I'm paid to have people stare at me." She looked past his shoulder and saw they had drawn the attention of Tom McCullough's lawyer.

Jessie saw the spark of curiosity in the lawyer's glance. Had he recognized her?

When he slid down from the bar stool and started toward them, her heart began to beat irregularly. The thought of talking to Tom McCullough's attorney was about as appealing as swallowing paint.

"It was nice seeing you, Aidan, but I really have to go," she murmured, avoiding his eyes.

As she hurried away she heard him say, "Jessie, wait!" But she didn't look back.

SLEEP DIDN'T COME EASILY for Jessie that night. When she wasn't thinking about her troubled niece her thoughts were filled with Aidan McCullough. Why did he have to keep turning up in her life?

Seeing him with his father's attorney had stirred feelings she didn't want disturbed. It reminded her of the trial, and how she hadn't been able to chase away the doubts that still plagued her.

Intellectually she could justify the decision she had made as a juror; emotionally she couldn't. It didn't matter that the evidence had pointed to Tom McCullough's guilt or that the general consensus was that the jury had reached the only possible verdict in the case. Deep in her gut she felt as though she had made the wrong decision.

On several occasions during the past week she had been tempted to call another of the jurors, Mrs. Abbott, to see if she was having any posttrial stress. She had even gone so far as to pick up the phone and start to dial. But each time she had stopped before making the connection, not wanting to upset the older woman with questions of whether or not justice had been served.

Instead she had gone to the library and thumbed through the periodical index in search of articles dealing with jury stress. She had been somewhat relieved to read that it wasn't uncommon for jurors to suffer emotionally from the experience. According to several studies, two-thirds of the jurors involved in trials of gruesome crimes were found to have suffered from anxiety and sleeplessness as long as four months after the trial had ended.

Jessie wasn't sure she'd be able to keep it all together for four months, especially not if she kept running into Aidan McCullough. The more she saw of him, the more heavily her decision in his father's trial weighed on her mind.

Sometime during the wee hours of the morning she decided that the next time she saw him she would make it perfectly clear to him she had no interest in him and would prefer that he not come by Braxton's anymore.

That opportunity came the following day. Just before the end of her shift, Aidan showed up at the window. She didn't see him at first, but she knew he was there by the way her skin was tingling.

As soon as the fairy dust fell and Jessie was allowed to move around she searched the crowd until she found him leaning up against a street lamp trimmed with green garlands. She gestured for him to get in line for the Santa phone.

When it was his turn to speak to Santa, Devony's eyes sought Jessie's in a knowing glance. "I think this one's for you."

She took the phone from Devony's outstretched hand, trying to ignore the heat spreading through her body.

"I'd like to talk to you," she told him, trying not to notice how the tiny white snowflakes were glistening like stars on his hair.

"You want to talk to me?" he repeated, obviously caught off guard.

"Is that possible?"

A look of satisfaction gleamed in his eyes. "Just name the time and place and I'll be there."

Jessie glanced at her wrist. "I get off work in about thirty minutes. You can wait for me at the guard desk near the employee entrance."

"Sure. I'll see you then." He smiled as he hung up the phone, a half smile that lifted one side of his mustache.

"Okay, Jessie. What gives?" Devony wanted to know as soon as the curtain had closed for the evening and they were free to leave. "What's going on between you and this Aidan character?"

"It's not what you think," she warned.

"You told me you weren't interested in him."

"I'm not."

"Then why did you ask him to meet you?"

Jessie sighed. "It's a long story, Dev." She started for the dressing room, hoping Devony would drop the subject. She didn't.

"Are you sure it's safe to be meeting him? I mean, just because the guy's been coming to the window every day..." She paused, waiting for Jessie to say something, but she didn't comment. "Do you even know his last name?"

"Yes, I do. It's McCullough."

"McCullough? As in the McCullough who killed Kathleen Daniels?" Devony grabbed Jessie's elbow, her mouth dropping open.

"Yes. Aidan is his son," Jessie confirmed.

"Then this *doesn't* make any sense. You shouldn't be seeing him." She shook her head. "Uh-uh, no way, Jessie."

"It's all right, Dev," Jessie tried to reassure her, but Devony was adamant.

"All right?" she shrieked in disbelief. "You're meeting the son of the man you sent to prison for murder and you say it's all right?"

"It's not what you think, Dev, and if you don't mind, I'd really rather not discuss this."

Devony held up her hands in mock surrender. "All right, all right. You don't want to talk about him. I won't press you."

Jessie felt a twinge of guilt. She and Devony were good friends, but as close as they had become, Jessie didn't feel comfortable talking about certain aspects of her life. She had always kept most of her personal life to herself.

As she made her way to the security desk at the department store entrance, she reminded herself that the only way to get rid of her anxiety over the trial was to get Aidan out of her life.

When she spotted him leaning up against Fred's desk, her skin tingled. His back was to her, so all she saw was a dark leather jacket, gray pant legs and black loafers. He was bent over the desk, his head close to the guard's grinning face.

"Here's our elf coming now," Fred said when he noticed Jessie approaching.

Aidan straightened and turned to face her. He looked pleased to see her, and Jessie felt a twinge of guilt in her stomach. How did you tell someone to get out of your life when he was looking at you as though you had asked him for a date?

"Is the North Pole closed for the day?" Fred asked, diverting Jessie's attention from Aidan's handsome face.

Jessie nodded. "Mmm-hmm. Devony should be coming any minute. She had to make a couple of phone calls before she left."

Fred looked at Aidan and said, "You remember what I told you, won't you?" He winked conspiratorially, then unlocked the door for the two of them to leave.

Jessie was curious to know what it was that Fred wanted Aidan to remember, but judging by the look Aidan gave the security guard, she decided it was better not to inquire.

A gust of wind greeted them as they stepped outside, and Aidan shivered, quickly zipping up the front of his jacket. He pulled a pair of leather gloves from his pocket. "Where to?" he asked, his breath forming a tiny white cloud in the cold air.

Another twinge of guilt skittered through her blood-stream. He had definitely misinterpreted her message. She wanted to tell him in one simple statement she didn't want him showing up at the window, that she didn't want him anywhere near her. She should have been able to tell him right here, right now on the sidewalk in the cold without feeling so much as a twinge of remorse.

Unfortunately, she couldn't. Or she didn't want to. She wasn't sure which was the case. So she said, "I'm not exactly dressed for going out."

"You look great to me," he said, looking down at her floral leggings and fuchsia tennis shoes. "What about that place across the street?" He nodded toward a small café on the corner whose green neon lights flashed invitingly.

Reluctantly she agreed, but only because he was shivering and she didn't feel comfortable saying what she had to say standing out in the cold. When they entered the café Jessie immediately felt underdressed.

The small restaurant was more of a coffeehouse where couples often gathered for quiet conversation and warm drinks on cold nights. Jessie hadn't been in the establishment for quite some time and had forgotten how intimate the atmosphere was with its dimly lit rooms and soft, unobtrusive music.

They were shown to a tiny table barely big enough for two people to sit at without bumping knees or elbows. When Jessie shrugged out of her coat, Aidan immediately took it from her and hung it up beside his on one of the coat hooks along the wall.

"Thank you," she said with a polite smile.

"You're welcome," Aidan answered, a bit bemused by her prim-and-proper manner. He was about to ask her why she was looking at him as though he were going to take a chomp out of her arm when the waitress arrived to take their order.

"I'll have espresso," Jessie told the slip of a girl.

"Make that two," Aidan seconded.

After an unsuccessful attempt to convince either of them to order a pastry, the waitress left. Aidan watched Jessie's eyes follow her back to the bar.

"This is an interesting place," he said, glancing around the café.

"Yes, it is," she agreed, her eyes, too, making a roving study of the coffeehouse. He could see that she wasn't as calm as she wanted him to think she was.

When she had asked him to meet her after work he had been so flattered that he hadn't given any thought as to the reason she wanted to see him. For days he had been wanting to pick up the Santa phone and ask to speak to her. Now she had made the first move and he wasn't sure how to respond.

He had never been a man who arranged words in his head before he spoke. He usually said what he was feeling, which is exactly what he did now.

"Why do you think I've been coming by Braxton's every day?" he asked, watching her steadily.

"You said it's on the way to your father's office."

"If you take the long way around." He flashed a reserved smile that exuded a kind of easy charm.

"What are you trying to tell me?"

"That I've been coming by the window because I think you're beautiful." To his surprise, she blushed. "You must be used to that kind of compliment by now."

"Just because I'm a model doesn't mean I'm comfortable with flattery," she said candidly.

"I'm not trying to flatter you, Jessie. I'm trying to tell you that for the past four weeks I've been behaving like those little kids who line up outside Braxton's with their noses pressed to the glass in order to see the man who's been occupying their thoughts almost nonstop. Only it isn't Santa who's been monopolizing my thoughts. It's been you.''

He waited for some reaction from her, but all she did was bite down on her lip. He could see by the expression in her eyes that he had definitely caught her off guard.

''I'd like to get to know you better, but I think you already realize that, don't you?''

She lifted her eyes to his and the beauty he saw there startled him.

''The signals you've been sending have been a little confusing,'' she answered with a lift of one eyebrow.

''Yes, well, the events of the past few weeks haven't exactly made communication easy, have they?'' His mouth curved ever so slightly.

She smiled weakly, but it was a smile and his heart swelled.

''If I were to ask you to have dinner with me, would you?''

''Probably not,'' she answered, and his heart plummeted.

''Because of my father?''

''Doesn't it bother you that I was one of the persons who sat on the jury that found him guilty?''

He leaned closer to her with both elbows on the table. ''Jessie, in the past week I've had to come to terms with the fact that my father was tried and found guilty. If you hadn't been sitting in that spot on the jury, then someone else would have been and the verdict would most likely have been the same.''

''Then you believe your father is guilty?'' she asked, her forehead wrinkling ever so slightly.

"If you want the honest-to-goodness truth, Jessie, I don't know." As soon as the words were out he was attacked by guilt. He should never have admitted that he had doubts about his father, even if it was true.

Doubts were what was causing the stress in his relationship with his mother. She couldn't understand why he didn't unconditionally believe in his father's innocence. The result was that he had been walking a tightrope, trying to believe in his father's innocence for his mother's sake, yet wondering if the jury hadn't been right in its conviction.

"I'm sorry, that was a totally inappropriate question to ask," she said, interrupting his thoughts. "I'm sure it hasn't been easy for anyone in your family to deal with your father's situation."

There was compassion in her eyes and Aidan revised an earlier opinion of her. Maybe she hadn't been so immune to the courtroom proceedings, after all. When the waitress arrived with their coffee he decided it was best to change the subject.

"Why don't we not talk about the trial. Tell me about Jessie Paulson. How did she become a mannequin in Braxton's window?"

"Contrary to what lots of young girls want to think, it's neither an exciting nor glamorous story." She took a sip of her coffee.

"I would think standing still for long periods of time would be hard on the joints."

"You get a little stiff, but it really isn't bad once you get used to it." She set her cup back down on its saucer. "I've done all sorts of modeling from posing with a pig in a farmer's field to passing out pamphlets at the convention center. Working at Braxton's is one of my better assignments."

"Then you've been modeling for a while?"

"Awhile," she murmured as she took another sip of her coffee, her attention on the porcelain cup.

There were several awkward moments of silence while he eyed her steadily before he said, "You just don't want to give me a chance, do you, Jessie?"

That brought her head up with a jerk and she reached for her purse. "Maybe this wasn't such a good idea."

"It was *your* idea," he reminded her. For once he had caught her by surprise, but she was still more poised than he was. "Just why did you ask me to meet you this evening?" he demanded out of curiosity.

She hesitated before answering. "I was going to ask you to stop coming by the window."

"I see." He glanced around the room, feeling like a first-class fool. He had been fantasizing that she was interested in him when in reality all she wanted was to tell him to get lost. "No wonder this is awkward. I'm sorry. My signals must have been crossed." He reached into his pocket for his wallet and pulled out several bills, which he tossed onto the table. "I didn't mean to be a nuisance."

He meant to make as quick a getaway as possible, but she stopped him. "Aidan, wait." She reached across the table and put her hand on his arm. "It's not what you're thinking."

"What should I be thinking?" he asked.

She shrugged and looked around uneasily. "You haven't been a nuisance. It's more like a distraction."

From the look in her eyes he could see that he hadn't had his signals crossed. She wasn't immune to him. "Weren't you the one who said you could tune out the distractions?"

"Most of them," she admitted, arching one eyebrow.

"But not me, eh?" His expression became thoughtful. "Just what is it about me that distracts you, Jessie?"

She bit down on her lower lip, debating whether she should say what was really on her mind. He had the sort of eyes that encouraged confidences, but years of keeping her emotions neatly under control had her reluctant to divulge too much of what she was feeling.

She compromised with "It wasn't easy sitting in judgment of your father, Aidan."

"I thought we had already decided that the trial was over and done with."

"You said you had come to terms with what had happened," she reminded him.

"And you haven't?" He looked surprised by her admission.

"Not exactly," she said hesitantly, wishing she hadn't given him any hint that she was suffering emotionally from having served on the jury. "It was a very stressful experience and one I'd like to forget."

"And as long as you see me, that won't happen?" he stated matter-of-factly.

"I don't think so," she said soberly.

He was quiet for several seconds before answering. "Jessie, the very first time I saw you in the window I wanted to get to know you."

"I thought maybe that was why you always seemed to be there," she said with a wry grin.

His grin was sheepish. "I guess I wasn't exactly subtle, was I? The point is, if the trial hadn't occurred, I would have found a way to introduce myself."

"But the trial did happen," she said with a dose of realism. "We can't pretend it didn't."

He sighed. "No, we can't." He reached out across the table and covered her hand with his. "I'm sorry you were put in a position to sit in judgment of someone close to me, but that was something neither of us had any control over. Jessie, the trial's over."

"And you think we should forget what's happened?"

"Would that be so hard to do?" he asked, surveying her thoughtfully.

She lifted her shoulders gently. "Maybe not with time."

"Time is one thing I don't have. I'm not going to be in Minnesota much longer, and before I go back to California I'd like you to have dinner with me."

When she didn't answer right away, his thumb gently stroked the back of her hand. "What do you say, Jessie?"

She looked around the room in bemusement. "I can't believe I'm even considering saying yes. It seems so unorthodox."

Pearly white teeth gleamed beneath his mustache. "My whole life has been unorthodox."

Just a glance into his dark eyes had her resolve weakening. "I work at Braxton's every evening until nine."

"That's early for me. I'm used to eating late."

Still she hesitated, mentally debating the wisdom of accepting his offer. There were more cons than pros on her mental list. An attraction to a man who was only going to be around for a short time was foolish. Even if he was going to stay in Minnesota, there was the matter of his father's conviction. As hard as she had tried to forget about the trial, she didn't need to have dinner with the son of the man she had found guilty. On the other hand, there was an uncontrollable curiosity inside her that wanted to know what was being done by Will Lepley's firm to prove Tom McCullough innocent.

If she had dinner with Aidan she would be able to find out where things stood with the appeal. It was for that reason Jessie decided to accept his invitation...at least, that's what she told herself.

CHAPTER EIGHT

BY SEVEN O'CLOCK FRIDAY evening Jessie was wishing that she had never agreed to have dinner with Aidan. She didn't see how it could be anything but awkward.

However, awkwardness wasn't her only concern for the evening ahead of them. There was something happening between her and Aidan that was separate from the role she had played in his father's life. There was a strong sexual attraction that had begun the first day he had stood outside Braxton's window.

Jessie knew she shouldn't be surprised it was there. Aidan was not only handsome, he radiated a lethal combination of sensitivity and masculine determination. It was a combination most women would find impossible to resist, and Jessie knew that she was no different from any other woman when it came to being attracted to the opposite sex.

All day long she expected him to show up at the window, but there was no sign of him until just before closing. And then it was only to briefly smile and wave at her before ducking into the store.

To Jessie's relief, Devony was going out with Nick after work and didn't hang around long enough to notice that her partner wasn't pulling on her old sweats, but a black turtleneck sweater and stretch pants. A mustard woolen jacket added contrast as well as sophistication.

After removing her stage makeup, Jessie reapplied her own cosmetics and left her hair hanging straight rather than sweeping it into a ponytail. As she glanced at her reflection in the full-length mirror she wondered what kind of women Aidan usually dated. Short? Tall? Blond? Brunette? Redheaded?

From the look he gave her when he saw her, she decided that it didn't matter. He had a predatory look—the kind every man gets when he sees a woman he finds attractive. His look made Jessie's skin tingle, and it took a considerable amount of self-control for her to act as though she wasn't feeling the same reaction to his presence.

"Where are we going?" she asked, setting her purse on Fred's desk so she could slip on her coat.

"You won't need that," he told her, gesturing to her fulllength woolen jacket. "I made reservations at Angelina's."

On the same city block as Braxton's was a sleek new skyscraper hotel whose lobby opened onto the same courtyard shoppers often used to enter the department store. Jessie had heard Devony speak highly of its Italian restaurant, Angelina's, but she had never been there to see if it was as good as its reputation.

"No point in going out in the snow if we don't have to," Aidan told her, glancing out at the flurry of flakes. With a hand gently resting on her elbow, he guided her toward the atrium.

"You're not very fond of winter, are you?" she commented, the memory of him shivering in the cold coming to mind.

"It's not so bad, but I'd be lying if I said I didn't enjoy living in a warmer climate." He gestured for her to precede him as they stepped onto an escalator at the hotel. "After four years in southern California, I'm not exactly prepared for snow and ice."

"You don't miss the dramatic change of seasons?" she asked, trying to ignore the pleasurable sensations that traveled through her as his hand once again gently sought her waist.

"Not really, although Christmas without snow still doesn't seem quite right to me," he admitted with a warm, almost nostalgic smile that only added to the confusion inside Jessie.

"Don't you come home for the holidays?"

He shook his head in regret. "Been too busy to take time off."

Any further conversation was preempted as they reached the entrance to Angelina's. A formally dressed maître d' showed them to a secluded table draped with crisp white linen. As he held the chair for Jessie to be seated, she noticed the single long-stemmed red rose lying across her plate and her eyes automatically sought Aidan's.

Any question she had as to why he had invited her to dinner was answered by the look on his face. She carefully picked up the flower and sniffed its fragrance.

"This is lovely. Thank you," she said quietly.

"You're welcome," he said in a mellifluous voice that melted against her skin like butter on a hot biscuit. He waited until the maître d' was out of earshot, then added, "I'm glad you're here with me, Jessie."

The atmosphere was much too intimate for her comfort. Her pulse started to pick up speed, so she steered the conversation away from the personal. "Tell me about California . . . why you like living there."

"You need to ask that when six months out of the year you can't venture outdoors without heated socks and thermal underwear?" he quipped.

"It's not that bad," she gently chided, unable to resist smiling at the image of him in long johns and electric socks.

"Twenty degrees below zero and a sixty-below windchill is bad," he insisted, his face twisting into a wry grimace. "It seems much colder than I remember. Maybe my blood's thinned or something."

She grinned. "You've just been spoiled by the warm California sun." And blessed, she added silently, noting how his skin boasted a healthy glow from living in the warmer climate.

His "Could be" was accompanied by a grin and a shrug.

"Are you planning to go back soon?"

"I'm not sure. Do you want me to leave?" he asked in the direct manner she was coming to expect from him. Suddenly there were undercurrents in the conversation.

She was excused from having to answer by the arrival of their waiter—a young man dressed in a black tuxedo who serenaded them with an operatic version of the menu. His performance lightened the atmosphere and eased the tension that was slowly creeping into their conversation.

To Jessie's relief, Aidan changed the subject once the waiter had gone. "Have you lived in Minnesota all of your life?"

"Mmm-hmm. I grew up in Morrison County on a dairy farm about a hundred miles north of here."

"A dairy farm?"

"You look surprised. Don't I look like a farm girl?"

"Not quite."

Jessie chuckled. "Come visit the farm when I'm mucking out the barn."

"I guess then you probably know how to milk a cow."

"And goats, too. I competed in lots of 4-H competitions at the county fairs. Of course, the milking on the farm s done by machines. It's been quite a while since I've sat on a milking stool.''

He tried to picture her in bib overalls sitting on a wooden stool, her long slender fingers squeezing the teats of a Guernsey, but the image escaped him. "So you really do come from hardy stock."

"The Paulsons are a pretty sturdy lot. They have to be, or else they wouldn't have been able to hang on to the farm as long as they have."

Aidan liked the way she looked when she relaxed. Gone was the haughtiness she usually presented to the world. In its place was a warmth that made her blue eyes sparkle with interest.

"It can't be easy being a farmer nowadays," Aidan commented soberly. Their salads had arrived and she was focusing on the plate in front of her rather than him.

"It probably never has been easy. Not many people would be willing to work ninety to a hundred hours a week, get up at four-thirty every morning and give up their summer vacation year after year to run a business."

"No, I don't imagine they would," he agreed, hearing the pride in her voice as she talked about a subject dear to her heart. "So how does being in the city compare to life on the farm?"

"It's like being in two different worlds," she answered, lifting her eyes to his.

"And which do you prefer?"

"There are advantages to both, which is why I compromised and moved in with my grandmother in Delano," she told him, breaking a bread stick in two. "I can still work in the city and enjoy all the conveniences, but it's a small enough town and far enough away from the urban sprawl that it feels like I'm in the country."

"Delano...isn't that about thirty miles from here?"

"Yes, it's straight out Highway 12."

"It's still a rather long commute to Braxton's," he observed. "Wouldn't it be easier to have an apartment in town?"

"Probably, but I don't mind the drive," she answered. "I had an apartment in Minneapolis when I first came to the city, but I like living with my grandmother much better."

"Have you lived anywhere else?"

She shook her head. "Right after I graduated from high school I went to the university—the St. Paul campus."

"The college of Home Economics?"

Again she shook her head. "Agriculture. I was in the nutrition science program for a while," she answered, spreading butter on one half of the bread stick. "Only, about halfway through the program I discovered it wasn't what I wanted to do, so I decided to quit school and get a job."

"Is that when you decided to pursue a career as a model?"

"Oh, no." She punctuated her answer with a laugh. "I never dreamed I'd be modeling some day."

"So how did you end up as a mannequin?"

"I guess you could say it was a case of being in the right place at the right time. After I left college I went to work as a receptionist at an advertising agency."

"And a talent agent walked in the front door and decided you'd be perfect as a store mannequin?"

"Not quite," she told him, taking a sip of wine before continuing. "It was an art director, and it wasn't me he was noticing, but my hands." She lifted them for his perusal. "He said they were exactly what he needed for his current project. So I auditioned, everyone liked the results, and the rest is, as they say, history."

"And that's how you got started—working as a hand model?" he repeated in amused wonder.

"Mmm-hmm. Holding pies and cakes for a cookbook. Before long I was doing display ads for jewelry and then television commercials for pizza."

Aidan reached over to take one of her hands in his. "I'm not surprised," he said, studying it as if it were fine china. "I'd buy a product this hand was selling. It's perfect."

"Not quite, but close enough to fool the camera," she answered, easing the slender fingers from his grasp. She immediately reached for the wineglass and raised it to her lips.

Aidan's eyes followed the elegant hand's progress, watching the flawless fingers wrap themselves around the crystal stem. Like the rest of her, her hands fascinated him, firing his imagination with all sorts of fantasies.

"Have any of your other body parts worked alone?" he asked with a devilish grin.

"No. My feet aren't the right size and my legs are too bony," she answered. "It's either my hands or all of me."

At this point Aidan wanted to say he'd take all of her, but refrained from making the remark. "What happens when the holidays are over and Braxton's no longer has a need for Santa and his elves?"

"I'll be moving across the street to Renae's Bridal Salon. Instead of dressing as an elf, I'll be a bride."

"In the window?"

"Yes. There'll be three mannequins, but I'll be the only live one."

"A model bride, eh? Won't there be a model groom to hold your hand?"

"Not according to my agent. Of course, they could spring one on me at the last minute."

Seeing that her glass was nearly empty, Aidan reached for the bottle of wine. "Have you ever been a bride, Jessie?" he asked, keeping his eyes on the glass as he poured.

"Hundreds of times," she answered, deliberately misunderstanding him.

He lifted his eyes. "I mean in real life."

"Only once in real life." She took a bite of a bread stick, but her gaze didn't falter from his. "You already knew that, didn't you?"

"It was in Will Lepley's juror profiles," he admitted with a sheepish lift of his brows. "I guess marital status is one of those statistics that shows up everywhere."

"Yes, well, during the juror interviews Mr. Lepley used that statistic to imply that my divorce left me hating men in general."

"Did it?"

"Only one in particular, and since he's of no consequence in my life anymore, I guess it doesn't really matter," she said easily—too easily for Aidan not to wonder if she really believed it.

"I take it the guy was a jerk," he surmised with a knowing grimace.

"Actually, most people like him, but then again most people don't know him the way I do." She couldn't keep the bitterness from her voice. "He's a tennis pro who believes marriage is just a game. Unfortunately, we weren't playing by the same set of rules."

"What are your rules for marriage?" he asked, leaning closer to her so she caught the scent of his after-shave.

"Fidelity is at the top of the list," she stated, a hint of a warning in her voice.

"I've never been married, but I would think that should be the number-one rule in any marriage," he told her, meeting her gaze.

Jessie was grateful for the reappearance of the singing waiter. The conversation had been much too personal, and she had revealed more than she had intended. As soon as the waiter had moved on, she decided to steer the conversation away from her private life and ask about his.

"Tell me about your work. What does a management consultant do?"

"In simple terms, teach people how to manage their employees. A company will hire me to evaluate its management strategies and then make suggestions for improvement."

"Sort of like a fix-it man?"

He smiled. "Sort of. People do hire me to fix any problems they have, but that's only one aspect of our business. We also give seminars and workshops on management techniques."

"And is business booming?"

"Actually, we have more business than we can handle, which is why I should be back in California helping my partner instead of here in Minnesota."

"I'm a bit surprised you are still here. I thought you would have returned by now."

"Until the doctors give us the word my father's going to be okay, I want to be here—for my mother's sake, of course," he answered.

Jessie wanted to ask about his father, but every time his name was mentioned there was a tightening in his features and she decided it was safer to ask about the woman who could make his dark brown eyes soften with tenderness.

"How is your mother holding up through all of this?"

"Better than I expected. Truthfully, I don't know how she keeps going."

"She must be a strong woman."

"One has to be tough to live with my father," he said with a derisive tilt of his brows. Seeing Jessie wince, he added, "You heard the testimony. It's hard not to be angry with my father after everything he's put my mother through this past year."

Although there was a gentleness in his eyes, Jessie couldn't help but notice there was an edge to his voice. As much as she wanted to avoid the subject of his father, she needed to find out what was happening.

"How is your father?"

"The doctors are optimistic. If he continues to improve, he should be back in prison before long," he said brusquely.

Guilt ricocheted through her conscience. "I'm sorry."

"You have nothing to be sorry about, Jessie," he told her, his eyes warming as they met hers.

Jessie knew that this was her opportunity to tell him that she was having doubts as to his father's guilt. "Aidan, there's something I need to tell you about the trial."

She licked her lower lip and took a deep breath, but before she could continue he reached across the table and stilled her fidgeting fingers.

"Jessie, don't apologize for doing what you thought was right. Every time the subject of the trial comes up there's this awkwardness between us, and I don't want it to be there."

"Maybe it's unrealistic to think it can be any other way," she suggested.

"No, I don't believe that and I hope you don't, either," he said firmly. "To be perfectly honest with you, Jessie, my father and I haven't exactly seen eye to eye in the past few years. Even before the trial there were problems between us."

"Your family appeared to be very close during the trial," she commented.

"That was the image we were supposed to present. Will Lepley wanted us to look like your all-American, happy family," he said mockingly. "We're hardly the Cleavers." He made a disgusted sound and said, "I'd say we're more like the Simpsons."

"It's only natural that there'd be some stress in your lives considering your father's situation," Jessie said diplomatically. "Sometimes crisis can bring a family closer together."

"Not in this instance," he said cynically. "Our family life has been splattered across the front page of every newspaper in this area."

"It must have been a terrible experience for all of you." Her eyes warmed to his with compassion.

He heaved a long sigh. "It wasn't so bad for Sean and me, but my mother was the one who suffered. I'm just glad that it's over and we can finally put it all behind us... at least, we should be able to if Will Lepley's hunches are right."

"Isn't there going to be an appeal?" Jessie held her breath, waiting for his answer. One of the reasons she hadn't come forward about her doubts as to the verdict was that she had assumed Tom McCullough's attorneys would file an appeal.

"Just because there's an appeal doesn't necessarily mean another trial will be granted," he answered, and Jessie's nerves began to dance. "The attorneys are waiting for the trial transcripts to be released and then they'll start writing their briefs."

"You don't seem very optimistic," she commented, hoping he would contradict her. He didn't.

"Will Lepley is one of the top criminal lawyers in the state, but he himself has admitted he doesn't have much to go on," he answered soberly.

"I'm sorry." Again she apologized, unable to think of anything else to say.

"Don't apologize every time the subject of the trial comes up, Jessie. You didn't do anything wrong." There was a sharpness in his voice that added to Jessie's discomfort.

She wanted to tell him that yes, she had done something wrong. She had voted guilty when she should have voted not guilty. She wanted to mention the feeling she had—the one that grew stronger with each passing day, the one that told her Tom McCullough was innocent. But she didn't.

Once more the waiter appeared, and talk of the trial ceased. During dinner their conversation centered around their tastes in books and movies, and to Jessie's surprise she discovered they agreed on many and argued about few. The rest of the evening passed quickly, and before she knew it they were the only two customers left in the restaurant.

A discreet cough by their waiter alerted them to the fact that everyone else had gone home. "I didn't realize it was so late," Jessie said apologetically.

"I enjoyed this evening," Aidan said, coming around to her side of the table to help her up.

"I did, too, Aidan. Thank you," she said sincerely, conscious of the fact that he didn't drop her hand as they walked out of the restaurant.

He insisted on seeing her home. He escorted her to her car, climbing into the passenger side so she could drive him to the spot where he was parked. Jessie expected him to kiss her good-night, but he simply touched her cheek with the back of his fingers and said, "You're a good listener, Jessie." Then he climbed into his white Lincoln and followed her all the way to Delano, making sure she was safely inside her grandmother's before driving away.

JESSIE EXPECTED AIDAN to turn up at the window sometime during her shift the next day, but there was no trace of him anywhere in the crowd. She wanted to think that his absence was due to the fact that it was Saturday and he hadn't been working at his father's office.

However, when Monday came and went with no sign of him, she began to think that he had been disappointed in their date. When he didn't show up on Tuesday, she concluded that she had definitely misread his interest in her.

On the Wednesday before Christmas the line to see Santa outside the window was longer than usual, despite the wintry weather conditions. Blustery cold winds and frigid temperatures didn't deter shoppers. Jessie had to smile at the bundled-up children who had barely any skin exposed between the knit caps and the woolen scarves.

Standing in the midst of three-feet-tall people who seemed to be all eyes and no faces was Aidan. He didn't wear a hat, his collar was turned up close to his jaw, and a pair of sunglasses covered his eyes.

When he finally reached the Santa phone his cheeks were cherry red and his lips were starting to turn blue.

"You're going to get frostbite," were Jessie's first words to him. "You'd better get inside."

"Can elves take sleigh rides on their coffee breaks?" he asked, nodding toward the mall where a horse-drawn sleigh was carrying shoppers up and down Nicollet Avenue. Actually, it wasn't a real sleigh with runners, but a wagon that had been converted so it would work on the city streets.

"This elf can't take a break until her shift ends at nine," Jessie replied apologetically.

"The sleigh's only running until five-thirty. Can't you get off early?"

She lifted her hand in a helpless gesture. "Sorry. Besides, you're not dressed for a sleigh ride."

He gave her a look of disappointment. "I'd better go. The kids are getting restless." He had barely said goodbye when the two boys behind him nearly bowled him over scrambling to get to the Santa phone. Aidan grimaced, then waved at Jessie as he pushed his way toward the department store's revolving door.

Jessie didn't see him the rest of the afternoon and hoped that he would be waiting at the guard desk when she was finished. When she rounded the corner and saw only Fred sitting at the exit, she was surprised at how disappointed she felt.

"How are you doing, Jessie?" the burly guard asked as he rose from his desk.

"I'm all right, Fred. How about you?" Jessie automatically started toward the door leading to the parking ramp, but he stopped her.

"I can't let you out that door tonight," he told her, searching through his ring of keys. "We need to use the Tenth Street entrance."

Puzzled, she asked, "But what about my car?"

"Don't worry about your car," he said with good humor. "Has good old Fred ever not made sure that you were escorted to your car?"

Jessie gave him an affectionate grin and followed him to the store's north entrance, which was on the corner of Tenth and Nicollet. As soon as Fred pushed open the heavy glass door she saw the reason he had been grinning. Just outside was the horse-drawn sleigh that had been carrying shoppers up and down the mall all afternoon. Waiting to help her climb aboard was Aidan.

A smile of delight spread across her face.

"Want to go for a ride, Jessie?" he asked with a charming grin that made her feel warm all over.

"You'd better say yes," Fred whispered in her ear. "It cost him an arm and a leg to get that fellow to work past five-thirty."

Jessie didn't want to say no. Evening had settled on the mall and thousands of tiny white bulbs twinkled from bare branches. Large, fluffy flakes of snow were gently falling from the darkened sky, and Christmas carols blared from loudspeakers on the lampposts.

Jessie offered him her hand.

"I haven't done this since I was a kid," Aidan told her as he eagerly helped her climb up onto the sleigh.

"Are you sure you're up to this? I wouldn't want you to get cold," she said saucily as he sat beside her on the wooden bench seat.

"I can think of a few ways to keep warm," he answered with a devilish grin, and Jessie's heartbeat accelerated. "This will help." He reached down to pick up a green-and-navy plaid lap robe, which he spread across their legs. "We should also sit close together and make the most of our body heat," he added, slipping his arm around her shoulder and drawing her closer to him.

Jessie didn't resist, but leaned into his warm embrace, thinking how strange it was to be riding down the Nicollet Mall in a horse-drawn sleigh.

"Well, what do you think?" he asked as the sleigh slowly made its way down the street trimmed with green garlands and the twinkling lights.

"I've never been in a sleigh with wheels," she confessed, enjoying the sound of horses' hooves clopping on the street.

"It's a city sleigh," Aidan told her. "What you need to do is imagine you're in the country traveling across fields of freshly fallen snow under a starry sky."

Jessie leaned back to look up at the sky but saw only glass and metal. "I think I just got hit in the eye by a star," she said as a drifting snowflake caused her to blink. She looked at Aidan, who was trying not to shiver as the wind picked up in intensity and started whipping icy flakes against their faces.

"And to think only yesterday I was walking around in shirt sleeves," Aidan said with a sigh of longing.

"Were you in California?"

He nodded. "I left last Saturday and returned this morning. Some urgent business came up that needed my attention."

Despite the cold, Jessie glowed inside. The reason he hadn't been by Braxton's had nothing to do with not wanting to see her.

"How long can you stay before you have to return again?" she asked, trying not to sound too interested in his answer.

"Through New Year's Day." He took her hand in his. Even though they were both wearing gloves, she could feel his fingers rubbing hers.

"Did you decide to spend the holidays with your mother?"

"That's only part of the reason why I came back," he said, his face close to hers so she could feel the warmth of his breath on her lips. "I wanted to stay away...I tried to stay away from you, Jessie, but I can't."

Jessie found it difficult to swallow. Not one to be coy, she simply said, "I'm glad you're back."

A gust of wind loosened a long strand of hair from her ponytail and he reached up to push it away from her face.

Then, with the snow gently falling, Christmas music playing in the background and lights twinkling around them, he kissed her.

He took his time, sliding his mouth over hers until he felt her respond. The heat that had been centered in her lower body was slowly building and spreading through each and every one of Jessie's bundled-up limbs.

Even though his hands touched no flesh, just the thought of what they would be like on her body made her weak with longing. She felt his mouth at her temple and then near her ear, searching and tasting.

''Whoa.'' It was neither Jessie nor Aidan who ended the embrace, but the driver of the sleigh.

Both of them looked at the man who had brought them to a halt at the same spot where their journey had begun. He was sitting a bit hunched over, nonchalantly waiting for the two of them to climb down.

''I think the ride's over,'' Jessie said huskily.

Aidan helped her from the sleigh, then spoke briefly to the driver, who tipped his hat and departed. Seconds later a large city bus pulled up to the curb, spewing forth a cloud of dark and smelly exhaust fumes.

Aidan looked at Jessie apologetically. ''Back to reality.''

She gave him a half smile, and for several moments they stood staring at each other, until he said, ''How about dinner? I know a *warm,* quiet little place not far from here.''

She didn't answer right away, for she was still trying to come to terms with the new emotions rushing around inside her heart. It had been a long time since she had made love with a man and she knew that if she was wise she would take things slowly where Aidan McCullough was concerned.

But desire had stirred in her, and for the first time in a long time she had found a man she really wanted to get to know better. So instead of saying no, she said, "That would be nice. I'd like to have dinner with you."

"Great." His response was accompanied by the sexiest grin she had ever seen on a man. It made her forget all her reservations about Aidan McCullough.

CHAPTER NINE

AIDAN TOOK JESSIE to a restaurant on the banks of the Mississippi that smelled of hot spices and barbecue sauce. As he had warned, the decor was almost bare-bone essentials—there were no linen tablecloths, formal place settings or flower centerpieces, just paper place mats on wooden tabletops scarred from years of use, stainless-steel forks and knives and candles burning inside amber globes.

It was exactly the kind of place Jessie wanted to be in considering she was wearing a pair of leggings and a baggy woolen sweater. It also had the best barbecued ribs she had ever tasted and a breezy atmosphere that allowed her to completely relax with Aidan.

Not once during the evening did they talk of the trial—much to Jessie's relief. Instead, they spoke about their childhoods, comparing their experiences growing up on a farm and in the city. Jessie discovered that despite their differences there was something intangible that connected them and she knew it wasn't simply sexual attraction.

During the next few days she spent most of her free time with him. They went to the movies to see a romantic comedy that had Aidan squeezing her hand as they laughed at the same scenes. He took her to Orchestra Hall to hear a holiday concert featuring a local college choir. And two days before Christmas he took her shopping so that she could help him select a gift for his mother.

"What are we looking for?" Jessie asked as they entered the crowded shopping mall. "Jewelry? Clothing? Perfume?"

"I'd like to give her something she can wear...like maybe a sweater?" he answered, a hint of a question in his tone.

"I think that's a great idea. I know several places we can look," Jessie told him, slipping her arm through his and steering him toward an escalator. "What's her favorite color?"

Aidan's grin was sheepish. "I'm not really sure, but she does wear a lot of navy blue."

Jessie recalled the times she had seen Helen McCullough in the courtroom and agreed. She led him to an exclusive boutique featuring imported woolens and in no time they were shown a variety of sweaters.

"What do you think?" Jessie held up a long white cardigan for Aidan's approval. "She could wear this with slacks or use it as a jacket for a dress. And it goes well with navy blue."

He eyed the sweater critically, stroking it with his fingers. "It's soft, isn't it?"

"That's because it's a blend of wool and mohair," the salesclerk explained, then pulled out several other sweaters, but in the end Aidan went along with Jessie's suggestion.

After having his package gift wrapped in silver foil and trimmed with a red velvet ribbon, Aidan moved purposefully toward another lane of the mall. "I always give my mother a box of truffles," he said as a candy store came into view. "She has a weakness for chocolate."

"Doesn't everyone?" Jessie tossed him a knowing grin. "I have absolutely no willpower once I get a whiff of the aroma in that store."

Amusement danced in Aidan's eyes as he urged her into the shop. "I think you can afford to give in to a little temptation. What's your favorite?" he asked as they stood in front of the glass case surveying the chocolate confections.

"It's a toss-up between the Turtles," Jessie answered, pointing to the chocolate-covered caramel-and-pecan candies on the lower shelf, "and the fudge." She looked dreamily toward the slab of dark chocolate at the opposite end of the case.

"We have samples," the salesclerk told them, gesturing toward a small glass dome on the counter where a dozen miniature squares were arranged on a silver serving tray.

"Ooh," Jessie crooned, reaching for a piece of the creamy smooth chocolate. "Umm...this is wonderful," she announced with a sigh, licking her fingertips as she glanced at Aidan. "You'd better try a piece."

Aidan reached for a sliver and offered it to her. "Here. You can have mine."

"You don't want it?" she asked in disbelief.

"I can't eat chocolate."

"You *can't* eat chocolate?"

"Uh-uh. I'm allergic to it."

"Oh, you poor man!" she crooned in sympathy, cheerfully polishing off his piece. "He doesn't know what he's missing," she said to the clerk, who simply shook her head and murmured, "What a shame."

"Well, what's it going to be? The Turtles or the fudge?" Aidan asked as the salesclerk waited for their order.

Jessie eyed the confections covetously. "I think I'd better pass on the Turtles and go with one small piece of fudge."

Aidan relayed her request to the clerk, who cut a generous portion of fudge from the slab.

"That's not exactly a small piece," Jessie murmured to Aidan.

"Whatever you don't eat now you can take home with you," he reasoned, then ordered an assortment of truffle for his mother.

By the time they reached the parking ramp the fudge wa gone. Aidan pretended not to notice, although Jessie wa certain he had.

As he drove her home she thought about how quickly she had become comfortable being around him. In just a few short days she had gone from being edgy in his presence to being completely at ease with him. Part of it was because he was a very easy man to talk to...so easy that she had told him more about herself than she normally told close friends.

Having been through a divorce, Jessie had vowed to be pragmatic when it came to men. She had learned to proceed slowly and think carefully about the consequences of any relationship.

However, with Aidan she found herself constantly tempted to ignore her intellect and let her emotions take charge. They were growing closer, and she knew that if they continued to see each other it wouldn't be long before their relationship would move on to a more intimate level. It was a step she needed to consider carefully.

That was why every time she saw him, she searched for a flaw in his character, hoping to find something that would put a halt to her growing attraction to him. She found nothing.

Except for the fact that he had a strained relationship with his father, there was little to criticize. And after all, his father *had* hurt his mother by having an affair. Unfortunately, it was partly because of his father that they would probably never have the opportunity to see if their relationship could develop into something more serious.

Consequently, she was a bit relieved to be going home for Christmas, far away from the charm of Aidan McCullough. She needed to put her feelings for him into perspective, and she couldn't think of a better place to do that than at the farm, where serenity and common sense prevailed.

ONLY, THE HOLIDAYS WERE not exactly serene in Harding. Nor was she able to forget about Aidan. When she arrived at the farm she was greeted by her mother, who promptly informed her a special delivery package had come for her.

Since she and Gran were the last ones to arrive for the holiday celebration, her entire family was present when she opened the parcel. Inside were two more boxes, each gold with a red satin ribbon.

Without even opening the enclosed card, Jessie knew who had sent them. A warmth spread through her from head to toe as a dozen pairs of eyes watched her fumble with the packages.

"Who are they from?" Carla demanded impatiently.

Jessie's fingers trembled as she pulled the small enclosure card from its envelope. In one corner of the business-size card was an embossed sprig of holly. But it was the bold, dark handwriting that held Jessie's attention.

"Since I can't be with you this Christmas, here's a little temptation. Aidan." Jessie silently read the greeting.

"Well, who's it from?" Carla repeated.

"It's . . . it's from a friend of mine. His name is Aidan," Jessie answered, tucking the card into her pocket.

"A friend, huh?" Carla studied her sister with obvious curiosity.

Before Jessie could answer, Gran spoke up. "He's that young man she met in the hospital the day I went to visit my friend Lorraine."

"You met a guy in the hospital? What is he—a doctor?" Carla asked.

"He's such a nice boy. Very polite. And tall, like Jessie," Gran announced to the room.

"How long have you been dating him?" Jessie's mother joined in the interrogation and Jessie began to fidget.

"We've only gone out a few times," she said on a note of boredom, trying to downplay their relationship.

"It must be somewhat serious if Gran's already met him," Carla remarked, and Jessie was grateful when her six-year-old niece, Kelly, tugged on her shirt sleeve.

"Aren't you going to see what's inside?" she asked in a child's voice of innocence, her small finger pointing to the boxes.

"Good idea," Jessie answered, untying the red ribbons. Inside one of the boxes was a large slab of fudge, which drew several "ahs" of appreciation from her family.

"Wow! Look at how big those Turtles are!" Jessie's twelve-year-old nephew, Chad, exclaimed when she removed the second lid. "Can I have one?"

"Chad!" Jessie's brother-in-law, Gene, quickly reprimanded his son. "Those are Auntie Jess's candies, not yours."

"No, it's all right," Jessie insisted. "There's enough here for everyone." She was about to pass the candy around when Gene stopped her.

"They're not going to eat their dinners if they start in on the candy."

Jessie shoved the boxes in her mother's direction. "You can be in charge of these."

"I'll put them in one of my candy dishes," Mrs. Paulson said, reaching for the boxes.

That brought a groan from several of the children, who knew that their grandmother's candy dishes were off-limits until after dinner had been served.

"So, come on, Jessie. What gives? Tell me about this new guy in your life," Carla urged as the female members of the family prepared the dinner table.

"Really, Carla. There's not much to tell. We've had dinner a couple of times—"

"She saw him every night this past week," Gran interrupted as she walked past with a loaf of rye bread.

"So what does he look like?"

Jessie shrugged. "Tall, dark hair, mustache. Just a regular-looking guy."

"It's not that guy you saw in the restaurant that night Missy and I were with you?" she probed, a frown puckering her brow.

"Yes," Jessie admitted begrudgingly, then escaped to the kitchen when Carla gushed, "Ooh, he's cute."

But the kitchen was no haven for Jessie. In between barking out orders her mother managed to say, "You could have invited your young man to dinner."

"I don't know him that well, Mom," Jessie said, then buried her head in the refrigerator.

"So when do we get to meet him?" Carla asked over her shoulder.

Jessie straightened, balancing a jar of pickled herring, a block of goat cheese and a pitcher of cream in her hands. "Did I do this to you when you were dating Gene?"

"Do what?"

Jessie simply looked at her sister and groaned in exasperation. It was a relief when Gran announced that dinner was ready.

Along with the traditional American stuffed turkey, a platter of *lutefisk*, boiled fish, strewn with melted butter was served with mashed potatoes and *lefse*. As all thirteen of them crowded around a table that should have seated twelve, a sense of closeness and of caring permeated the dining room that had been the site of Paulson celebrations for over a hundred years. Even Missy appeared to relax during the meal, perhaps picking up on the happiness that everyone seemed to feel.

As the food was passed around the table, the same comments Jessie had heard all of her life filled the room. None of the younger Paulsons could understand Gran's penchant for *lutefisk*, nor could Gran understand how the young folks could ruin the taste of her *lefse* by adding sugar.

Jessie sampled everything, smiling as her grandmother told stories of what Christmas had been like for her as a child. They were stories she had heard many times over, but she cherished the expression on her grandmother's face as she spoke of her Norwegian heritage, especially the lighting of the Christmas tree.

"As soon as dinner was completed, my aunt and uncle would go into the parlor and shut the doors," Gran told them, her eyes twinkling wistfully. "All of the children had to wait patiently in the dining room so that none of us would see them lighting the red candles on the tree."

"Did you know what they were doing?" Kelly asked.

"*Ja,* that's what made it so exciting. We knew that as soon as they opened the doors the Norwegian spruce tree that was as tall as the ceiling would be aglow."

"What else did you put on the tree?" Missy asked, even though everyone seated at the table already knew the answer.

"There'd be tiny Norwegian flags, small apples, colored paper chains and little heart-shaped baskets filled with nuts and raisins," Gran answered, relishing the memories. "But it was what was underneath the tree that had all of us so excited."

"The presents?" Kelly's eyes widened at the thought.

"That's right. Everyone gathered around while the littlest of the cousins played gift bearers."

"Just like we do?" Kelly again spoke up.

"*Ja,* just like you do. Only back then Christmas gifts were not bought at a shop, but were made at home. New mittens or a scarf...maybe a dress." A tiny tinkling laugh accompanied her grin.

As the stories continued, other members of the family contributed their memories of Christmases gone by. Voices were happy, full of caring as the holiday spirit pulled everyone together in a special way that only occurred at this time of year. All problems and disappointments seemed to fade into insignificance.

By the fourth day of her visit, however, Jessie was beginning to notice some undercurrents of tension among her family. Despite the festive spirit, she sensed an anxiety pervading the atmosphere. There was an edge to her father's voice, and even her mother lacked her usual good nature. Jessie suspected the cause was related to the farm, but was uncertain how to approach the subject without offending her parents.

She finally decided the best way to get to the heart of the matter was to talk to her brother, Jim, who had become her father's partner after graduating from college. He and his wife, Mary, had bought the small farm bordering the Paulson land and had gone into partnership with her parents to make Pine Crest one of the largest and most successful dairy farms in the county.

Waking early one morning, Jessie pulled on an old parka and a pair of rubber boots, then headed out to the barn where she knew Jim would be milking. As she tramped across the packed snow, the lighted windows of the white-washed barn beamed out a welcome to her, reminding her of other mornings when as a child she had staggered out of bed before the sun had even peeked over the horizon to help her father with the milking. Now the muffled sounds of cattle grunting and groaning gently called her back to her roots, to those days when life had seemed so simple.

Before she had even stepped inside the barn, the scent of hay and cattle teased her nostrils. For Jessie it had never been an unpleasant odor but an honest smell that spoke of hard work.

The first person she saw when she entered the building was her seventeen-year-old nephew, Erik, who was coaxing one of the Guernseys into its stall. Tall and lean, he reminded Jessie of Jim when he had been that age.

"I see Candy still hasn't learned which stall is hers, has she?" Jessie commented, giving the cow a gentle pat on the head.

"I don't think it's ever going to change, Auntie Jess. Candy comes in and moseys into Delilah's stall, backs up and out, and then goes into her own. She does the same thing twice a day," Erik explained.

"I know. It's been going on for years. I suppose it doesn't matter as long as Delilah doesn't get to her stall first," Jessie said with a knowing grin. "Where's your dad?"

"He's over there," he said with a gesture toward the far end of the barn.

Jessie could see her brother's lanky form crouched beside a Guernsey. As she walked down the aisle, one of the barn cats followed close on her heels.

"Good morning," Jessie called out, and Jim glanced up at her.

"What are you doing up so early?" he asked, returning his attention to the Guernsey.

"I couldn't sleep so I thought I might as well get dressed and help out," Jessie answered, bending to scratch the cat. It put her at eye level with her brother.

"Mom could probably use your help in the kitchen and then you wouldn't have to get dirty," he told her.

"You never used to worry about me getting dirty when we were kids," she reminded him. "Quite the opposite if I remember correctly."

They shared a nostalgic smile, then he asked, "Why couldn't you sleep?"

"I've been worrying about you and Dad," she said, coming straight to the point.

"Me and Dad?" He cocked an eyebrow.

"There's no use in pretending there's nothing wrong. I can tell by the way the two of you have been looking at each other that something's going on, and I want to know what it is."

He didn't answer right away, but continued working for several moments before saying, "I told Dad I thought I should get a job."

"You want to quit farming?"

"Not quit, Jess. I could never quit," he said with a quiet determination. "I want to hold on to the farm…keep it so that a fourth generation of Paulsons will be farming in the future." He glanced toward Erik, who was at the opposite end of the barn.

"Are you saying you need to get a job to subsidize farm income?" she asked, her voice a mixture of concern and disbelief.

"The majority of farmers in this area work, Jess. They have to if they want to keep their land." He finished hooking up the Guernsey, then rose to his feet.

Jessie stood, too. "But Pine Crest has always been one of the most successful farms in this county."

"And it will be again if milk prices ever go up to where they should be. But for right now, our income has been cut and our expenses keep going up." He moved on to the next cow and Jessie followed him.

"No wonder Dad's so upset."

"You know what his opinion is of farmers working."

She nodded in understanding. "The day I have to take a job to support my farm is the day I call it quits." The words she had heard so often over the past twenty-six years rolled off her lips with ease. "You're not considering selling, are you?"

"We don't need to sell. We just need some additional income."

Jessie sighed. "I knew milk prices were down and that times were tough, but I never guessed it would be this bad."

"It isn't just Pine Crest, Jessie. Anyone who says he's making a good living farming is a liar." An undertone of hostility crept into his voice.

Jessie folded her arms across her chest. "It's sad to see what's happening. Mom told me that the Emberson farm went up for sale last week."

"Farmers are getting tired of being the only businessmen in the world who have to buy retail and sell wholesale." This time there was no mistaking the bitterness in his voice.

"Are you tired of farming?" she asked, unaware that she was holding her breath as she waited for his answer.

"Frustrated would be a better word. Like I told you, Jess. I want my sons to take over this place some day, but unless there are better times ahead..." He trailed off in uncertainty.

"But Dad's talking about doubling the herd," she said, puzzled.

"That's his solution to our financial problems. But I think that if we double the herd we'll only be taking on more headaches." He adjusted his cap. "I'd rather get a job."

"And therein lies the problem," she concluded aloud, then sighed. "No wonder Dad's been so somber. It's a blow to his pride to think that you have to go to work to support the farm."

"I realize that, Jess, but what's more important? Pride or hanging on to the farm?" He didn't wait for her to answer, but continued. "I don't like it any more than Dad does, but I don't want to lose this place, either."

"Times have got to improve," Jessie said hopefully.

"We've been saying that for the last couple of years," he said cynically. "We're running out of time for a miracle."

"Where is Dad, anyway?" She looked up and down the aisle.

"He's out rounding up the rest of the herd," Jim said, referring to the cattle that were still needing to be milked.

Deciding to wait for him, Jessie plopped herself down on one of the cots in the rear of the barn. She stretched out her legs, pulling an old red blanket up over them, her thoughts on the conversation she had just had with her brother. Even though she no longer lived on the farm, she felt as if it were a part of her and she didn't want to consider that it might not be in the Paulson family some day.

There was something oddly comforting about this big old barn with its animals continually moving around, Jessie thought as she listened to the familiar sounds around her. Maybe it was because the cows weren't simply milk-producing machines. They were living, breathing creatures christened with names carefully selected to match their personalities. Three generations of Paulsons had cared for Guernseys with heartfelt husbandry.

A chill rippled through Jessie as she thought about the possibility of some big conglomerate buying out their family tradition. As a child she had often heard her father voicing his fear of corporations, with farm managers taking the place of the family farmers. Now she wasn't so sure that his fear wasn't grounded in reality.

As she stared up at the hayloft overhead, she thought about all the times she had played in the barn with her brother and sister. The hayloft had seen its share of laughter, including one particular night when she had been fifteen and had climbed the loft's rickety wooden steps with Dennis Emberson, the cutest boy in the sophomore class. It was in the hayloft that she had received her first kiss, not the most memorable experience of her life, but important in its own right.

Jessie closed her eyes and smiled as she thought about other childhood memories. It wasn't long before the soothing noises inside the barn had lulled her to sleep.

"JESS, THERE'S SOMEONE here to see you."

A hand on her shoulder gently nudged Jessie awake. She squinted in the bright stream of sunshine pouring in through the window. Partially blocking the sunlight was her brother's lanky frame, but it was the man behind him who caused her to scramble to her feet.

"Aidan!" His name came tumbling out in a tone that was somewhere between surprise and horror. "What are you doing here?"

"Hello, Jessie. I was on my way to St. Cloud so I thought I'd stop in and say hello," he said with the most handsome smile Jessie had ever seen.

"But St. Cloud is fifty miles from here."

"Fifty-three point five, to be exact," he said with an engaging grin.

Jessie stood staring at him in disbelief, unaware that her brother was moving out of sight. All she could see was an impeccably dressed businessman who looked as though he should be in a boardroom rather than a barn.

The white shirt and patterned tie peeking out of his cashmere overcoat reminded her that she was dressed in her usual farm outfit—faded blue jeans, a ragged sweatshirt covered in stains and an ugly old green army jacket. In one simple fashion statement, she was a joke.

To make matters worse, while she had been sleeping her woolen stocking cap had come off, and she could imagine the tangled mess her hair was in. Added to the fact that she wore no makeup and had on a big pair of rubber boots caked with mud and...

It didn't bear thinking about. She glanced down at his feet. "You shouldn't be in here. You're going to get mud and...and...farm...stuff all over your shoes," she stuttered.

"When your father said you were in the barn, I thought it would be an opportune time to see what a dairy barn looks like," he said, obviously amused by her appearance.

"You're not exactly dressed for a farm tour," she snapped, annoyed by his amusement.

"I'm willing to risk a little mud and stuff if you are," he drawled with a lecherous grin.

This was awful, Jessie thought. Why had he come? She was supposed to be forgetting about him, putting things into perspective and now here he was in her barn, looking gorgeously handsome and sending her emotions on a rocket ride.

She glanced at her watch, then said, "It's only nine-thirty. What time was your business meeting?"

"I haven't had it yet. It's later this afternoon. I came here first because I have a question to ask you."

He had driven all this way to ask her a question? She felt as if she was fifteen again and waiting for her first kiss in the hayloft. "You could have telephoned," she said, rubbing her palms on her thighs.

"It wouldn't have been the same," he said with a disarming smile that had her heart tumbling out of rhythm.

"You could have at least warned me you were coming. I'm not exactly dressed for company."

"It's a little different from what I'm used to seeing you wear," he said with a smile. "But I have to confess, I like the farmer's daughter look on you."

Jessie didn't want to look down for fear she'd see traces of the "farm stuff" she had avoided mentioning. It was one thing to be wearing old ratty clothes that were clean, quite another to be wearing ones splattered with manure.

"Why don't we go back to the house. If we're going to take a tour, you'd better borrow a pair of boots or else they won't want you in the meeting room this afternoon—business or no business," she told him.

Once they were inside the farmhouse Jessie saw that it was time for the morning coffee break. Seated around the kitchen table were her dad, Jim, Erik and a couple of hired hands, all ready to dig in to the basket of muffins and sweet rolls her mother had baked. Jessie introduced Aidan, then disappeared upstairs to shower and change.

When she came back down, all the men were gone except for Aidan, who had taken off his cashmere coat and was sitting at the table talking to her mother and her grandmother. Both women were captivated by what he was saying and didn't even notice her enter the room.

It was only when she cleared her throat that any of them looked up. "Sit down, Jessie. Aidan was just telling us about California," her mother said, her usually pale cheeks flushed with color.

Aidan stood to pull a chair out for her, and her grandmother said, "Has he told you about the time he stopped to help someone on the freeway who had a flat tire and it turned out to be a celebrity?" When Jessie indicated he hadn't, she said, "You're never going to guess who it was."

"Bob Hope?" Jessie said weakly, thinking there weren't many celebrities who could make her grandmother's cheeks turn pink in excitement.

"Oh, no!" Gran brushed away Jessie's answer with a flap of her hand. "It was Burt Reynolds! Can you imagine that?"

"And he had Loni Anderson in the car with him, too," her mother added, equally impressed. For Aidan's benefit she added, "She's originally from Minnesota, you know."

"As a matter of fact, I did know that," Aidan confessed, meeting Jessie's eyes.

"I hope Burt appreciated your help," she commented with a lift of one slender eyebrow.

"Oh, he did. As a matter of fact, as a way of saying thank-you he sent me tickets to some big celebrity charity event they were having in Hollywood," Aidan told them smoothly. "Only I didn't go."

"You didn't go?" both her mother and grandmother repeated in unison with a collective sigh.

"I couldn't. It was the same night as my partner's wedding. I did give the tickets to a friend, though, and he told me they were excellent seats, right down in front of the stage."

There were more sighs from her mother and grandmother. Jessie could hardly believe that these were the same two down-to-earth women who pooh-poohed any Hollywood gossip that appeared on TV and seldom went to the movie theater.

"We invited Aidan to stay for lunch, but he says he wants to take you out," her mother announced.

"There aren't many places around here where you can get a decent lunch," Jessie warned. It wasn't that she didn't want to eat at one of the local lunch counters, but she could just imagine the talk their presence would generate if Aidan were to stroll in dressed in his cashmere coat and Italian leather shoes.

Her mother clicked her tongue. "Now, that's not true, Jessie. This may not be the city but there are some fine cafés in Pierz," she gently scolded her daughter, then added for Aidan's benefit, "that's the next town over."

"Yes, and they serve home-cooked meals, not that fast-food junk," her grandmother added, and Jessie felt duly chastised. "The chili's quite good at Doreen's."

"But you'll want to go early," her mother advised, gathering the empty cups from the table. "She often runs out before the lunch hour's over."

"Actually, I already made reservations for lunch," Aidan said, getting to his feet.

She saw her mother and grandmother exchange curious looks. Each of them was wondering where in the world he was planning to eat that he needed reservations for lunch. Certainly not in Harding or Pierz.

"I was hoping to get a tour of the farm before we left." Aidan looked at Jessie, who was retrieving her jacket from the coat tree.

"It's awfully cold outside," she told him as he held the navy blue parka for her while she slid her arms into the sleeves.

"I'm willing to risk it if you are," he said close to her ear.

Jessie's heart raced at his nearness. "I'm not sure it's safe to take a farm tour dressed the way you are."

"I've always said, you never get anywhere by playing it safe." He gave her a devilish grin.

"Then we'll tour the farm," she said and tossed him a clunky old pair of rubber boots and the order, "Put these on."

Because it was winter, Jessie made it an abbreviated tour, explaining the basic operation of the farm and introducing him to the fundamentals of dairy farming. By the time they were through, he had a better understanding of milk prices and she had a glimpse into the insight that made him a management consultant.

As they drove the short distance into Harding, they talked about the difficulties the traditional family farm was facing. So caught up was she in her litany of frustrations on the subject, she didn't realize that they had passed through town without stopping.

"You missed Pierz," she told him as the big white Lincoln ate up miles on the country road.

"No, I saw it. I just didn't stop." He glanced sideways at her, a hint of amusement dancing in his eyes. "I thought we'd eat at a place I found a little farther down the road. You don't mind, do you?"

"No, but what about your meeting? Won't you be late?"

"It's not until this afternoon. We'll have plenty of time for lunch," he assured her, then changed the subject. "You haven't told me about your Christmas."

"Oh, it was nice," she replied, not wanting to tell him that it had been filled with stress and she had missed being with him. "Thank you for the chocolates. They were delicious."

"I'm glad you enjoyed them," he said in a velvety-smooth tone that made Jessie want to lean over and press her cheek up against his cashmere coat.

"How was your Christmas?" she asked, stifling the urge.

"Mine was nice, too."

Immediately Jessie was swamped with feelings of guilt. How could Christmas possibly be nice with your father in prison? Lingering in the back of her mind was the idea that had there been a different verdict, Tom McCullough would have spent his holiday with his family. She pushed such thoughts aside and asked, "Did your mother like the sweater you gave her?"

He smiled at her then. "Yes, and I'm sure she knew that I had help selecting it. She did everything but come out and ask me if I'm seeing someone."

She shot him a sideways glance. "You didn't tell her about me, did you?"

"No. I only said that I had met a model who posed as an elf in Braxton's window and that she had helped me pick out the gift."

"I'm glad that's all you told her," Jessie said on a note of relief.

"Why?"

"Why?" she repeated sarcastically. "Because I'm sure she had enough on her mind at Christmas without knowing that one of the women who sent her husband to jail helped pick out her Christmas gift."

"You're not the one who has caused her suffering, Jessie. My father is," he reminded her a bit more sharply than he intended, but he couldn't help himself. It angered him that the trial always managed to come between them. "I thought we were going to try to forget about the trial."

"How can I when every time you mention your family I think of the part I played in their lives?" she argued.

"You're not to blame for the problems my family's had face this past year," he stated firmly.

"Maybe we'd better change the subject," she suggested, her shoulders stiffening.

"That's fine with me," he agreed through narrow lips.

From that point on, their conversation centered around her family, the farm, the weather—all nice, comfortable social topics of conversation on a nice, comfortable social level. They were safe topics and Jessie was beginning to wonder what the big question was he needed to ask her. He certainly didn't seem to be in any big hurry.

Not once had he made so much as a flirtatious gesture toward her, and she was beginning to think that Jessie the farm girl didn't attract him the way Jessie the model did.

She found out how wrong she was just a few miles down the road when he pulled the car off the highway at a roadside rest.

"I didn't drive all the way up here to take you to lunch and talk about the price of milk," he said, removing his leather gloves and dropping them in his lap.

Prickles of awareness danced along the back of her neck. "I didn't think that you had."

He reached over and pulled her into his arms, tipping her face with one hand. Her body tingled in anticipation as he tenderly traced her cheekbone and the shape of her mouth before claiming her lips with his.

It was a long, slow, seductive kiss that made Jessie remember why she had needed time away from him. Her body was willing to forget that there were reasons she shouldn't give in to the desire he stirred in her.

When he finally lifted his mouth from hers, his breathing was as uneven as hers and the desire that burned inside her was shimmering in his eyes.

"That is why I didn't telephone," he murmured, his mustache tickling her lip. "I couldn't have done that over the phone." He kissed her once more, then said, "I've missed you."

Everything inside her was shaking, but she managed to say in a small voice, "It's only been four days."

"Are you sure? It seems much longer than that," he said, his eyes studying her face. "I went by Braxton's yesterday and there's a big sheet over the corner window."

"I'm on to new things," she said lightly, trying to ignore the weak sensation his fingers were creating as they wove themselves in her hair.

"I want to be one of those new things, Jessie," he growled close to her ear, planting a trail of tiny kisses on the warm flesh beneath the curtain of blond hair.

"I thought you were going back to California," she said weakly as his lips blazed a hot trail across her neck.

"Not for another week."

Jessie sighed as feelings stirred deep inside her, like smoldering embers coming to life with a fresh gust of wind. "But I'm staying in Harding till after New Year's."

"I was hoping I could convince you to come back with me." His lips found hers. "Tonight."

"I promised Gran I'd stay," she said, her voice now coming out in uneven breaths as his hand worked its way inside her jacket until it found the soft flesh beneath her sweater.

"And you don't think she'd understand if you said you wanted to go back a few days early?" His eyes met hers as his fingers found the hardened peaks of her breasts.

"I'm not sure I understand, Aidan," she told him, easing herself away from him. When she turned her head away from him he put a finger under her chin and guided it back.

"Maybe I don't, either, but I do know what's important and it's this." He cupped her face in his hands and kissed her, a deep, probing kiss that left little doubt as to his intentions.

Jessie responded to his caresses, pressing closer to him as she realized that his touch was what she had been missing, what she had been craving...what she had been afraid to admit she needed. She could feel her resolve weakening, and it was both frightening and exciting.

"There's something happening between us, Jessie, and I don't want to pretend it isn't there," he whispered against her lips.

"Neither do I, but I can't leave tonight," she told him, pressing her hands against his chest as a means of putting a halt to something that could easily get out of control.

He kissed her again and asked, "Can you be home for New Year's Eve?"

She could only nod.

Satisfaction gleamed in his yes. "How would you like to go to a party?"

Not one for crowds, Jessie seldom spent New Year's Eve on the town. However, the thought of being with Aidan was a temptation too great to resist. "I'd like that."

"Good." He smiled, then he kissed her, slowly and deliberately. When he finally lifted his mouth from hers there was no doubt in Jessie's mind that she had made the right decision.

CHAPTER TEN

As JESSIE EXPECTED, her mother sighed when she announced she wouldn't be spending New Year's Day with the family. Her grandmother, on the other hand, grinned—a silly little close-lipped grin that told Jessie she knew exactly why she had changed her plans.

Since Jessie wasn't going to be around for the family celebration, her mother suggested everyone come over for dinner on Jessie's last night at the farm. The party was smaller than usual, however, since her brother's family all had the flu and were unable to attend.

If Jessie had any regrets about cutting her holiday short, it was that she hadn't had any time to spend alone with her sister. When dinner was finished and only the cleanup remained, Jessie automatically joined Carla in the kitchen to help with the dishes.

From the little she had seen of Missy, Jessie knew that the relationship between Carla and her daughter hadn't improved. Missy had hardly been visible over the holidays, spending most of her time separated from the rest of the family. Neither Gene nor Carla commented on the fact that she was rather withdrawn, and Jessie wondered if they thought it was a typical teenage attitude.

When Missy didn't offer to help with the dishes, however, Carla did make an effort to draw the girl into the family circle. She shouted up the stairs several times, ordering the teenager to come down.

A few minutes later a pair of feet came bouncing down the stairs. Only they weren't Melissa's feet, but her brother's. From the scowl on Chad's face Jessie knew something was wrong.

"For Pete's sake, Mom. How long is Missy going to be in the bathroom?" he complained as he bounced into the kitchen. "Can't you make her come out?"

Trailing behind Chad was Kelly, who said, "I think she's throwing up."

"Oh, no! I hope she hasn't caught the flu that Jim's family has," Mrs. Paulson stated uneasily, worry creasing her forehead as she looked up over the rims of her glasses.

"I'd better go up and check on her," Carla said, untying her apron. "Chad, pick up a towel and help Auntie Jess," she ordered on her way out of the kitchen.

"But Ma, the football game's on," he protested with a groan.

"It won't hurt you to miss a few minutes," Carla retorted before disappearing up the stairs.

Again Chad groaned, making a face at the offensive dish towel Jessie dangled from her finger. Before he could reach for it, her mother said, "You don't need to help, Chad. You can go watch the game with the rest of the men."

Chad quickly escaped, tossing a "Thanks, Grandma" over his shoulder.

"You know, Mom, it wouldn't hurt to have a couple of your grandsons out here helping with the dishes," Jessie pointed out as her mother sprayed a fine mist over soapy glasses. "This is the nineties. Men *can* do dishes."

Her mother dismissed her criticism with a sigh. "The men have enough chores to do around the farm without doing the dishes."

Jessie knew that to a certain degree that was true, but still, the feminist side of her couldn't help but think it was rather unfair that after spending hours in the kitchen preparing the food, the women herded their way back out into the mess to clean up while the men all parked their sated bodies in front of the TV.

"I can help," Kelly offered eagerly. "I can't reach the cupboards, but I know how to dry."

"Good point, Kelly," Jessie said, giving her niece a smile as she handed her the towel meant for Chad. "I'll tell you what. You dry them, then hand them to me and I'll put them away."

"I sure hope Missy's all right," Mrs. Paulson said as the three of them worked together. "Jim says the flu bug is a nasty one."

"She looked all right at dinner, Mom," Jessie noted.

"She gets sick a lot," Kelly said with a roll of her big blue eyes.

An uneasiness settled in Jessie's stomach. She stole a glance at her mother to see if Kelly's statement had aroused the same suspicion that she had—that Missy's upset stomach might have been self-induced. Apparently it hadn't, for she continued to scrub the enamel roaster with the same deliberate motion.

Within a few minutes Carla returned, her face guarded as she entered the kitchen.

"How is she?" Mrs. Paulson asked immediately.

"She's okay," Carla answered, not elaborating on her daughter's condition.

"Did you tell her she could lie down on my bed?"

"She's in one of the spare bedrooms," Carla replied, taking the dish towel from Kelly's hands and busying herself with the dishes. "She'll be all right."

Jessie wasn't so sure. She doubted that her niece's upset stomach was due to the flu as everyone seemed to believe. Yet she knew Carla would be reluctant to talk about Missy in front of her mother and consequently decided to wait until she and Carla were alone before inquiring about her niece's health.

Only that time never happened. If Jessie hadn't known better, she would have thought that her sister was deliberately avoiding her the rest of the evening.

As a result, Jessie didn't get the opportunity to talk to Carla about her suspicions. Not wanting to go back to the city without discussing the subject, Jessie decided to stop by Carla's on her way home the following morning.

When Jessie arrived at the Collins farm she found her sister alone in the kitchen kneading bread dough. Gene had taken Chad into Brainerd to get parts for his truck and Kelly had gone to play at the neighboring farm.

"I thought you were leaving this morning." Carla's greeting was reserved, confirming Jessie's suspicions that her sister had been avoiding her.

"I am. I have my stuff in the car." She gestured toward the driveway. "I thought I'd stop in on my way home and see how Missy is."

"She's fine," Carla said curtly. "She's upstairs in her room. I'll get her." With her floured hands raised in the air, Carla stuck her head around the corner and called up the stairway to the teenager, but there was no answer.

"Maybe she's still sleeping," Jessie said tentatively.

"She better not be. If Gene gets back from town and sees that she's still in bed, he'll have a fit," she said uneasily. Again she hollered up the stairs.

"I'll be down in a minute," came the muffled reply.

Jessie sat at the kitchen table and watched as her sister continued to punch and roll the mound of dough. Her mother had often told her that kneading dough was good therapy, that it helped to work out the stress in a woman's life. Judging by the look on Carla's face, it was working out something, only Jessie wasn't sure exactly what.

"There's fresh coffee," Carla said over her shoulder, nodding toward the coffeemaker on the counter.

"Oh, no, thanks," Jessie said with a shake of her head. "Mom filled me with *julekake* and coffee before I left."

"It figures," Carla retorted.

They made small talk as they waited for Missy to come down. Several times during the conversation Carla paused to look toward the stairs. When she had finished her kneading and there was still no sign of Missy, she again hollered upstairs to the teenager.

"I don't know what's taking her so long," she said apologetically, pouring herself a cup of coffee.

"Teenagers can spend hours getting dressed. Putting on makeup and fixing hair are the number-one priorities in their lives," Jessie said with an understanding smile.

Only it was obvious when Missy came downstairs that she hadn't spent the time on personal grooming. She was dressed in an old pair of jeans with a black leather vest. If she had showered, she hadn't washed her hair, for it lay flat against her scalp, looking as though it hadn't seen a comb for several days. But it was her arms that had Jessie's jaw dropping open in surprise. They were covered with tattoos—a snake, several roses, the peace symbol and her initials.

"Auntie Jess came to see how you are," Carla explained as the teenager ambled into the kitchen.

"I'm fine," Missy announced, slouching onto a chair.

It took Jessie a moment to find her voice. "Good." She flashed her niece a warm smile, then added, "Maybe you'd like to come back with me for the remainder of your school break? We could go to the Mall of America."

For a moment Jessie saw a flicker of interest in the pale face, but it was soon gone. "Thanks, but I've already made plans with my friends."

Jessie kept the smile in place. "Maybe another time. When did you do this?" she asked, unable to resist pointing at the tattoos.

Missy looked at her arms and said, "Oh, these aren't real. They're those temporary ones that wear off in a couple of days, but they look real, don't they?"

Jessie could only nod.

"Would you like some fruit?" Carla asked as she set a bowl of raisin bran in front of Missy.

To Jessie it looked as if Missy wanted to say no, but nodded for her mother's sake. While Carla pulled a grapefruit from the refrigerator and sliced it into small pieces, Jessie watched her niece eat her cereal as though it were gruel.

She was about halfway through the bowl when the phone rang. When Carla announced that it was for Missy, she jumped up. "I'll take it in my room."

"Don't be long. Jessie's going to be leaving," Carla reminded her.

Missy spun around and ran back to Jessie, giving her a quick hug. "Have a safe trip home, Auntie Jess. 'Bye."

"What about your breakfast?" Carla called out to Missy's departing figure, but she paid no attention. At the sound of footsteps on the stairs, she heaved a sigh of frustration and grumbled, "Teenagers."

For Jessie it was the opening she had been waiting for to bring up the subject of Missy's dieting. "She didn't eat much," she said, watching Carla clear away the dishes.

"You know how it is when you've had a touch of the flu. It takes a while to get your appetite back."

"Did she have the flu?" Jessie asked boldly.

Carla spun around and faced her with her hands on her hips. "You know she did. It was the same bug that kept Jim and his family away from Mom's last night." There was a nervous little chuckle at the end of her statement.

Jessie didn't press the issue. "Is she better?"

"Yes. She's fine." There was a crispness to her tone that warned Jessie she didn't want to be discussing her daughter, yet Jessie was too concerned about her niece's health to let the subject drop. "You never did tell me what the doctor said when you brought her to Minneapolis for her physical."

The dishes clanged as Carla dropped them into the sink. "Because it was rather personal and I didn't think I should talk to you about it."

Carla sought Jessie's advice on nearly everything in her life. Now her reluctance to talk about Missy gave Jessie a sense of being left out.

"Did Missy ask you not to say anything?" she wanted to know, trying not to sound as hurt as she was feeling.

"I think that in this case, the fewer people who know, the better," Carla answered coolly.

Jessie could feel her annoyance growing. "Carla, I'm the one who set up the appointment for you. You came to me because you were worried about her dieting."

"Well, you don't need to be concerned about it. We're taking care of it," she said stiffly.

"Taking care of what?" When Carla didn't answer, Jessie got up from the table and crossed to where her sister stood. "What did the doctor say?"

"Keep your voice down or she'll hear you." Carla glanced over her shoulder to see if Melissa was around.

"All right," Jessie said in a near whisper, "but will you please tell me what's going on?"

Carla hesitated for only a minute, then said, "The doctor thinks she's bulimic."

Jessie slumped back against the cupboard. Finally her suspicions were confirmed that her niece was experimenting with unsafe dieting habits. She felt a horrible helplessness.

"How serious is it?"

"Missy denies there's a problem. She admits she's made herself sick when she's overeaten, but she says it's something she's only done a couple of times."

"And you believe her?"

Again Carla looked over her shoulder before saying in a low voice, "At first I wanted to, but then the doctor ran some tests...." She trailed off uneasily.

"And?"

"Her sodium and potassium levels are low. Dr. Marek says that happens when girls binge and purge."

"Then he's pretty sure she has a problem."

"All the signs are there," she said somberly.

Jessie tried to be optimistic. "At least now you know what it is you're dealing with."

"Yes, someone who wants to stay thin so badly she'll do the most awful things," Carla said with a shudder. "Every time I think about what she's been doing in the bathroom my skin wants to crawl right off my bones."

"It must be difficult for all of you." Jessie tried to comfort her, putting a hand on her arm. "Is there anything I can do to help?"

Carla stepped back so that Jessie's hand dropped away. "I think you've done enough already," she answered, not with gratitude but with anger.

Bewildered, Jessie asked, "What's that supposed to mean?"

"Surely you know why Missy's obsessed with her weight?" Carla asked angrily.

"You think this is my fault?" Jessie had a sinking feeling in the pit of her stomach.

"Missy's only doing what she thinks will make her look like you. She wants to be thin and beautiful...to have a model's figure."

Shaken by the accusation, Jessie fought for composure. "No, that's not true," she said uneasily, a sliver of guilt wedging its way into her conscience.

"Isn't it? Ever since Missy was a little girl she's idolized you. It was Jessie this and Jessie that—always parading around in your old clothes and posing in front of the mirror. Is it any wonder she thinks that if she diets until she's pencil thin she'll be just like you?"

Stunned by her anger, Jessie could only stare at her sister in disbelief. When she did find her voice, it was unsteady. "If that's true, then I'm sorry. I'll talk to her." She started toward the stairs, but Carla stopped her.

"Jessie, don't!" she ordered, the power of the command stopping Jessie in her tracks.

"You don't want me talking to her?"

"I told you, Missy doesn't want you to know about this."

Jessie paused at the foot of the stairs, a lump in her throat preventing her from speaking. Was there any truth to what Carla had said? Had she unintentionally encouraged her niece to focus on her body image?

"This is why you've been avoiding me, isn't it? You blame me for Missy's illness," she said shakily.

"I haven't been avoiding you," Carla quickly denied. "It's simply been easier for me and Missy to stay home."

"I'm sorry." Jessie found herself apologizing. She looked down at her hands, fighting for composure. "I wish you'd let me help."

"You don't need to. I told Missy I'd help her and I will," she said with determination.

"I guess you know what's best for your daughter," Jessie said unevenly, still stinging from the accusation.

"I can see that she chooses the right foods to eat and watch to make sure she doesn't overeat. I'll even hide some of the goodies if I have to."

"Is that what the doctor recommended you do?"

"It's what Missy needs for me to do," she said firmly.

"Yes, I'm sure it is, but what about professional therapy? Shouldn't she be getting treatment somewhere?"

"Dr. Marek did say there's a clinic in Minneapolis especially for teenagers with eating disorders, but it's an in-patient program."

"Are you going to admit her?"

She shook her head. "Missy got real upset when he suggested it. She doesn't want to go into the hospital."

"But if it's what's needed to get her well…" Jessie trailed off.

"Jessie, if she goes into the hospital, everyone at school is going to know what's wrong with her. I told you, Missy and I are working together on this. She wants to do it at home and I'm going to give her all the support I can."

Jessie wasn't as convinced as Carla that she had chosen the best plan, but she nodded in understanding. "I'd better get going." She walked over to the coatrack and pulled on her parka. "You'll call me if you need anything?"

"Yeah." Although Carla stood with her arms crossed, her shoulders stiff, Jessie could see that she was fighting back the tears, as well.

She wanted to give her sister a hug, but the air between them still vibrated with accusations and anger. So she simply said, "I'm sorry. I love you both," and ran out the door on a sob.

NORMALLY AIDAN LOVED a party as much as any other thirty-year-old bachelor. However, when he arrived in Delano and saw Jessie in her party clothes, the last place he wanted to take her was to Rick Fenson's New Year's Eve party. She looked stunning, and he found himself regretting not arranging a romantic, private dinner for two instead of accepting an invitation to a party where she would be the object of lots of attention—particularly men's.

Every other time they had been out together Jessie had worn very little makeup and had dressed casually, so that he often forgot she was a model.

But tonight, from the rhinestone comb in her hair to the patent leather heels on her feet, she was all glamour, and it was enough to dazzle any eyes. Wearing a turquoise-sequined slip of a dress that accentuated her shapely figure and left her shoulders bare except for the narrowest of straps, she looked like a dangerous combination of innocence and glamour.

"Where's your grandmother?" he asked, tearing his eyes away from the glimmering sequins to glance around the room.

"Oh, she didn't come back with me. She decided to stay an extra week with my parents," Jessie explained, tucking her house key into a tiny beaded purse that matched her dress. "Would you like something to drink before we leave?"

"Ah, no...no, thanks," he said, having to clear his throat as he answered.

"I'll get my coat, then," she said and started up the stairs. "Make yourself at home. I'll only be a minute."

Aidan watched her slender silk-stockinged legs ascend the staircase and thought that if he didn't ignore the impulses his hormones were conveying to his brain he would soon be stuttering like a high school kid on his first date. It wasn't as though he hadn't seen a beautiful, sexy woman before. The world was full of them, only none of them had quite the same effect on him as Jessie did.

He managed to curb some of his erotic thoughts so that by the time she came back down he didn't feel as if he was back in puberty. She was carrying a tailored black wool coat, which he helped her slip on over her dress.

"You look good tonight," he said huskily.

Her eyes met his and she smiled politely as she gave him a routine "Thanks."

Disappointment settled around Aidan. He hadn't expected her to exactly glow with pleasure, but he had thought his compliment would warrant more than a polite smile. Did she get so many compliments that his was just one more to be added to the pile?

"Actually, you look better than good. You look great." He couldn't help but try again.

"I didn't want to overdo it with the glitter, but when you said the Riverfront Hotel I figured I'd better put on my party clothes," she told him, this time with a warmer smile that made up for her earlier reserve. "I want to make a good impression on your friends."

"Trust me. You will," he murmured, watching her fold her long, slender form into the Lincoln.

They hadn't been at the party for more than a few minutes when Aidan saw just how true that was. Jessie attracted attention, not only because she looked like a blond goddess in turquoise sequins, but because she also had that aloof look that challenged male egos.

Although several men flirted with her, Jessie didn't seem to notice. Aidan wasn't sure if it was from years of being the object of attention or if she had eyes only for him. He preferred to think it was the latter, for watching other men trying to make time with Jessie made him aware of animalistic tendencies he thought he had left behind in his youth.

When the dancing began, he became acutely aware of just how possessive he had become with his date. The thought of Jessie in another man's arms made every jealous bone in his body ache.

Much to his chagrin, Rick had hired a rock band to entertain his guests. Aidan had hoped to hold Jessie in his arms—or even more importantly, keep others from holding her in their arms.

Only he didn't get to hold her, for the band played a series of fast numbers in which it was nearly impossible to tell which wriggling bodies were partners on the dance floor. When the band finally played a slow, romantic ballad, a short, thick man with leering eyes tried to cut in. Before Aidan could tell him to beat it, Jessie gave the stocky man an apologetic grin and announced that she was going to take a break.

Aidan ushered her over to the bar, where he handed her a glass of champagne. Instead of returning to the table where they had been sitting with three other couples, he suggested they step out into the hallway for a breath of fresh air.

"It's so noisy in there you can't even talk," he told her after the door had closed behind them, muting the sound of the band.

"It's a nice party," she said, her cheeks lightly flushed from the dancing.

"Are you having a good time?"

"Mmm-hmm," she answered, but Aidan wasn't sure she was being honest. He wished she wasn't so adept at hiding her emotions.

"You have a curly paper thing in your hair." He reached up to pull a tiny spiral of pink confetti from a blond tress.

"Every few minutes someone seems to be throwing this stuff."

"It'll probably get worse as it gets closer to midnight."

He nodded in agreement. "I had forgotten what it's like to be in a room full of horn-blowing, confetti-throwing party animals."

"Don't you usually spend New Year's Eve shaking rattles and blowing party makers?" she asked.

He didn't want to admit that he had spent three of the past four New Year's Eves working. "I think I prefer to party on a little less grand scale. Like maybe a few good friends . . . or even just one special person."

"I know what you mean. I feel that way, too."

Her comment took him by surprise and he thought about asking her whether or not she wanted to leave. But just then the elevator bell gave a little *ping,* announcing the arrival of more guests. Automatically Aidan and Jessie turned toward the sound. In the small group of people who filed out of the elevator were Aidan's brother, Sean, and his wife, Giselle.

It was the only time the entire evening that Aidan saw Jessie's composure slip. A look of anxiety crossed her face and he found himself feeling extremely protective of her. Automatically he slipped his arm around her waist.

"Well, well, well. If it isn't my little brother," Sean said, steering his wife toward them. "I didn't expect to see you here tonight." Judging by the way he was looking at Jessie, Aidan knew that his surprise had more to do with his choice of date than his appearance at the party.

"Happy New Year." Aidan greeted them both, shaking his brother's hand and giving his sister-in-law a kiss on the cheek before introducing Jessie.

For several minutes the four of them made small talk until Sean suggested they go into the ballroom before all the champagne was gone. He held the door open, but Aidan indicated they were going to wait a few minutes before joining the others.

"Are you all right?" he asked Jessie as soon as Sean and Giselle had disappeared.

"Yes, I'm fine," she answered, but Aidan wasn't so sure she was telling the truth. He had caught a glimpse of the anxiety his brother's appearance had created.

"I didn't know Sean had been invited tonight. I'm sorry," he apologized, wishing he could always protect her from life's unpleasant moments.

"It was obvious he wasn't expecting to find you with me," she said uneasily. "You haven't told him we've been dating, have you?"

He shook his head, then took her hand in his. "I haven't talked all that much with Sean lately, and when I have seen him, we've usually discussed business."

She didn't say anything, her face masking her emotions. He wished just once she would stop trying to hide her feelings.

"Would you like to leave?" he asked, gently rubbing his thumb across the back of her hand.

"Why? Do you think your brother's uncomfortable because I'm here?" Her blue eyes were clouded with uncertainty.

"It's not my brother I'm worried about," he said a bit impatiently, then looked at his watch. "I think we ought to continue our celebrating elsewhere."

"I thought you wanted to dance again?"

"Not really. Do you?"

She shook her head. "I'm not much of a dancer."

"Me, neither." He pulled her by the hand. "Come. I'm going to take you away from here."

"You don't have to leave for my sake, Aidan."

"I'm not doing it for you, Jessie. I'm doing it for us." He gave her a quick kiss on the lips, then led her back into the ballroom so they could say their goodbyes.

Rick didn't seem too disappointed that they were leaving, thrusting an open bottle of champagne into Aidan's hands as he wished them a happy New Year. Sean, on the other hand, looked displeased, and Aidan guessed that he had expected to talk to them.

Out in the corridor waiting for the elevator, Aidan lifted the champagne bottle and said, "I guess we'll have to have our own private celebration."

"It's probably not wise to take an open bottle in the car—especially not on New Year's Eve," Jessie told him in her usual pragmatic manner.

"Oh, we're not going anywhere in the car," Aidan told her as the elevator doors slid open and they stepped inside. Instead of pressing the button for the lobby, he inserted a key in the console that allowed them access to the private suites in the hotel.

"Is the key compliments of Rick also?" she asked as the elevator surged upward.

"This key is mine," he answered, tossing it in the air and capturing it within his fist.

"You have a room here?"

"Mmm-hmm. I thought it would be easier for my mother."

"Easier for your mother?" She raised one eyebrow.

"Yeah. Despite the fact that I'm thirty years old, she still waits up for me to come in at night. I figured I'd save her a lot of worrying if I simply spent the night here."

"How thoughtful," she said sweetly, but her eyes held amusement.

The doors slid open and he gestured for her to step out. "You're not thinking I have ulterior motives, are you?"

"A girl can hope, can't she?" she quipped, surprising him with a sly grin.

Either the champagne was starting to relax her or she was revealing the warm, funny side of her personality he had only glimpsed previously. Whatever it was, Aidan couldn't get the key in the door fast enough.

"Nice place," Jessie commented as he ushered her into the elegant suite.

"No paper streamers, confetti or balloons, but it is quiet," he said, taking her coat.

"It's big, isn't it?" she said appreciatively as she looked around.

"We won't be bumping into any bodies if we want to dance," he replied, walking over to the stereo system and pressing a button. The jazzy sounds of Wynton Marsalis softly broke the silence.

Jessie walked over to the floor-to-ceiling windows and looked out at the city skyline. "This is a wonderful view."

"The bellman said we'll be able to see the fireworks at Riverplace when the clock strikes midnight. Why don't you sit down and I'll get us some glasses," he suggested, taking the bottle of champagne over to the marble-topped bar.

Jessie looked at the assortment of furniture in the room and ended up on the white leather sofa, knowing perfectly well that sitting in one of the chairs wasn't going to keep her out of Aidan's arms.

He brought in two glasses of champagne and handed one of them to her. "Are you hungry? I have some stuff in the refrigerator."

"Oh, no. I'm fine. That was a lovely buffet," she told him, then took a small sip of the champagne.

"Rick always does everything first class," he said as he sat down beside her. "The best food, the best champagne, the best music ... well, at least what he thinks is the best music."

"You don't like rock and roll?"

"I like some of it, but mostly I listen to jazz. It's better for dancing." He got to his feet and reached for her hand. "Come. I'll show you." His voice was as smooth and as coaxing as his smile.

Jessie went into his arms in the traditional manner, putting her left hand up around his shoulder, her right hand inside his left. With her heels on, she was the same height as he was, her eyes meeting his.

"What's so funny?" he asked when she hid a smile.

"Nothing. I was just thinking how nice it is to be able to dance cheek to cheek with a man and not have to stoop over."

His hand curled more tightly around hers, drawing it closer to his chest. "There were plenty of tall men at that party tonight who would have gladly challenged me to a duel to be able to dance with you."

"But you noticed it was a short one who tried to cut in," she reminded him.

"Is that why you declined? Because he was a pip-squeak?"

She giggled. "He wasn't exactly a pip-squeak, and no, it wasn't the reason I declined. I just thought that if I was going to dance with anyone, I wanted it to be with you," she answered without any coyness.

"I'm not much of a dancer," he admitted, barely moving in rhythm with the music.

"You seem to be doing all right," she said sexily.

"That's because this is Wynton Marsalis." He softly hummed the melody the trumpeter was playing and her body relaxed against his.

Their feet barely moved across the plush carpet, yet their bodies swayed back and forth, letting the sensual music speak for them in a language that needed no words.

"You're right. Jazz is much better for dancing," she said huskily, the hand she had placed on his shoulder creeping higher to slip around his neck.

"Much better," he agreed, pulling her even closer so that she could feel the effect her closeness was having on him.

Any doubts she had as to what his interest was in her were erased. Jessie had thought that she would need more time to make the decision as to whether she should become intimate with Aidan, but now that she was in his arms, feeling his desire, she knew how foolish she was to think that they could keep their relationship platonic. The longer they danced, the slower they moved, the greater the ache she felt to let her feelings take control.

She could feel his warm breath near her ear. It sent tingles of pleasure up and down her before she realized that it was his lips sending the tingles. He was kissing her on her neck and she was melting. Before his mouth could reach her throat, several loud bangs had them both turning to face the window.

Off in the distance fireworks lit up the sky in a burst of sparkling color.

"It must be midnight," she exclaimed.

Aidan lifted her chin and gazed into her eyes. "Happy New Year, Jessie," he said, then claimed her lips in a wild, hungry kiss.

She loved the velvet pressure of his mouth against hers. With lazy, sensuous strokes he moved his tongue over hers, causing her body to respond to the not-so-subtle messages being transmitted in his kiss.

Because they were so close in height, their bodies matched up perfectly. Chest against chest, thighs pressed to thighs, they were in tune with each other, encouraging further exploration.

She clung to him as he bent her backward, her hips arching into his as he trailed kisses down the column of her throat. When his lips reached the gentle swell of her breasts, she gasped as desire went racing through her.

She wanted him. Every nerve ending in her body was announcing to her brain that she wanted him. Slowly and rhythmically her hips moved, not in time to the music but in response to the primal instinct that was causing her to slip her fingers inside his evening jacket and run them over the muscles hidden beneath crisp white cotton.

He lifted his head for a moment to draw a ragged breath, his eyes looking into hers, seeking an answer to the unspoken question between them. It was her opportunity to wish him a happy New Year and suggest he take her home—which is what logically she knew she should do.

The only problem was she didn't want to go home. She wanted to stay right here with Aidan and explore the pleasures now teasing her senses. Inside her there was another kind of fireworks exploding. This man made her feel good, so good she needed to ignore the logic threatening to end their evening. She looked into his smoky, promise-filled eyes and, smiling, began to undo the pearly white button studs on his shirt.

He stilled her hands, then carried them to his lips, pressing a kiss onto her knuckles before leading her into the bedroom. The room was as elegant as the rest of the suite, but Jessie saw none of the exquisite furnishings, for her eyes were pinned to Aidan, who was taking off his clothes as if they were burning his body and needed to be quickly discarded.

When he was naked except for a pair of designer boxers, he asked with a teasing grin, "Do you need any help?"

"I believe I do," she said with a sensuous pout, lifting her curtain of blond hair off her neck as she turned around so that he could undo the zipper on her dress.

From the way his eyes were devouring her she expected him to tear her clothes away as fast as he had rid himself of his, but to her surprise he stood back and watched as she stepped out of the dress.

"You ever do any lingerie modeling?" he asked when she was down to her bustier and garters.

"I'm not the right size," she answered, bending over to remove her shoes, one at a time, her eyes still holding his.

"I find that hard to believe," he murmured huskily.

Slowly he circled her, studying her from all angles. When she would have undone the clasp at the front of her bustier, his hand stopped hers.

"Some things a man likes to discover for himself," he told her, his voice raspy. He cupped her hips and pulled her closer.

She could feel the enormous passion in him, and she wet her lips as his fingers left sparks of desire wherever they touched her skin. The look on his face as her breasts were released from the confining bustier nearly caused her knees to buckle.

When he bent down to touch his tongue to her nipple, her knees did weaken and she leaned against him. He wrapped an arm around her waist and suckled her until her heart was racing.

When he lifted his head he smiled at her, saying, "You are definitely the right size." Then he explored her satiny flesh, taking his time as his hands and mouth found every sensitive area of her body.

Just when Jessie thought she would melt from the ex-quisite pleasure, he lifted her and carried her to the bed.

When he would have slipped out of his shorts, her hand stopped him.

"Allow me," she said, sliding her hands seductively down his sides until they were inside the elastic waistband. His sudden intake of breath told her that her touch was as electric as his.

For several long seconds she stared at his naked form, then boldly traced a path from the small dark mat of hair on his chest down across his abdomen. Lower and lower her hands moved until they reached their destination.

With one smooth movement he had her flat on her back and was poised over her. Then he lowered his head and began a deliberate seduction with his lips and hands.

Weeks of wanting and needing each other made them both burn with desire, making a slow seduction impossible. They came together in a sweet, hot explosion that was such a perfect union they both cried out in wonder.

"Ahh, Jessie, I knew it would be this good."

She was with him all the way, the heat spreading through her until she thought she wouldn't be able to take any more. When the explosion of ecstasy came, it shook both of them to their very souls.

As passion subsided, Aidan rolled onto his back, pulling Jessie close beside him. Neither spoke while their hearts slowed and bodies cooled.

Aidan was content to lie back and listen to the sounds of passion spent—the heavy intermittent breathing, the sighs of satisfaction. Jessie was so still he thought she might have fallen asleep until she propped herself up on one elbow and looked down at him, a smile on her face.

"Happy New Year."

"I'll say." He tangled his fingers in her damp hair, delighted with the way the evening had ended. She was everything he had imagined she'd be and then some. And now she was bending over him, her hands moving over his flesh, her eyes glistening with pleasure.

"Did this New Year's Eve live up to the ones from years gone by?"

He captured one of her roving hands and brought it to his lips. "If you're asking me whether I usually spend it making love with a beautiful woman, the answer is no."

She playfully tapped his lips with her finger. "Uh-huh," she drawled sarcastically.

"All right, so there've been a few women in my past, but none of them has ever made me want to quit my job and leave sunny California for the frigid temperatures in Minnesota."

"Is that what you want to do?"

"You tempt me, Jessie," he said with a groan as his hands resumed their playful exploration. "And while we're on the subject, maybe you ought to tell me about the broken hearts Jessie Paulson has left behind."

"What makes you think I did the breaking?" she purred innocently.

"Because any man that would let you go would have to be either dead below the waist or mentally impaired."

A chuckle accompanied her feathery-light kiss. "The list of men in my life is pretty short. One ex-husband who should be dead below the waist and several ex-boyfriends who were definitely mentally deficient."

"What was this ex-husband of yours like?" he asked, wishing he wasn't jealous of a man he knew nothing about.

"If I told you, then it would mean he was worth mentioning and he's not," she said quietly.

"Did he hurt you?" He reached up and wrapped a silken tress around his finger.

"I doubt there is such a thing as a painless divorce," she reflected solemnly. She shook her head as if trying to chase away the memories. "It doesn't matter. It was a long time ago and I know now that he wasn't worth the tears I cried."

"Do you still see him?" he asked, the very idea provoking an ache in his jealous bones.

She shook her head. "I don't think he even lives in Minnesota anymore."

"Good."

She pressed up closer to him, until her nipples were flattened against his chest, her legs enticingly tangling his. "As I said, he's not worth discussing."

"Then we won't." He gave her a quick kiss on her lips. "Besides, I have other plans for us."

"Such as?"

She was stretched out now, astride him, her blue eyes seductively inviting.

"I'm going to make you forget every other man you've ever known," he told her, loving the feel of her warm flesh against his.

"Is that a promise?"

"You bet. I can't believe I ever thought you were a cold woman," he said, groaning as she ran her hands teasingly down the length of his body.

"Cold? Me? Why did you think that?" she asked, surprised.

"You have a way of shutting out the world, remember?"

She chuckled huskily. "Yes, well even an ice cube melts in the presence of fire... and this feels as though there's a mighty hot fire burning somewhere deep inside." Her fingers gently massaged his inner thighs and all around his manhood.

"I don't think you know what you're doing to me," he warned as desire flared once more.

"Oh, I think I do," she said with an innocence that was masterfully tinged with temptation. And then she proceeded to show him that she knew exactly what she was doing, taking him on an erotic journey that lasted far into the night.

WHEN AIDAN AWOKE he was alone in the big bed, and his stomach contracted at the thought that Jessie might have gotten up and gone home. But then he realized the sound that had awakened him was the shower, and he relaxed against the pillows, resisting the temptation to join her.

Her scent still lingered in the covers, reminding him of the pleasures they had shared. A look at the clock told him it was early. The turquoise-sequined dress was still draped over a chair, the bustier and her stockings carelessly strewn across the floor. Would she want to go home right away or could he talk her into spending the day with him?

When she came out of the bathroom she was wearing a black-and-red satin kimono the hotel had provided. To Aidan she had never looked sexier.

"Good morning," she said upon seeing him propped up in the bed. Her smile was almost shy, endearing her all the more to him. "I'm sorry if I woke you."

"You didn't wake me. I'm glad to see you're still here. I was beginning to think I had dreamed last night happened."

"It was no dream," she said, walking across the room to sit on the edge of the bed. "I'm here and I need a ride home."

He reached for her hand and said, "I was hoping I could talk you into spending the day here with me."

"I don't have any clothes but that dress," she said, gesturing toward the sequined shift.

"What I had in mind for today didn't involve clothing," he said with a wicked grin, and she snatched her hand
away from his with a playful clicking of her tongue.

"What time do you have to check out?" she asked,
picking up her scattered lingerie.

"I have this place until noon tomorrow."

She looked up at him and smiled slyly. "Confident,
weren't you?"

"No, just optimistic." He swung his legs over the side of
the bed, draping a sheet across his stomach.

"We could always run back to your place and you could
pick up a few things," he suggested.

"If you had told me you had a room, I could have
packed a bag," she retorted with a candidness that was de-
void of any sarcasm.

"I didn't think that logical brain of yours would agree to
spend the night with me," he returned with equal candor.

She smiled. "You're probably right."

He couldn't help but touch her, gently laying his fingers
on her cheek. "You're not regretting last night, are you?"

"I have a feeling I should be, but I'm not."

"Good. Because now we can spend the rest of today and
all of tonight together." His mouth nibbled hers, gently
drawing her lower lip between his.

"But what about your family? I thought you said your
mother always invites people for dinner on New Year's
Day. Won't she be expecting you?"

The backs of his fingers swept blond tendrils of hair away
from her cheeks. "I don't want to think about my family,
Jessie. I only want to think about us."

Jessie wasn't so sure that was such a good idea. To pretend that his family wasn't an obstacle to their deepening
relationship was inviting trouble.

But Aidan's power of persuasion was strong, and she ended up spending not only New Year's Day but the following night with him, too, as he extended his stay at the hotel an extra day. Most of that time was spent in the hotel room, where they not only made wild, passionate love, but talked for hours and hours, becoming intimate in a way Jessie had never been with any man. The moment they had stepped into the hotel suite they had found their own private Shangri-la.

It was only when the telephone rang on their final morning together that reality intruded. Jessie had just finished showering when she found Aidan sitting with the receiver in his hands, a faraway look on his face.

''Is anything wrong?'' she asked.

''No.'' He slowly replaced the receiver back on the cradle. ''That was my mother.''

''Oh.''

There were several moments of silence before he said. ''She wanted to let me know that my father's being released from the hospital. He's going back to prison.''

A chill settled in Jessie's bones. For three days they had managed to avoid the subject of his father. Now it was there between them like a detour sign, refusing to let them continue on the road to bliss without going over a bumpy stretch.

''What's happening with his appeal?'' Jessie asked cautiously.

''The trial transcripts have been released and Will Lepley is writing up the briefs.'' He got up and walked over to stare out the window, his hands in his pockets.

''What does that mean?'' Jessie followed him, slipping an arm inside his.

"Will's hoping either to find evidence that was con-
aled or else discover something new that will convince the
dge to grant another trial," he said uneasily.

Jessie studied the serious face she had come to love in
ch a short time. "You look as though you're not happy
at he might be given another trial."

"I'm not happy," he admitted candidly. "I don't see
hat good is going to come out of it other than to raise false
opes in my mother. You should hear the optimism in her
oice when she talks about all of this," he said, running a
and across the back of his head.

"Maybe she has reason to be optimistic," Jessie sug-
sted tentatively.

"She doesn't," he snapped. He looked at her as if she
dn't understand any of this. "You don't need to look at
e as though I'm some kind of coldhearted son, Jessie. The
an hasn't exactly done things that merit loyalty."

"I didn't know that fathers needed to earn loyalty," she
id quietly, then immediately regretted it. Aidan's face
arkened. He turned away from her and she stepped
ound him to face him, reaching for his hands.

"I know you're angry over what he's done to your
other, and I understand that. But haven't you even con-
dered the possibility that he might be innocent?"

"Innocent? How can you even suggest that?" He shot
er a look of disbelief. "You were there for the trial. You
ere on the jury that convicted him."

This was the opening she had been waiting for. "I fol-
wed the instructions given to me as a juror, but some-
ing happened to me, Aidan, during the trial."

He raised one eyebrow. "What are you saying?"

"I know this is going to sound crazy, but several times
uring the trial I had this feeling that your father was in-

nocent. I didn't act on it because we were instructed
judge by the evidence, not by our emotions.''

''So you think he's innocent?''

She could see the idea didn't please him. ''Yes,'' sh
stated firmly. ''I do.''

''Jessie, just because he's my father doesn't mean yo
need to wish he was innocent,'' he warned in a danger
ously calm voice.

''I'm not saying that because he's your father, Aidan
Haven't you ever wondered if there might not be more ev
idence out there somewhere? I mean, there was no confes
sion of guilt, no eyewitness who saw what happened.''

He eyed her suspiciously. ''What are you getting at?''

''If his lawyer is going to appeal, maybe there's some
thing we didn't hear about…something that will shed new
light on the case,'' she said evenly.

''The only reason he'll be given an appeal is because h
has expensive lawyers who know how to get an appeal,'' h
said cynically. ''He's hurt people, Jessie.''

The bitterness in him frightened her. She knew he sti
harbored a great deal of anger over what had happene
between his mother and his father. That anger fueled hi
suspicions about his father's guilt and justified his accep
tance of the verdict. It was also causing him to put her o
the defensive whenever she brought up the possibility tha
his father might be innocent.

''Maybe it would be better if we didn't discuss this,'' sh
said, dropping her hands from his and taking a step back
ward.

With a groan he reached for her and pulled her close
''I'm sorry, Jessie. You're right. We shouldn't be discuss
ing this. My problems with my father are my own and
don't want them coming between us.''

His body was warm and comforting against hers, and once again she melted into his embrace. She wanted to ask him to confide in her about those problems, but a little voice warned her that they were going to end up on conflicting sides if they discussed his father. Once more she wondered if her guilty verdict would continue to haunt her in more ways than one.

CHAPTER ELEVEN

MUCH TO JESSIE'S SURPRISE she was actually relieved when Aidan left for California. In just a few days they had gone from getting to know each other to sharing the most intimate aspects of their lives and she felt in need of some breathing space. During the two weeks he would be gone she planned to think seriously about their relationship. To use intellect rather than emotion in deciding where they were headed.

However, she found it difficult to be intellectual when the very first night he was gone she pulled back the covers of her bed and discovered he had sprayed her bed linens with his after-shave. She couldn't think one logical thought that night as she lay between the scented sheets.

After only a few days without him, she admitted to herself that she had been bitten by the lovebug. She knew she had been bitten badly when after missing several of his phone calls she checked into the cost of getting a cellular phone.

Of course it would have been easier to put him out of her thoughts if she wasn't pretending to be a model bride at work every day. Normally she wouldn't have paid much attention to white-lace-and-satin wedding gowns, but every time she stood in front of the dressing-room mirror she found herself fantasizing what it would be like to have Aidan beside her in a morning coat and tails.

Unlike the Christmas window, which drew a steady stream of shoppers, the bridal display seldom held anyone captive. Occasionally, passersby would stop and point a finger as they realized Jessie was a live person and not a mannequin. But none paused for more than a few seconds—with the exception of the brides-to-be who were more interested in the dresses than the mannequins.

Jessie wasn't surprised. Even for January, the weather was exceptionally cold and most of the postholiday shoppers stuck to the skyways rather than walk the sidewalks out of doors. Most activity occurred during the lunch hour, which was when she first noticed Sean McCullough staring at her through the glass.

Despite the jolt to her nervous system, Jessie gave no indication that she recognized him or that she had even seen him. However, the longer he stood on the outside looking in, the more difficult it became not to be affected by his presence.

It wasn't long before he moved directly into her line of vision and rapped on the glass with his gloved hand. "I need to talk to you," he mouthed with exaggerated motions.

Jessie paid no attention. Then he disappeared into the bridal salon only to reappear a few minutes later. Using pantomime, he told her he'd be back.

When she had finished posing for the day, she found him sitting on one of the velvet upholstered salon chairs, looking as uncomfortable as she was feeling. Seeing her, he immediately rose to his feet.

"Ms. Paulson," he said with a curt nod.

"Please, call me Jessie," she told him, doing her best to maintain her composure as she shook his outstretched hand. "What did you want to see me about, Mr. McCullough?"

"It's Sean." He was holding his overcoat, and shifted it uneasily from arm to arm. "I was hoping I could convince you to have a cup of coffee with me."

"I'm afraid I'm rather busy," she answered politely, a knot forming in her stomach.

"I'm sure you are, but I promise I won't keep you long," he responded with a persuasive smile. "I'd just like a few minutes to talk to you."

Jessie felt the knot in her stomach tighten. She really couldn't think of anything they might have to discuss, yet she couldn't help but be curious as to why he was interested in her.

When she didn't respond right away, he added, "Please, it's rather important."

"All right," she reluctantly agreed. "There's a coffee shop right around the corner. Why don't I meet you there in half an hour? I need to change." She glanced down at the bouffant wedding dress.

He nodded and the tilt of his head reminded Jessie of Aidan. Sean wasn't as tall or as broad through the shoulders as his brother, but he had a similar physique, and many of the same mannerisms.

It was because of his looks that Jessie found herself wary of him as they sat across from each other in the coffee shop. He had warm, seductive eyes, the kind of eyes that encouraged people to trust and confide in their owner, and Jessie knew that she needed to be cautious with what she told him.

"What did you want to talk to me about?" she asked as she stirred sugar and cream into her coffee.

"I believe I owe you an apology," he said, pouring a liberal amount of cream into his own cup. Up close, he reminded Jessie even more of Aidan.

"An apology?" She looked at him warily.

"Yes. That day I stopped by Braxton's and spoke to you on the telephone . . . I was totally out of line and I'm sorry. I really have no excuse for what I said except to tell you that I was extremely upset because of my father's situation and I'm afraid I took it out on you. I don't know what else to say but I'm sorry."

"Apology accepted," she said pleasantly, trying to ignore the uneasy feeling that warned her he wasn't as sincere as he wanted her to believe.

Again he smiled, and she responded with her own guarded but polite smile. There were several moments of awkward silence before he said, "Since you're dating my brother, I thought it would be best to clear the air, so to speak." He stared straight into her eyes. "I don't want either of us to feel uncomfortable around the other."

She tried not to squirm under his scrutiny, and chose her words carefully. "I'm not sure that's possible, considering the circumstances."

"You mean because you were a juror at my father's trial?"

She nodded solemnly.

"You were only doing what you thought was right," he said smoothly . . . too smoothly for Jessie's peace of mind.

With Aidan, she was beginning to feel less defensive about her position on Tom McCullough's jury, but it was different with Sean. His words did little to ease her guilty conscience or to convince her that he didn't hold her responsible for his father's incarceration.

"It isn't easy sitting in judgment of another human being," she told him, trying to keep the defensiveness from her voice.

"I'm sure it isn't," he said grimly, then sighed. "I was in the courtroom and I heard the evidence. I'm not sure that if I had been in your position I wouldn't have come to the same conclusion as you did."

She could see that as much as he wanted her to believe that he didn't resent her for being a juror, he wasn't any more comfortable with her presence than she was with his. "That doesn't change the fact that you're unhappy with the verdict."

She could see that she had hit a nerve by the tiny pulse throbbing in his forehead. Like Aidan, he didn't try to hide his emotions.

"Yes, I am unhappy, but it's with the system that sent him to prison. If the police hadn't been so eager to get a suspect in the case, they might have spent more time looking for the real murderer."

"You're convinced your father's innocent, aren't you?" she remarked pensively, thinking how different his attitude toward his father was from Aidan's.

"You don't know him the way I do. He's not the monster the D.A. wanted you to think he is," he pleaded passionately.

"You don't need to defend him to me," Jessie said, wishing she could get up and leave. The vibrations she was getting from Sean were unpleasant—very unpleasant. As much as he professed not to feel anger toward her, she knew he couldn't be indifferent.

"My father didn't kill Kathleen Daniels," he said with a strong conviction. "And I'm not just saying that because I'm his son. He couldn't kill anyone."

Jessie wanted to tell him she agreed with him, that she had her doubts about the verdict, but caution held her tongue. "Isn't there an appeal?" she asked weakly, hoping to add a ray of optimism to the conversation.

"Yes." He paused to take a sip of coffee, then said, "We're hoping to get his conviction thrown out and have him granted a new trial. Will Lepley's convinced that someone knows about the murder and hasn't come forward...someone who has a good reason to keep silent."

There was something about the look on his face that elicited sympathy from Jessie. Unlike Aidan, who always had so much anger in his eyes whenever he spoke about his father, Sean looked forlorn, as though the thought of his father never being free was unbearable.

"I hope you're successful," Jessie said sincerely.

He looked at her over the rim of his cup. "Do you really?"

"Yes." She held his gaze.

"Are you saying you've changed your mind about him being guilty?"

Suddenly she felt trapped, as if he was ready to pounce on any information she might divulge. Brian's reminder to be careful as to what she said regarding the trial flashed in her mind. "What I'm saying is I'd like to see your father out of jail, too."

"Why? Because you're dating my brother?" he asked suspiciously.

"It would make things easier for me and Aidan," she admitted candidly. "But I also believe in justice, and if your father's innocent as you say he is, then of course I hope he's freed."

He took another sip of coffee, then folded his arms and leaned up against the table. "But in your eyes justice means my father stays in prison."

Jessie reached for her things.

"Please, don't leave."

She paused with her hand on her purse, her coat over her arm. "I don't think there's any reason for this discussion to continue. You've made your point, Mr. McCullough."

"Point?"

"You're not happy that I was on your father's jury." She shoved her arms into the sleeves of her jacket. "And you're not happy that Aidan and I are seeing each other."

Sean raked a hand through his thick, dark hair. "The reason I wanted to talk to you was to get past all of this."

"Well, you haven't and I doubt you ever will," she said, rapidly losing her self-control. She bent over to search for a glove that had fallen on the floor.

"I'm sorry...really."

When Jessie straightened she saw something in his eyes that elicited sympathy. It was a combination of sincerity and frustration. She debated whether she should make another attempt to be pleasant.

"Do you know when Aidan's coming back?" he asked.

"Don't you?"

"No. Aidan and I haven't been communicating very well lately," he admitted, not with sarcasm but with regret.

Jessie could see the stress on his face and felt her anger dissolving. "He said he was going to try to make it back by next Friday."

"Then he'll be here."

"You sound awfully confident of that."

He chuckled sardonically. "It bugs the hell out of him that my father's case isn't settled."

Jessie knew what he said was true, but she didn't want to get into any sort of discussion about Aidan. "I have to go," she said, getting up from the booth.

He, too, stood, a look of apology on his face. "I'm sorry, Jessie. Honestly. I didn't want to make you feel uncomfortable."

Jessie shrugged off his apology, thanked him for the coffee and left, giving him the impression that she wasn't upset by their conversation. Little did he know that her insides were shaking and her conscience was fighting off a tidal wave of guilt.

However, no one would have guessed the emotional turmoil Jessie was experiencing, for just like the mannequin she pretended to be, she only showed one expression to the rest of the world. Indifference.

THERE WERE TWO phone messages waiting for Jessie when she arrived home. Neither was from Aidan, the one person she needed to talk to. Before Jessie had the chance to return either of the calls, the phone rang again. This time it was Devony, calling to remind her of the party she was giving that night.

Jessie hadn't seen Devony since Christmas Eve, when they had posed for the final time in Braxton's window. While Jessie had gone to Harding for the holidays, Devony had flown to Pennsylvania to spend Christmas with her grandmother, and then on to Hawaii for an assignment.

As soon as she had returned from the islands she had called to inform Jessie she was having a party and would accept no excuses as to why she couldn't come. Jessie's first inclination had been to say no, knowing that Devony's parties were not for those who preferred peace and quiet.

However, Devony was her closest friend, and after much cajoling she managed to convince Jessie that sitting home pining over a man and waiting for the phone to ring was not the way to beat the January blahs. Jessie did put one condition on her acceptance, and that was that she be allowed to help with the food. This way she could always retreat to the kitchen should the need arise.

As Jessie expected, Devony's apartment was like a scene out of a movie, with people crammed from wall to wall and an eclectic collection of music playing in the background. Most of the guests were connected to the modeling profession, including a number of actors and actresses who often did television commercials as well as theater work.

Jessie circulated freely, refilling hors d'oeuvre trays and picking up empty glasses, stopping to chat with people she knew from her work. It was while she was gathering discarded plates that she overheard several women discussing a model who had been abused by her boyfriend.

"A lot of good a restraining order does," a svelte redhead commented sarcastically. "There has to be a better way of protecting women from men who have already proven they are violent."

"Personally, I think women need to be more careful in choosing whom they get involved with. I mean, that animalistic behavior is often there from the start, but women ignore it," a blonde said critically.

"That may be, but a lot of men don't become violent until a woman wants to call it quits," the redhead insisted stubbornly.

"Isn't that what happened to Kathleen Daniels?" a third woman asked. "That guy who murdered her didn't have a history of beating her up or anything."

At the mention of Kathleen Daniels's name, Jessie moved a bit closer.

"Maybe *he* didn't, but she didn't exactly run around with a tame crowd," the redhead answered.

"Was she a friend of yours?" the blonde asked in surprise.

"No, but you know Mike Sampson, the photographer? He used to date her, and he told me she was impressed by men with money who could afford her expensive habits."

"Oh, was she into that stuff?" the third woman asked, her face wrinkling distastefully.

At that point the conversation switched to the subject of women making foolish choices involving wealthy men.

Jessie discreetly retreated to the kitchen where she contemplated what she had heard.

"Are you hiding in here, or what?" Devony asked a few minutes later when she strode through the doorway with an empty serving tray.

"Dev, do you remember when you told me you thought you had met Kathleen Daniels at a party a few years back?" Jessie asked, her brow furrowed as she rinsed out glasses.

"What about it?" Devony countered, reaching into the refrigerator for a container of cheese.

"Do you think she was into drugs?"

"I suppose she could have been, but I told you, Jess, I really didn't know her." She gave her friend a puzzled look. "Why are you so interested in her, anyway? The trial's over."

Jessie shrugged. "It was something I overheard out there that made me think about her," she said, nodding toward the living room.

"I think it's because you're dating Aidan McCullough," she stated confidently. "You wouldn't even be thinking about that trial business if you weren't seeing him."

Jessie didn't comment, but asked, "Do you know Mike Sampson?"

"Sure, doesn't every model?" She reached into a cupboard for a mixing bowl.

"Do you know if he dated Kathleen Daniels?"

"No, but there's an easy way to find out. Ask him." She opened a can of chili, mixed it with the cheese, then popped it into the microwave. "But I still don't see why you're so concerned about someone who's dead." She whispered the last three words, as if out of reverence for the deceased.

Jessie dismissed her comment with a wave of her hand. "It's just something that I've been curious about. That's all." Devony was frantically opening and closing cupboard doors and Jessie asked, "What are you looking for?"

"That green bowl I always use for dip."

"I think it's already in use," Jessie told her, relieved that the subject of Kathleen Daniels had been dropped.

At that moment someone poked his head around the door and said, "Dev, we need more napkins."

"I'll get them. You wait for the dip," she ordered Jessie, gesturing toward the microwave whose digital clock indicated there were still two minutes to go before the dip would be ready.

The longer Jessie thought about what she had overheard, the more determined she was to find out more about Kathleen Daniels. The medical examiner had testified that the autopsy had revealed no traces of any drugs in Kathleen's body, yet the women at the party had hinted she was into illegal substances.

The following Monday Jessie decided to pay a visit to Mike Sampson after work. When he saw her enter his studio, he grinned broadly.

"Jessie. Long time, no see." He welcomed her with open arms, giving her a kiss on each cheek. "What brings you here?"

"I need to ask you about something, Mike," she answered, taking the stool he offered.

"You don't mind if I put away this equipment while we talk, do you?" he asked, unplugging a cord from the wall.

She shook her head. "I didn't mean to interrupt, but I wanted to ask you about someone."

"Male or female?" he asked with another grin.

"Female. A woman named Kathleen Daniels. Did you know her?"

The broad smile slowly slipped away. "I dated her a few times. Why?" he asked cautiously, wrapping the electrical cord around his elbow and his fist.

She briefly explained why she was interested, telling him that Tom McCullough's son was a friend of hers and she wanted to help him prove his father's innocence. She omitted the fact that she had served on the jury that had found Tom McCullough guilty.

"I'm not sure that I can tell you anything that will be of any help," he said, pushing aside a cardboard backdrop that had been painted to look like an ocean. "Besides, from what I heard about the trial, Jess, I have to say I believe the old guy did it."

Jessie thought how strange it was that so many people believed Tom McCullough to be guilty, yet she had sat on the jury and she was the one questioning his innocence. She simply shrugged and said, "A while back I would have agreed with you, but now I'm not so sure."

"And you want me to give you the good stuff that will fuel your uncertainty, right?" he asked with a sly grin.

"I guess I just want to understand what kind of person Kathleen was," she said honestly.

Mike hooked his leg around a chair and straddled it, resting his arms across the back. "I'm not sure anybody ever really understood Kathleen," he said with a sigh. "She came here wanting me to do some photographs of her."

"She was a model?"

He shook his head. "Uh-uh. Not that she wasn't endowed with all the right stuff," he said wistfully. "Lenore Green sent her here. I think you know Lenore...a tall brunette, does a lot of runway work." Jessie nodded and he continued. "Anyway, Kathleen wanted the photos for her boyfriend. She said she had seen the work I had done for the Chantal catalog and wanted the same effect."

Everyone in the modeling profession knew that Chantal was an intimate apparel designer whose fashions often appeared in men's magazines. "She wanted to be photographed in lingerie?"

"Very skimpy lingerie," he confirmed.

"Did you do it?"

"Of course," he said with an amused chuckle. "The shots were great...she was a beautiful woman. A little messed up in the head, but beautiful," he reflected wistfully.

"How messed up?"

"Too messed up for my taste," he said evasively.

"Which is?" she inquired, her eyes pleading with him to continue.

"For one thing, unlike a good portion of the adult population, I believe in monogamy."

"And Kathleen Daniels didn't?"

"She had several sets of prints made of each shot," he said dryly.

Jessie didn't know why she should have been surprised by the information, but she was. "Did you know any of the other men she dated?"

Mike shook his head. "We didn't exactly run around in the same social circles—if you know what I mean."

"You mean men like Tom McCullough?"

"And a few silver spoons, as well. She needed to date men who could afford her," he said matter-of-factly. "Even had I wanted to continue dating her, I wouldn't have been the only man in her life because she had expensive tastes."

"Are you talking about drugs?"

"I'm not sure she was hooked on them, but she liked to go to parties where the coke was served alongside the nuts and mints on the coffee table. When I told her I wasn't interested, I never heard from her again."

Jessie was silent for several moments, contemplating everything Mike had told her. ''It seems odd that none of this was brought out at the trial,'' she said, puzzled.

''Like I said. She moved in a pretty snazzy social circle. My guess is that the kind of men she dated kept their mouths shut out of self-preservation.''

''Could be,'' she conceded, a frown knitting her brow. After looking at some of the proofs Mike still had from the Kathleen Daniels photo shoot, Jessie went home and tried to make sense out of everything she had learned about the dead woman.

More than ever, her instincts were strongly telling her that there was more to Kathleen's death than had been presented in the courtroom. Even though she wasn't sure the information she had uncovered would be useful in Tom McCullough's appeal, she knew that she had to tell someone what she had learned.

The question was, whom? Brian had warned her against going to see Tom McCullough's attorneys. If Aidan had been here and she could have explained to him face-to-face what she had found out, she might have told him, but it wasn't anything she wanted to get into over the phone, not when the mere mention of his father's trial caused such friction between the two of them.

That left only one person. Sean McCullough. Jessie knew he hadn't given up hope of finding new evidence that would prove his father was innocent. But this wasn't new evidence—or was it? She knew there was only one way to find out. She needed to go to see him.

It wouldn't be easy, and if Brian knew what she was doing he'd probably disapprove. Yet Jessie couldn't worry about the legal ramifications of her actions. Something wasn't right with Tom McCullough's conviction and she was going to find out what it was.

As she walked to McCullough Enterprises she told herself that she was doing the right thing. Sean McCullough—despite his initial attitude toward her—would be grateful she had come. In a way they were allies—they both wanted the same thing. To prove his father was innocent.

Jessie reminded herself of that common goal when she was shown into Sean's office and saw the daunting look on his face.

"Jessie." He stood behind the massive mahogany desk, gesturing for her to take one of the leather chairs across from him.

"Thank you for seeing me," she said politely, giving his office a quick perusal as she sat down. Everything spoke of money—the plush carpet, the mahogany furniture, the artwork on the walls. She saw several photographs on the credenza behind his desk—all family portraits, which reminded her of why she had come.

"What can I do for you?" he asked, leaning back in his chair.

"I have some information I thought you might be interested in."

One eyebrow arched and he tipped his head forward inquisitively. "About?"

"Kathleen Daniels."

That brought his whole body forward, and he placed his hands in front of him on the desk.

"You said you were looking for information that might help your father's appeal. I think I might have some."

He listened intently as she explained what she had learned about Kathleen Daniels from Mike Sampson. Any tension that he had previously exhibited was replaced by a curiosity that became hopeful enthusiasm as he questioned her thoroughly to make sure he understood what she was saying.

"I don't know if this is anything your father's attorney can use in the appeal, but I thought I should pass it on," she said when she was finished.

Sean seemed cautiously optimistic. "I'm not sure, either, but at least it's more than what I've been able to come up with," he admitted. "Does Aidan know about this?" he asked, watching her carefully.

She shook her head. "I figured since he's away it would be better to come to you," she told him, although she was certain that he knew her reluctance to tell Aidan had more to do with his attitude toward his father rather than with his being in California.

"I'm glad you came, Jessie," Sean said, coming around to the front of the desk.

Jessie stood, suddenly feeling awkward. "If there's anything else I can do…" She trailed off, debating whether she should confide in him her own reasons for believing in his father's innocence.

She decided not to tell him of the uncanny feelings she had about his father. For now it was enough that she had provided information that might help in the appeal.

IF JESSIE HAD HAD ANY worries that the intensity of her relationship with Aidan would change after being away from him for two weeks, they were quickly dispelled the very first night he arrived back in Minnesota. Aidan booked a suite at the Riverfront Hotel, just as he had on New Year's Eve, ordering room service so they could eat a quiet dinner for two before spending the rest of the night making love.

When she awoke the next morning she found him standing over her with a breakfast tray. On it was a basket of croissants, a bowl of strawberries, two glasses of orange juice laced with champagne and a red rose. Jessie pushed herself up against the pillow and said dreamily, "This could be habit forming."

Aidan sat on the edge of the bed and placed the bed tray in front of her. "Are you talking about me or the room service?"

"Both," she answered, leaning forward to give him a peck on the cheek.

"I'd like to go to bed with you every night and wake up with you every morning." He gave her a long, slow, seductive kiss, then said, "I missed you like crazy."

"I missed you, too," she told him, laying her palm against his cheek.

He turned his lips into it. "I never thought I'd see the day when I couldn't wait to hop a plane to Minnesota in January."

"Maybe you ought to move back here," she suggested lightly, her fingers traveling up and down his arm seductively.

"The thought has crossed my mind lately," he admitted, climbing into bed beside her.

"Really?" she asked.

"My mother's mentioned it to me on several occasions, but I'm not sure I could get used to the cold again," he answered, spreading raspberry jam on a croissant.

"There are ways of staying warm." As if to prove her point she reached out to touch the most sensitive areas of his body.

"There is always that challenge to stay warm, isn't there?" he murmured on a sigh of satisfaction.

"There is, isn't there," she agreed with a slow grin, her hands continuing to caress him.

"There's only one problem."

"What's that?"

He raised the croissant to her lips and she took a small bite. "I like California better."

Jessie sank back against the pillow with a groan.

"I also have a great job there," he added, giving her a sip of the sparkling orange juice. "On the other hand—" he took a bite from the other side of her croissant "—I'm lonely in California."

"You wouldn't be lonely in Minnesota," she told him, sitting forward. "And your mother would be happy."

"There's only one woman I want to make happy, Jessie." He raised the champagne glass and tipped it toward her.

A warm, tingly sensation rushed through Jessie's body. She was about to shove the bed tray aside and show him just how happy she was when the phone rang.

As soon as Jessie heard Aidan say, "Oh, hi, Mom," she wanted to get up and go into the other room. But Aidan's hand stopped her. While giving quite a few one-word answers such as "fine," "uh-huh" and "good," he gestured for her to stay where she was.

Jessie munched on strawberries while she waited for Aidan to finish, trying not to focus on his end of the conversation. When he closed with "We'll be there," she couldn't help but wonder who the "we" was and where the "there" was.

"That was my mother," he stated as soon as he had hung up the phone. "The family's getting together for brunch on Sunday and she wanted to know if I was planning on being there."

"Are you?" she asked, a sinking feeling in the pit of her stomach that the "we" he had mentioned included her.

"I told her I'd be there." He reached for her hand, and tightened his fingers around hers. "I'd like you to come with me. I think it's time you were introduced to my mother."

Jessie's eyes were filled with anxiety as she looked into his. "Have you told her about me?" she asked apprehensively.

"I'm sure she's already guessed there's someone special in my life. Mothers have a way of knowing about such things."

"I know, but does she know who I am?"

He gave her fingers a comforting squeeze. "She knows that you were on the jury."

"It's going to be awkward," she said uneasily.

"Jessie, I wouldn't take you if I thought there was the slightest chance that anyone would say anything to make you feel uncomfortable." He kissed her, a tender, reassuring kiss that had Jessie clinging to him. "I want you with me."

"All right." The words tumbled out despite the little voice that warned her it was not a good idea.

CHAPTER TWELVE

BRUNCH WAS SERVED at the McCullough family home, which was a sprawling manor set in the rolling countryside of suburban Minneapolis. Although Jessie knew Aidan's family was wealthy, she hadn't given much thought to the differences in their backgrounds until she saw his family home.

According to Aidan, Sunday brunch was his mother's way of bringing the family together on a regular basis. Besides Sean, Giselle and their two children, Mrs. McCullough had invited Aidan's grandmother plus an aunt and an uncle.

Jessie found it difficult to relax at the elegant dining-room table. Although no mention had been made of her role in the trial when introductions had been made, she sensed that everyone knew exactly who she was and that it was only a matter of time before one of them mentioned Tom McCullough.

As if he could sense her uneasiness, Aidan leaned close to her and whispered, "There's no need to be nervous. The McCulloughs haven't bitten a guest in years."

She smiled at him. "You have a nice family."

"What have you been saying to Uncle Larry? I've never seen him laugh so much." He refilled her cup with coffee.

She looked sideways at him and gave him a sly smile. "I guess we share the same sense of humor."

He placed his hand on her thigh. "I'm glad you came with me today."

"I am, too," she told him, wishing she could dispel her uneasiness.

"Did you get a chance to talk to my grandmother?"

She took a sip of her coffee. "Mmm-hmm." She glanced over to where an elderly, white-haired woman sat beside Mrs. McCullough. "As a matter of fact, we talked about you."

He grimaced good-naturedly. "Do I want to know what was said?"

Jessie chuckled. "Probably not."

His grandmother, having overheard bits of their conversation, spoke up. "It was simply girl talk, Aidan. Nothing you need to be concerned about."

Then Sean made several jokes regarding Aidan's bachelor status, which brought laughter from Sean and his uncle and a couple of chuckles from his mother and grandmother, as well.

"It's good to see smiling faces around this table again," Aidan's grandmother said.

"We haven't had much to smile about, have we," Sean remarked. Looking around the table, he added, "Since everyone's in such a good mood, this is probably as good a time as any to share some news I have regarding Dad's case."

Jessie's stomach muscles tightened. The moment she had been dreading had arrived. When she glanced sideways she noticed Aidan's smile had slipped from his face and his shoulders had stiffened.

"What news is that?" Mrs. McCullough asked with obvious interest.

All eyes were on Sean as he spoke. "There've been some developments in Dad's case. I didn't want to mention this to anybody until Will Lepley had checked into it, but it's possible there may be a witness who could testify that Dad didn't murder Kathleen Daniels.''

His announcement sparked a flurry of questions as eyes turned in his direction and voices demanded an explanation.

Sean leaned forward on his elbows, his face intent. "We all know that Kathleen Daniels was in Dad's car the night she was killed. It was the main piece of evidence the D.A. used to convict him of the crime.''

"So what are you saying? That someone saw her get out of Dad's car?" Aidan inquired, his fork poised in midair.

"No, but it's possible that she went to a party after she left Dad. If that's the case, all we have to do is find someone who was at this party who can testify to seeing her alive.''

Aidan's next comment thickened the air with tension. "You're assuming that she did get out of Dad's car.''

"Why is that so hard to believe?" Sean demanded in an accusing tone.

"Aidan, please." Helen McCullough's plea quieted both men.

Aidan apologized to his mother, then said, "If she had gone to a party, don't you think someone would have come forward by now?''

"It depends on the kind of party it was . . . and whether she left alone," Sean answered. "Maybe whoever was with her that night has a good reason for remaining silent.''

"This sounds like an awful lot of speculation to me," Aidan stated dubiously.

"Why don't you just let me explain what we found out before you pass judgment," Sean suggested, unable to keep the annoyance from his voice. Aidan gestured that the floor was all his.

"The D.A. wanted everyone to think Kathleen Daniels was a churchgoing, law-abiding citizen who was as sweet and simple as the girl next door. Well, thanks to Jessie, we found out that she wasn't quite the innocent the D.A. painted her to be. Actually, she was just the opposite."

Jessie swore she could feel a shock wave travel from Aidan's body to hers. When she looked at him, he was staring at her in a way she had never seen before.

"You knew Kathleen Daniels?" It was more of an accusation than a question.

She shook her head. "No, but I know someone who did." She explained about Mike Sampson, finishing up by saying, "I thought the information might help your father in his appeal so I went to see Sean."

"Yes, and it's a good thing she did," Sean said gratefully. "Will hired a private investigator to follow up on the information Jessie gave me. Although we've found several people who have told us Kathleen Daniels often went to parties where drugs were available, so far none of them will admit to seeing her on the night of the murder."

"Drugs?" Aidan's face registered his disbelief. "The medical examiner testified there were no traces of chemicals found during the autopsy."

Sean rubbed his jaw pensively. "All right, I admit that piece of the puzzle doesn't quite fit, but she still could have gone to a party that night."

"So your theory is she got out of Dad's car, went to this party, then hooked up with the wrong person who offered her a ride home and killed her?" Aidan posed the question as though it were rather absurd.

"It could have happened that way," Sean insisted. "Or maybe she was on her way home alone and was murdered by some stranger. It really doesn't matter as long as we can prove that she was alive after the time Dad says he last saw

er. That would mean Dad was telling the truth when he
said she got out of his car a little past eleven and he never
saw her again.''

"This is all speculation," Aidan protested irritably.

"Maybe it is, but considering Dad's situation, we have
to choice but to check out every possibility. Sitting in
prison for a crime you didn't commit can do things to a
person—mentally and physically." There was genuine
concern in Sean's face and Jessie felt herself softening toward him.

"It is awful there," Aidan's uncle agreed. "I was ap-
palled when I went to visit Tom.''

Talk then turned to the subject of living conditions in the
jail, with Mrs. McCullough relating several stories of her
husband's hardship. Although no one at the table appeared to notice how subdued Aidan was for the rest of the
meal, Jessie knew that he was upset and it was because of
the news about his father.

Jessie felt a wave of relief when it was finally time to
leave, for she wasn't sure how much longer she could stand
the tension that had pushed its way between her and Aidan. Although he hadn't questioned her as to why she
didn't tell him about the information she had given Sean,
he knew he wasn't happy with her.

However, it wasn't only Aidan's attitude bothering Jessie. Ever since she had arrived she had wanted to speak
privately to his mother about her role as a juror. Despite the
graciousness of her hostess, she could sense a reserve in the
older woman's demeanor that she could only attribute to
the trial. As awkward as it was, Jessie knew she couldn't
leave without bringing up the subject.

"Mrs. McCullough, there's something I want to say to
you before I go. It's about your husband's trial," Jessie
began, and she could see Aidan's brow furrowing as it al-

ways did whenever the trial was mentioned. "I know yc must realize that I was on the jury that convicted your hu band."

"Yes, my dear, I do," she said quietly. Her eyes were lighter shade of brown than Aidan's, but glimmered wit the same emotion.

Jessie took a deep breath and said, "I'm sorry. I kno that it doesn't do much good, but there's not much else can say."

Hearing her apology, Aidan frowned, but Jessie didn notice, for there was such a sadness in his mother's eyes sh didn't notice the man at her side.

"Jessie, it's not your fault that the district attorney pr sented a convincing case," Mrs. McCullough said in a voic that sounded tired. "Besides, we still have the appeal, an thanks to you, that's looking much brighter."

"I hope the information I gave Sean will be of som help," she said earnestly, aware that Aidan was scowlin beside her.

Mrs. McCullough forced a weak smile. "I learned a lon time ago, Jessie, that we have to accept that some things a simply meant to be."

When Jessie thought of all the pain Aidan's mother ha experienced because of the trial, a lump rose in her throat She would have liked to have hugged her as she thanked he for brunch, but she had never been one to show her emo tions easily, and so she settled for a handshake.

Jessie expected Aidan to explode the minute they got int the car. He didn't. He started up the engine without sayin a word and drove toward her grandmother's.

When they had driven several miles and he still hadn' broken the silence, she finally said, "You're upset about th news concerning your father, aren't you?"

"Maybe it's better if we don't discuss my father's situation. We don't seem to share the same opinions," he said polly.

Jessie sensed a criticism in his answer, which only made her want to pursue the subject. "Aren't you in the least bit happy that your father might be cleared of murder charges?"

"I'd say he's a long way from being cleared," he snapped irritably. "If you ask me, Sean is grasping at straws with his party theory of his."

"From what I heard, I think it's plausible."

He didn't comment, but concentrated on the road, which was slick with freshly fallen snow.

Jessie was not about to let the matter drop. "At least there's a little more optimism now than there was when you left for California."

"I wouldn't have gone if I had known that you and Sean would be playing amateur detective while I was away," he said irritably.

"I wasn't playing amateur detective!" she denied, stung by the criticism.

"What would you call your snooping around?" Aidan grumbled.

"Snooping?" Her mouth dropped open. "You make it sound as though I was doing something illegal. All I did was ask a few questions. Why are you so upset about this?"

"I don't like the fact that my brother's dragged you into this mess."

"He didn't drag me into this. I wanted to help, Aidan."

He stole a glance at her and his voice lost some of its hardness. "Fine. You've helped. But in the future, I'd prefer you to leave the investigating to the investigators."

"Why?"

"Because there are things you don't understand, Jes sie . . . private family things," he answered in a deceptivel calm voice that warned her to tread carefully.

They had reached her grandmother's house and Aida had pulled into the driveway, but he did not turn off th engine.

"You're right about that, Aidan. I don't understand. She sat stiffly, unwilling to make any movement towar him. Neither one said anything for several awkward mc ments. Then Jessie made another attempt. "I don't under stand why you're so opposed to anyone trying to help you father."

"Because all this is doing is prolonging the agony we'v been going through ever since he was arrested." Aida raked a hand through his hair. "What if Kathleen Daniel went to a party? What if she was with someone other tha my father? What good are all the what ifs?" he pleade emotionally. "Don't you see? Without any concrete evi dence, the what ifs are useless . . . except for raising fals hopes in my mother."

"What would you rather everybody do, Aidan? Give u and let your father spend the rest of his life in prison?"

"Maybe that's what he deserves," he said soberly. "Dc I have to remind you that you were on the jury that founc him guilty?"

His words were like an arrow that had been aimed at target and had hit the bull's-eye. "This is getting us no where." She reached for the door but he was too quick fo her, trapping her with his arm.

"It bothers you that you found him guilty, doesn't it? he charged. "Isn't that why you're getting involved in ol this?"

"I don't have to listen to this," she said, pushing his arn away.

But he refused to be thwarted. "Why don't you just admit it? You're not doing this for my sake, but for yours."

Jessie's heart drummed relentlessly in her chest. She wanted to deny the accusation, but how could she deny the truth? He had reached right in and stripped away a layer of self-protection she thought she had safely anchored in place. She threw open the car door and tried to scramble out, but he grabbed her by the arm.

"Let go of me," she demanded, piercing him with a look that made Aidan's heart sink in his chest. He released her just as quickly as he had caught her.

"Jessie, wait!" he called out before the door slammed shut, but she didn't stop. Without so much as a glance backward she went running into the house.

He sat in the car for several minutes, replaying all the accusations and angry words that had flowed between them. It wasn't so much what she had said that had angered him, but the look that had been in her eyes—as though she was suppressing a shudder.

She truly didn't understand him at all. Couldn't she see the emotional toll the trial had taken on him? Her eyes filled with sympathy for his mother and admiration for his brother, yet when they looked into his, they clouded with disappointment because he couldn't rally behind a man who had hurt the people he loved the most.

He shifted the car into Reverse and backed out of the driveway, thinking how different the day had ended from the way it had started. And all because of his father.

For four years he had stayed away from the people he loved because of his father, hoping that time and distance would allow him to forget the reason he had fled Minnesota. But now as he drove home, the past flashed before him crystal clear, as if it were only yesterday.

If it hadn't been for his reluctance to let go of the past he never would have introduced Kate to his father that day at the Uptown Art Fair. Aidan had wanted to ignore her but she had a way of getting under a man's skin and staying there, like a wood tick sucking a man's blood, and he hadn't been able to resist speaking to her. She had been searching for just the right watercolor for her new apartment; he and his father had come to soak up the atmosphere and browse through the hundreds of artisans booths.

Mesmerized by her beauty, his father had been the one who had invited Kate to have a drink with the two of them. Aidan had tried to signal to his father that Kate was a former girlfriend he'd rather not encourage, but Kate's charm was strong, and before he knew it they were seated at Figlio's drinking Mai-Tais.

Aidan had been cool toward her, thinking she wanted to start something up with him again. He had even chewed out his father afterward for his halfhearted attempts at matchmaking. Now he could only chuckle in self-derision. Little had he known that Kate was no more interested in rekindling their affair than he had been. It was his father who had caught her fancy.

An unpleasant feeling settled in his stomach as he remembered the day he had made that discovery. It had been a billing error that had raised his suspicions. A statement from the florist listed a charge for a dozen roses sent to K Daniels.

At first Aidan had thought it was simply an old charge that had somehow managed to show up on a current statement. However, when he had called the florist to straighten out the matter he'd learned the flowers had indeed been sent recently, but that the charge should have been on his father's account, not his.

Aidan had left the office immediately and gone to Kate's apartment. He had pounded on the door but there had been no answer. So he had waited. And waited. Until finally she had arrived.

Aidan had felt sick to his stomach at the sight of the man whose arm was at her waist possessively. Not because he still had feelings for Kate, but because for twenty-six years the man at her side had been his hero, a man he had proudly called "Dad." A man who was cheating on his mother.

Aidan had refused to listen to any explanations. For his mother's sake he had pretended there was nothing wrong with his relationship with his father, but after only a couple of weeks of hypocrisy he'd been unable to take any more. When the job offer had come from California, he'd packed his bags and left.

Now, four years later, he couldn't help but wonder if he hadn't made a mistake in leaving. Maybe if he had stayed and exposed his father, the affair would have ended and there would have been no murder trial to tear his family apart.

Guilty. The verdict echoed in his mind. Guilty. But who was the guilty party? His father? Him?

He couldn't think about it. It was a subject that had already caused him enough grief with his family. Now it was threatening to drive a wedge into his relationship with Jessie.

A pain knifed through his heart at the thought. He couldn't lose Jessie because of his father. He wouldn't lose her. But all he could see was that look of revulsion in her eyes as she had hurried to get away from him.

JESSIE WAS FULL of self-recrimination that evening. She had known from the start that it wasn't wise to get involved with Aidan, yet she had let the powerful sexual attraction she felt

for him overpower her intellect. Now she was having to pa
the price.

How quickly everything had changed. This morning sh
had thought that she and Aidan were on their way to mak
ing a commitment to each other. Now she wasn't sure if sh
even wanted to see him again.

As soon as the thought entered her mind she knew i
wasn't true. She wanted to see him...more than she ha
ever wanted to see any man. *That* was the problem.

She sighed as she rolled over on her bed to stare at th
ceiling. If only she could understand why he was havin
such difficulty in believing in his father's innocence. Sh
knew there were problems between Aidan and his fathe
problems he didn't want to share with her. That was wha
disturbed her most. She could accept that he was havin
trouble dealing with his feelings toward his father. Sh
couldn't accept that he wouldn't share those feelings wit
her.

When the doorbell rang later that evening, Jessie's hear
skipped a beat at the thought it might be Aidan. It wasn't
It was Missy. She looked haggard and drawn, a backpac
in her hand.

"What's happened?" Jessie asked, knowing immedi
ately from the look on her face that something was seri
ously wrong.

"Please let me stay with you, Auntie Jess. I can't live a
home anymore." Before Jessie had a chance to ask an
questions, Missy broke down in tears.

Jessie put her arm around Missy's shivering form an
pulled her into the living room, where she took the back
pack from her arms and helped her out of her coat.

"How did you get here?" Jessie asked, noticing that th
legs of her niece's jeans were covered with snow.

"I hitchhiked."

Jessie suppressed a groan. "You must be half-frozen. Why don't we go into the kitchen and I'll make you a warm drink. Gran's in Florida, but my hot chocolate's almost as good as hers."

Missy shook her head. "I'm really tired. Can I just go to bed?"

Jessie wanted to ask her questions, to find out what had prompted her to leave home, but the teenager was trembling so badly she decided explanations could wait for the morning. "Sure. Let's go up and I'll get you the electric blanket and a warm flannel nightgown." She gave her niece a comforting squeeze, then helped her wobbly figure climb the stairs.

Jessie quickly made up the guest bedroom, while Missy sat trancelike on the old-fashioned boudoir chair. By the time Jessie had plugged in the electric blanket, Missy still hadn't made any effort to remove her wet clothes.

"Why don't you change into this nightgown and I'll go get you something warm to drink." She passed her niece the floral-print nightgown she had dug out of her drawer.

"You aren't going to call my mom, are you?" Missy called out.

Jessie paused in the doorway. "She's going to be worried about you, Missy," she said gently. "I have to call her."

"Then I have to leave," she said, scooping up her backpack.

Jessie couldn't let her go in the condition she was in. "No, it's all right." She held up her hands in supplication. "I won't call her right now if you don't want me to, but we'll need to talk about this tomorrow."

Missy stared at her suspiciously. "You won't call her?"

"No. I promise." Jessie moved over to the nightstand and took the telephone receiver from its cradle. "There. We'll leave it off the hook for now, okay?"

Missy nodded uneasily and sank back down onto the chair. Jessie sighed with relief.

Instead of hot chocolate, she warmed up a can of chicken noodle soup and toasted two slices of bread. She hoped that Missy wouldn't be sleeping by the time she was finished.

She wasn't. She was in the middle of changing her clothes when Jessie entered the room with the serving tray. Immediately the teenager grabbed the nightgown and draped it across her bare chest.

"Oh, I'm sorry," Jessie apologized, setting the serving tray on the nightstand and turning her back to her niece. While Missy was blushing with embarrassment, Jessie was white with shock. In just a few seconds she had seen enough of her niece to know the doctor had been right with his diagnosis. Protruding bones and sunken flesh had changed a healthy body into a picture of horror.

Within seconds Missy had slipped the nightgown over her head, and a pile of wet clothes was pooled at her feet. "It's okay, Auntie Jess."

Even with the nightgown covering her arms and legs she still looked horribly thin, and Jessie could see that her hair was brittle and dull. The first word that came to Jessie's mind was malnourished.

"I brought you some soup and toast," she said, indicating the tray near the bed.

"Thanks." A hint of a smile curved her mouth.

Jessie had the overwhelming urge to sit beside her and spoon-feed her, but to her surprise Missy didn't need any encouragement.

"This tastes good," she murmured in between sips of the broth.

"Are you still cold?" Jessie asked, trying not to stare at her as she ate. Large, dark crescents shadowed eyes that mirrored trouble.

"A little, but I don't want to climb into bed until I'm finished eating, otherwise I'll get crumbs in the covers," she said in a small voice.

As soon as she was finished, Missy climbed under the thick woolen electric blanket and sighed. "This feels good."

Jessie sat on the side of the bed. "We need to talk, Missy," she said gently as she tucked the covers up close to her chin.

Uncertainty clouded the tired eyes. "I can't go back to the farm, Auntie Jess," she said grimly.

"Why? What's happened?"

She chewed on her lower lip before answering. "It's my mom. She's driving me crazy."

"Doing what?" she gently probed.

"She watches me…all the time. What I eat, what I drink. She even stands by the door when I go to the bathroom." She played with the satin hem on the blanket. "I mean, can you imagine what it's like to have your mother waiting outside the bathroom door for you?"

"She's only trying to help," Jessie said in her sister's defense, despite the rush of sympathy she was feeling for her niece.

"I don't need any help. I'm all right, Auntie Jess."

"Are you?" Jessie asked, reaching for her hand.

"You saw me eat."

And I also saw your bones sticking out of your flesh, Jessie said to herself. "You're awfully thin, Missy." It wasn't a chastisement, but an expression of concern.

Missy immediately withdrew her hand from Jessie's "You're going to call Mom, aren't you." It was an accusation, not a question.

"Only to let her know you're safe."

"Please don't." Her hands twisted the hem of the blanket. "She'll make me go in the hospital."

"Would that be so bad?" Jessie asked gently.

"I don't feel sick," she exclaimed.

Jessie looked at her emaciated frame and wanted to cry. "Don't get upset thinking about it," she said soothingly. "Get a good night's sleep tonight and tomorrow we'll worry about what happens next, okay?"

"I'm not sick," she repeated adamantly. "Bring me more food and I'll eat it. You'll see. I'm fine."

Jessie wanted so badly to believe her niece, but the memory of how she had looked undressed haunted her. "All right. Don't worry about it, just go to sleep." She leaned over and kissed her on the forehead.

Jessie wanted to believe that Missy would be fine without professional treatment, but there was no denying the physical evidence before her. After depositing the dishes in the kitchen, she went back upstairs to her room.

As she passed the bathroom she noticed the door was shut. Unable to resist, she pressed her ear up against the wood, then immediately chastised herself. If Missy caught her spying on her she'd be gone in a flash.

She quickly stepped away, but not before she heard evidence that Missy was purging. Sickened, she moved over to the telephone to call her sister.

Jessie wasn't sure if she was relieved or anxious when Carla agreed not to drive down until the following morning. As much as Jessie didn't want to alienate her niece, she was rapidly coming to the conclusion that the sooner Missy was hospitalized, the better.

Ever since Christmas Carla and Jessie's relationship had been strained. Several times Jessie had phoned her sister, and each time Carla had been polite, but distant.

Jessie didn't sleep well that night. She couldn't help but keep one ear open just in case Missy decided to leave, and she couldn't stop thinking about the way things had ended with Aidan.

By the time Carla arrived the next morning Jessie's stomach was agitated, her body ached from a lack of sleep and her nerve endings felt as though they were poking through her skin. She braced herself for another tongue-lashing from her sister, but it never came.

"We're taking her to the hospital," Carla said calmly when Jessie opened the door to her the next morning. Standing behind her was Gene.

"I think that's best," Jessie told her as she ushered them into the house. "She's upstairs in the shower."

Both her sister and her brother-in-law looked as though they had been through an emotional wringer. Jessie briefly explained what had happened the previous night and watched their faces become more grim.

"You know she doesn't think she needs to be hospital-ized," Jessie said apprehensively.

"She's afraid they're going to force-feed her until she gets fat," Gene said with a disbelieving shake of his head.

"The doctor says eating is the one thing she can control in her life," Carla added. "If she goes into the hospital, she thinks she'll lose control of her life."

"Are you taking her this morning?" Jessie asked.

Carla nodded soberly. "It has to be done."

"Would you mind if I came along?"

"Are you sure you want to? Missy still considers you one of her allies. If you come along, that'll probably change," Carla warned her.

"I'm not doing it for Missy. I thought you might wan me there," Jessie said, swallowing back the emotion tha had suddenly clogged her throat.

Carla didn't say anything for several seconds, then reached over and hugged Jessie. "Thanks," she said, he voice a half sob. "I'd like you there."

As Carla had predicted, Missy didn't appreciate Jessie going along to the hospital. In fact, she was downright angry that her aunt had sided with her mother.

Jessie tried not to let Missy's anger affect her, but by the time visiting hours were over that evening she was worn out. But as bad as she was feeling, she could see that Carla's suffering was worse.

While Gene went to get the car, Jessie tried to comfort her sister outside the hospital. "She'll be fine. You did the right thing," she told her, giving her a reassuring squeeze.

"Then why do I feel so crummy? I feel like all of her problems are my fault." She looked at Jessie, her face blotchy from crying.

"You wouldn't be human if you didn't blame yourself. All mothers feel responsible for their children, but this is not your fault, Carla," Jessie said firmly.

"That's what the doctors said, but I keep thinking back to when she was small and how I used to make such a fuss over the way she looked. Remember how I made her take dance lessons even though she hated them? And then there were those kiddie beauty pageants I entered her in." She shook her head in self-recrimination.

"Lots of mothers put unwilling daughters into dance lessons and beauty pageants, but that doesn't cause them to have eating disorders," Jessie said, trying to console her.

"I just wish I had never harped at her about her weight. Ever since she was small I cautioned her about eating the wrong kinds of foods, but that was only because I didn't want her having to battle her weight the way I've had to all these years." Carla twisted her hands in her lap.

"Let's face it. Ours is a society that puts an enormous amount of emphasis on how a woman looks. Look at me. I make my living on my looks."

Carla blew her nose, then shook her head. "I should never have blamed you for this, Jessie. You've been a positive influence in Missy's life and I should have never said those things to you at Christmas. I'm sorry." Her voice broke and she reached into her purse for another tissue.

Jessie gave her shoulder a gentle squeeze. "When something like this happens, all of us wonder if there wasn't something we could have done to prevent it. It's only natural because we care about Missy."

Carla suppressed a sob. "Did you hear what the doctor called it? He said she has a communication problem."

"Mmm-hmm. She needs to learn how to express the feelings she's been keeping locked inside her."

Carla nodded. "I guess that's one of the advantages of hospitalization. She'll be able to attend group therapy with other girls who have the same problem she has. That way she won't feel so alone."

"I've heard good things about the program," Jessie commented.

Carla sighed. "I hope it works. We have to do family therapy—all of us. Me, Gene, Chad and even Kelly."

"Are you worried about that?"

"It isn't going to be easy for us to get away from the farm."

"In this instance, you don't have any choice," Jessie stated in her usual pragmatic tone. "Talk to Dad and Jim. I'm sure they'll help you out." She deliberately put an extra dose of optimism in her voice, but she knew that there were difficult times ahead for her sister and her family. An eating disorder was not a problem that could be easily cured with a hospital stay.

It was quite late by the time Gene's pickup pulled into their grandmother's driveway. Sitting in front of the house was a big white Lincoln, its windows covered with frost.

"Looks like someone's waiting for you." Although Gene hadn't shut off the engine, Carla had climbed out of the truck with Jessie. "Do you want us to stick around?"

"No, it's all right," Jessie answered, her heart beating wildly in her chest. "You've got a long drive ahead of you. Go on. I'll be fine." She gave her sister a hug, eyeing the Lincoln apprehensively.

Carla and Gene started to drive away, but paused when they saw Aidan get out of his car. It was no wonder, Jessie thought. He looked awful. Besides not having shaved, he looked as though he had been ill.

Jessie waved at her sister, gesturing that everything was okay. Then she turned toward Aidan.

"How long have you been sitting in the car?" she asked.

He shrugged. "I don't know. A couple of hours."

"A couple of hours! Aren't you cold?"

"I had the car running, but it ran out of gas. I didn't want to leave to go get some more in case I missed you. Jessie, I need to talk to you."

She quickly climbed the porch steps and inserted her key into the lock. "Come on in," she instructed, pushing the door open.

He followed her into the kitchen, and in the bright light he looked even worse than he had outside beneath the street lamp. She gestured for him to sit while she heated a cup of water in the microwave.

"You should have called me," she gently reprimanded him, slipping out of her coat.

"I did, but there was no answer. Where's your grand-mother?"

"She's in Florida on vacation." When the microwave beeped she removed the cup and poured a heaping tea-spoon of coffee granules into the steaming water.

"Who were those people you were with?"

"That was my sister and my brother-in-law," she answered, setting the coffee in front of him. "You'd better drink this, your lips are blue," she said, folding her arms across her chest.

He took several sips, wrapping his large hands around the dainty china cup.

"Why did you come, Aidan?"

He set the cup down. "I need to know where things stand with us."

"Where do you want them to be?" she asked cautiously, standing far enough away from him so that he couldn't touch her.

"Can we forget yesterday ever happened?"

"I don't think so," she answered quietly.

"Then what do we do?" he asked, a hint of anxiety in his voice.

"Maybe it would be better if we quit seeing each other," he said in a low voice that was barely above a whisper.

"No! Don't say that," he begged, jumping to his feet. He started toward her, but she stepped back and he halted in his tracks. "I love you, Jessie."

His declaration brought a lump to her throat. When she lifted her eyes and saw the tenderness in his, it was more than her battered emotions could take. "Oh, Aidan," was all she managed to say before the tears came.

Aidan wanted to gather her into his arms and comfort her, but he wasn't sure that she wasn't crying because of him. He had come with the hope that she shared his feel-

ings and would want to continue their relationship. Now h
wasn't so sure. When she turned her back to him, his hear
contracted painfully.

"I'm sorry, Jessie. I shouldn't have come." He picked u
his jacket and started toward the door. His fingers were o
the knob when she stopped him.

"No, don't go." She wiped at the tears with the back o
her hand.

He turned to face her. "I don't want to make you un
happy."

"You don't. I'm not crying because of us," she said wit
a sniffle. "I mean, I am upset about yesterday, but I haven'
had much sleep in the last twenty-four hours and then to
day I spent all day at the hospital."

"Hospital?"

"We had to put my niece in an eating disorder clinic,'
she told him, feeling another surge of emotion. Jessie trie
to stop the tears that trickled from her eyes, but it was a
though one huge ball of emotion was tumbling out of con
trol. "That's why my sister and her husband were here."

"No wonder you're so upset," he said soothingly, mov
ing closer to her. "Do you want to talk about it?" he asked
slipping his arm around her shoulder.

Jessie nodded, sliding onto his lap as he sat down. Sh
meant to tell him only the medical details, but before sh
knew it she was confiding in him, explaining how Carla ha
blamed her for Missy's illness. By the time she was fin
ished she had revealed things she hadn't even admitted t
herself.

"So all of this has caused you to reflect about what yo
do for a living," he surmised in understanding.

She nodded. "Intellectually, I know I'm not responsibl
for Missy's behavior, but I can't ignore the fact that I'r

part of an industry that encourages women to go without food simply to look good to others.''

''Maybe that's true,'' Aidan agreed. ''But you also stay healthy by eating right. You haven't let your job distort your priorities.''

The longer they talked, the better Jessie felt. Never would she have imagined that she would be able to tell him her innermost fears and anxieties, and now that she had, the wonderful security blanket intimacy provides settled around her.

She studied the face that she had come to cherish more than any other she had ever known. ''I love you, Aidan.''

He tightened his hold on her, his mouth finding hers with undisguised relief.

''Oh, Jessie,'' he said on a heavy sigh when the kiss ended, pressing his forehead to hers. ''I don't want to argue with you...especially not over my father. I don't know why things got so crazy at my mother's the other day, but I'm sorry.''

She lifted her head and stared into his eyes. ''Won't he always be between us?''

''No.'' His answer was a sharp retort. ''I know I said some things I shouldn't have said Sunday, and I'm sorry.'' He lifted her hands to his lips and kissed each knuckle. ''It was sweet of you to try to help.''

''But you resented my interference.''

Again he sighed. ''No, it's just that I've seen what this trial has done to my family, and I don't want you to get caught up in the same kind of heartbreak.'' He held her tightly, as though protecting her from harm.

''But I like your mother and I want to help if I can.''

''And my mother likes you. She scolded me for the way I behaved on Sunday. Made me feel like I was twelve in-

stead of thirty." He planted tiny kisses on her wrists, the
traveled up her arms until he was at her shoulders.

"Aidan, you have got to resolve whatever it is that'
keeping you and your father apart...not just for you
mother's sake, but for you, as well," she advised him in
husky voice.

"I'm trying, Jessie, but it's not easy." The muscles in hi
body stiffened as he spoke. "He risked everything that wa
important to our family, and all for a relationship with
woman who was young enough to be his daughter."

"He's still your father, Aidan," she said gently.

His eyes darkened with emotion. "That's what makes m
so angry."

"Oh, Aidan" was all Jessie could say. She pressed he
forehead against his and closed her eyes.

"I can't just forgive and forget, Jessie," he said throug
clenched teeth.

Jessie pressed his head to her breast, not knowing wha
else to say. Finally she said, "Maybe time's the only thin
that will help."

He lifted his head. "It bothers you that there's discor
in my family, doesn't it?"

Jessie nodded. "You have to work it out, Aidan. And no
just for your mother's sake, but for ours."

"I will," he told her. "But you have to promise me you
won't go off playing detective. If Kate Daniels moved i
social circles where drugs were freely exchanged, it's not th
kind of people I want you to be around."

Kate Daniels. For just a moment it struck Jessie as rathe
odd that no one else had referred to Kathleen as Kate, wit
the exception of a couple of witnesses who had been friend
of hers. But then dark brown eyes gazed lovingly into her
and she pushed the thought aside, as well as all the argu-

ments she had formed as to why they didn't have a future together.

"All right, we'll leave the investigating to the professionals," she told him as his lips found the bare skin at her throat. "If we're going to make our relationship work, Aidan, we have to be honest about our feelings...and that includes yours toward your father."

"I don't want to talk about my father, Jessie." While his mouth blazed a trail of desire, his hands slid inside the bodice of her blouse and cupped a breast.

Jessie had told herself that if she made amends with Aidan, she would demand that he tell her what it was that had caused so much bitterness between him and his dad. But as his touch worked its magic on her body, all thoughts of his family disappeared, and all that mattered was that she was back in his arms where she belonged.

CHAPTER THIRTEEN

WHEN AIDAN ANNOUNCED that he'd be staying on for a couple of weeks to help Sean with McCullough Enterprises, Jessie felt as though she had been given a reprieve as to making a decision regarding the future.

Although she and Aidan hadn't made any long-term plans, they were rapidly approaching the point in their relationship where the next step would require a commitment between them. For now they could tolerate the long-distance love affair, but sooner or later the time would come when either she would have to move to L.A. or he would have to come back to Minnesota. On more than one occasion Aidan had hinted that he wanted her to move to California.

Jessie knew it was impractical to think that he would want to leave a successful business to return to Minneapolis. Although he was confident she'd have no trouble finding work in Los Angeles, Jessie knew the market in L.A. was much more competitive than it was in the Midwest, and the thought of leaving a city where she was already established was unsettling.

Despite agreeing not to speak of the trial or the pending appeal, Jessie couldn't put it from her mind completely. As hard as she tried to ignore the impulses regarding Tom McCullough, they continued to haunt her, pushing their way into her conscience.

Besides the fact that she was convinced that Tom McCullough was innocent, she found it troubling that Aidan and his father had such a strained relationship. And the fact that Aidan refused to talk to her about it simply made her more curious. It was the only sore spot in their relationship and it was a nasty one.

Like Aidan, Jessie wanted the entire mess resolved. She preferred that it would end with Tom McCullough being found innocent, but she told herself that if another jury convicted him of murder a second time, she would accept that she had been wrong about her feelings.

One bitterly cold afternoon when she was nearing the end of her shift at Renae's Bridal Salon, she noticed Sean outside the window. With his face tucked into the collar of his coat and a hat shielding his forehead from the cold, she almost didn't recognize him. But then he waved and smiled at her, motioning that he'd see her inside.

"What brings you here?" Jessie asked when she found him a short time later in the salon.

"I'm bringing a message from Aidan," he said with a friendly grin. "He had to drive to St. Cloud this afternoon and won't be able to have dinner with you this evening, but he will be back tomorrow morning and hopes you'll meet him for lunch at the Loon Café, twelve-thirty."

When Jessie frowned slightly, he added, "I'm sure he'll call you this evening."

They made small talk for several minutes, with Jessie resisting the urge to ask about his father. Just before Sean was going to leave, she gave in to the temptation.

"By the way, how is your father?" she asked, ignoring the guilty sensation fluttering like a caged butterfly inside her.

"Actually, he's in pretty good spirits. Things are looking brighter than they have in several months. I'm just on my way to see him."

"You're going to the prison?"

"Yeah. Want to come along?" It sounded like an innocent enough question, but Jessie couldn't help but wonder about Sean's motives.

Suspicious, she asked, "Are you serious?"

"Is there any reason why I shouldn't be?"

She wanted to say yes, there is. One big one named Aidan, but the longer she thought about it, the more intrigued she was by the idea. She hadn't seen Tom McCullough since that fateful day in the courtroom. Maybe if she were to meet him face-to-face she could better understand why she thought he was innocent.

"Do you really think it's a good idea?" she asked, apprehension furrowing her brow.

"Only if it's something you want to do."

For a brief moment Jessie thought about Aidan and how angry he would be when he found out. But then she remembered the guilt she had been suffering over her role in the trial and she decided that if nothing else, she wanted to see Tom McCullough to judge for herself whether she had made a mistake on the verdict.

"All right, I'll come with you," she told Sean.

Jessie had never visited anyone in jail before. Just driving into the prison complex was an unnerving experience that caused her stomach to jiggle in an unfamiliar way. When they stepped into the visitors' room and the door locked behind them, the seriousness of Tom McCullough's predicament was put into perspective.

She could see why Sean was so anxious to get him released. The man who had sat so tall and distinguished at the defense table in the courtroom had become a shell of his

ormer self. Jessie guessed that it was due partly to his
health, but she couldn't help but wonder if morally his
spirit hadn't been broken. When her eyes met his, she felt
a trembling sensation and knew that he didn't belong in this
prison.

After an affectionate embrace from his father, Sean
urged Jessie forward and made the appropriate introductions.

"So at last we get to meet," Tom McCullough said, extending his hand to Jessie. When he smiled, she could see
his resemblance to Aidan, for he had perfectly straight teeth
and a small dimple in his cheek.

Jessie took a deep breath. "Mr. McCullough." She
took the hand he offered. "I'm glad we finally have a
chance to talk."

"I've heard a lot about you," he told her as they all sat
down.

"You remember me from the trial, don't you?" She
didn't need to ask the question, for the answer was in his
eyes as he stared at her.

"Oh, yes. Aidan pointed you out to me because he
thought you looked like Kathleen," he said bluntly.

Jessie couldn't have been more surprised had someone
thrown a bucket of cold water in her face. Was that why
Aidan had stared at her so relentlessly in the courtroom?
Because he thought she had resembled the murder victim?

"Do I look like Kathleen Daniels?" she asked weakly,
her eyes moving inquisitively from Tom McCullough to his
son.

Sean's response was immediate. "Not at all. You may
have the same color of hair, but that's where the resemblance ends. I never could understand why Aidan thought
you did."

His father continued to study Jessie pensively befo
saying, "No, I don't believe you do, either." Jessie wasr
so sure he was telling the truth, but was relieved when
changed the subject. "Aidan tells me you're a model."

"Yes, I am," she confirmed, surprised that Aidan ha
talked to his father about her. From his attitude she ha
assumed he didn't visit the prison.

They talked briefly about her career, then moved on
the topic of what it was like growing up on a farm. The
was something gentle about Tom McCullough that ma
Jessie warm to the man. It also reaffirmed her earlier i
stincts that he was no killer.

When the guard informed them there were only a fe
minutes left to visit, Jessie said, "Mr. McCullough, there
something I want to tell you before I go." She took a de
breath to steady her nerves. "Ever since I first saw you si
ting at the defense table in the courtroom, I had this stran
feeling that you were innocent. Unfortunately, as jurors, v
were all instructed not to go by instincts or emotions, b
by the evidence presented during the trial."

"And the evidence did little to prove my innocence, d
it?" he said soberly.

"I'm sorry—" she began, only to have him cut her off
raising his hand.

"You don't need to apologize, Jessie. Eleven other pe
ple saw things the same way you did."

"That doesn't make what we did right."

He looked her squarely in the eyes and again she was r
minded of Aidan. "I've made some foolish mistakes in n
life and done some things I'm not proud of, but I'd nev
murder anyone, Jessie," he said with an integrity she b
lieved was genuine.

"I believe you," she told him. "I only wish there wa
something I could do to help prove your innocence."

"From what Sean tells me, you're already responsible for nformation that may help the appeal."

"That's true," Sean interjected. "Will Lepley said Jessie's tip may be what we need to convince the judge you hould be granted a new trial."

However, it wasn't Tom McCullough's plea of innocence that occupied her thoughts on the way home. It was hat one statement he had made regarding her appearance. *Aidan thought you looked like Kathleen.*

Jessie wasn't quite sure why it bothered her that Aidan had thought she looked like the murder victim. At least, not until her brain scanned its memory files and found Aidan's voice saying, *You remind me of someone I used to know.*

He had said that to her in the hospital coffee shop. Jessie had thought it was a line men often used when they wanted to meet women. Now she realized that for Aidan it had been the truth. The reason he had stared at her in Braxton's window and during the trial was because she had reminded him of Kathleen Daniels.

An unpleasantness swelled in the pit of her stomach. Aidan had never mentioned that he knew Kathleen Daniels. Yet he had called her Kate when everyone else referred to her as Kathleen. Could it be that he had known the woman well?

Ignoring her promise to him that she wouldn't go looking for information about the dead woman without his knowledge, she called her agent to find out how to contact Lenore Green. As it turned out, Lenore was doing a fashion show at a Minneapolis shopping mall the following afternoon. Forgetting about her lunch date with Aidan, Jessie made the long trip across town to see her.

Although they had never been formally introduced, Jessie had worked with Lenore on several occasions, mostly doing runway modeling. She had always been cool and aloof, and consequently Jessie hadn't made any effort to get to know her.

Instead of going into the dressing room, Jessie waited at the foot of the stage for the models to leave. When Lenore Green stepped out from behind the heavy curtain, she would have walked right past Jessie if she hadn't spoken to her.

"Hi. I'm Jessie Paulson. We've worked a few shows together—one was at the Galleria last spring." She extended her hand and the other woman took it cautiously.

"Lenore Green," she said, eyeing Jessie curiously.

"Yes, I know. I wonder if I could talk to you for a few minutes?"

The tall, slender brunette shrugged. "Sure. What about?"

"It's about a friend of yours...Kathleen Daniels."

Any softening in the woman's face quickly disappeared. "If you don't mind, I'd rather not," she answered stiffly and started walking toward the mall's exit.

Jessie walked alongside her. "Please. It'll only take a few minutes."

"The woman's dead. What could you possibly need to know?" she asked without stopping.

"I think the wrong man is in jail for her murder."

That made her stop and face Jessie. "And you want my help in proving that this 'wrong man' didn't do it, right?" she asked in disbelief. "You are the second person this week who has been after me to talk about Kate."

"You've already spoken to the private investigator?"

"Yes, and I'm going to tell you the same thing I told him. There's no way I would lift a finger to help any of the McCulloughs."

"Any of them?" Jessie repeated in confusion.

Lenore had started walking again and Jessie had to grab her arm to get her to stop. "Wait! Why did you say you wouldn't help any of the McCulloughs?"

"I told you I really don't want to discuss this." She shook her arm free of Jessie's grasp.

"I'm sorry. I'm sure it's not easy talking about a friend you've lost, but this is really important to me. I need to know about Kathleen's relationship with the McCulloughs...for personal reasons," she added in a quieter voice.

"Which one are you involved with? Aidan or the old man?" the brunette asked, her face twisting into a frown that almost looked like pity.

"Aidan's a friend of mine." Suddenly Jessie's lungs refused to operate normally. "Were he and Kathleen...?"

"Lovers?" the other woman finished for her when she stopped, short of breath. "He never told you, did he."

By now Jessie's heart was banging out of rhythm and her stomach was like an angry sea. She thought about turning and leaving before Lenore could tell her any more, but some perverse curiosity made her stay.

"Aidan's been in California for the past four years," she said weakly.

"Yes. The reason he left was because he broke up with Kate."

Jessie couldn't think clearly. She knew she should be asking more questions, but all she could think about was the fact that Aidan and Kathleen Daniels had been lovers.

Lenore Green continued to make disparaging comments about Aidan and his father, but Jessie's head was pounding and her thoughts were scattering in all directions. She needed to get away, to get fresh air, to think through what she had learned.

She held up her hand in protest. "It's all right... yo don't need to tell me any more."

Lenore shrugged. "It's your life. But if I were you, wouldn't be so quick to defend either of them. You say yo don't think Tom McCullough is guilty. Well, maybe I isn't. Personally, I wouldn't have been surprised if they ha told me Aidan had done it."

"No!" Jessie denied strongly. "No, he couldn't have. Her arms and legs began to tremble.

"Think what you like," the other woman said with shrug.

Perspiration was starting to bead on Jessie's forehead. She needed fresh air. "I'm sorry about what happened t Kathleen... really, I'm very sorry," she murmured, the rushed to the door, stumbling onto the snow-covered walk.

The cold air burned her lungs as she took several dee gulps, but she didn't notice. Nor did she see the puddles c slush or feel the wetness seeping through her shoes as sh made her way to her car. Once inside, she took several dee calming breaths, then grasped the steering wheel with he trembling fingers and headed for home.

As soon as Jessie was able to get past the feelings c jealousy Lenore's revelation had caused, she started piec ing bits of information together in her mind. Until now sh had thought Aidan's hostility toward his father was due t the pain he had caused his mother. But after learning abou his involvement with Kathleen, Jessie couldn't help b wonder if his anger wasn't due partly to the fact that he sti had feelings for her long after she had become his father mistress. Maybe Helen McCullough hadn't been the onl one hurt by Tom McCullough's affair with the younge woman.

The more Jessie thought about the triangle, the mo uneasy she became. Pieces of the puzzle she had been tr

ng so hard to put together began to fall into place, and she
didn't like the way those pieces were fitting together.

One thing became startlingly clear. The reason Aidan had
objected to her digging up information about Kathleen
wasn't because he was concerned for her safety. He was
worried she would find out about his relationship with the
dead woman.

How long had he known Kathleen Daniels before his father took her for his mistress? Had he ended his relationship with her or had she been the one to toss him aside?
Had they ever talked about marriage or had she simply
been a woman he had briefly dated?

Over and over Jessie rearranged the puzzle pieces in her
mind, yet she couldn't come up with the right fit. If Aidan
had been the one to break up with Kathleen, then why was
he so angry with his father that he was willing to blame him
for her murder?

Maybe he had been in love with Kathleen and she had
chosen his father over him. That would explain the es-
trangement between father and son... and why Aidan
hadn't testified at his father's trial. And why he wanted to
believe his father was guilty of her murder.

When Jessie arrived home the light was blinking on her
answering machine. She depressed the Play button and
wandered into the bathroom to get some aspirin from the
medicine chest.

She was about to pop a couple of white tablets into her
mouth when she heard Aidan's voice say, "Jess, it's me.
Where are you? I'm at the Loon Café, and I thought we
had agreed that twelve-thirty would work for both of us.
Was I wrong? I'll wait here another fifteen minutes or so
and then I have to get back to work."

There was a beep followed by several clicks indicating hang-ups on the answering system before she heard his voice again.

"Jess, it's me. I'm back at McCullough Enterprises. Obviously we had our signals crossed about lunch. Since you're going to be downtown this afternoon, why don't you meet me here around five-thirty and I'll take you to dinner instead. Love you."

Jessie washed down the aspirin with a glass of water, then walked back into her bedroom where she fell on the bed, her hand on her forehead. She had completely forgotten about her date with Aidan. She glanced at the clock and reached for the phone.

But she didn't pick up the receiver. She couldn't talk to him. Not yet. She needed more time to sort through everything she had discovered.

However, the longer she lay on the bed, the more troubled she became. Any way she looked at it, Jessie was not happy with what she had discovered.

At four-thirty Jessie knew she had to make a decision. Either get dressed and go to dinner with Aidan, or call him and plead a sick headache. Even though the headache was real, Jessie decided the only way she would get anything resolved would be to confront Aidan with what she had discovered.

As she drove to his father's office she thought about how every time she had tried to bring up the subject of the appeal, he had become angry. He hadn't wanted her investigating Kathleen's background. It was almost as if he didn't want any evidence uncovered that would absolve his father of guilt.

If she didn't know better, she would have reason to believe that he knew something about the murder he didn't want revealed. *Will Lepley's convinced that someone knows bout the murder…somone who has a good reason to keep lent.* Sean's words echoed in her mind.

Trotting right behind those words was something Lenore ad said to her. *I wouldn't have been surprised if they had ld me Aidan had done it.*

Jessie mentally shook herself at the bizarre direction her houghts were taking. That someone couldn't be Aidan. It as absurd even to think he was capable of such a thing. Tot to mention the fact he wasn't even living in Minnesota t the time Kathleen Daniels was killed. Or was he?

She pushed all such thoughts out of her mind as she arked her car in the ramp connected to the office building ousing McCullough Enterprises. The closer she got to the ffice, the faster her heart beat.

She knew Aidan was going to be angry when she told him he had contacted Lenore Green. Apprehension dampened er palms and she wished she had called and canceled their inner date.

When she reached the reception area, her head was hrobbing so badly she decided it was a bad idea to see Aidan. She was about to leave a message for him with the eceptionist when Sean walked by and called out to her.

"Jessie! You're just the woman I want to see." He lipped his arm around her shoulder and led her toward a mall lounge.

"Do you know what I know?"

For a moment Jessie was wondering if he was referring o the information Lenore Green had shared with her, but hen he said, "Will Lepley thinks we might be able to get nother autopsy done."

"He wants to exhume the body?" she asked, her face vrinkling at the thought.

"They don't have to. Apparently it's a common practice o save frozen tissues and body fluids from murder vic-

tims. If Will can convince the court that the medical ex
aminer missed signs of drug use, there's a possibility c
getting another opinion on the autopsy."

"Is that good news?"

"It's about as good as any we've had lately."

She reached over and squeezed his hand. "I'm reall
happy for you, Sean. I know how important this is to yo
and your family. What does Aidan think about it?"

Sean sighed. "It's probably better if you don't ask, Jes
sie."

"He's not happy about getting another autopsy?" sh
asked, uneasiness finding its way into her voice.

"He thinks we're building up false hope and that Mom'
going to be the one who suffers."

"I don't think he realizes how strong your mother is,'
Jessie said with admiration in her voice.

Sean shrugged. "Or else he has some other reason un
known to us as to why this whole mess has him in a fou
mood."

Another uneasy tremor traveled up and down Jessie'
spine, but Sean didn't seem to notice her reaction to th
statement.

"Anyway, I'm glad I ran into you. I wanted to tell yo
about the birthday party we're planning for my mother."

"It's her birthday?"

"Mmm-hmm. Next week. Giselle and I are having a
small party for her on Friday evening at our place and w
want you to be there. Can you make it?"

"Can I let you know? My niece has been in the hospita
and I'm not sure what the family plans are," she said eva
sively.

"Sure. I hope you can come. You probably don't realize
this, but it'll be one year ago next Saturday that Kathleer
Daniels died."

She frowned. "I didn't realize that," she said pensively.
"That's what made this whole incident even uglier than
already was. Anyway, I'll let Aidan fill you in on the de-
tils about the party."

She nodded in understanding. Sean rose and was about
o leave when Jessie stopped him. "I would imagine that
his is going to be a special birthday, especially since
Aidan's here."

"Yeah, as long as he doesn't leave," Sean retorted. "Last
ear no one expected him to come, and he showed up. This
ear we're all expecting him to be here, so I suppose he'll
ave to go back to California."

Jessie's mouth became dry and her heart felt as though
were going to leap out of her chest. "He was here last
ear for her birthday?" she repeated in a daze.

"Yup. You wouldn't have believed the shock it was for
veryone."

CHAPTER FOURTEEN

"DARLING, ARE YOU all right? You look a little pale." Aidan had come up behind Sean and was standing over Jessie solicitously.

"I . . . I have a bad headache," Jessie told him, her hand shaking as she pressed her fingers to her forehead.

Aidan hunched down beside her. "Do you want me to see if I can find you some aspirin?" he asked, his voice full of tenderness.

"I'm sure my secretary must have some," Sean offered.

"It's all right. I've already taken something," Jessie told them, holding her head in her hands.

"Maybe you ought to lie down for a few minutes. There's a couch in Dad's office," Aidan offered.

Jessie couldn't look him in the eyes. She stared down at the hand that rested on her knee. It was tan and smooth and caring . . . not the kind of hand she could imagine suffocating someone.

A violent shudder made her hug her arms around her body. "No. I've been resting all afternoon and it hasn't helped," she replied weakly.

Sean and Aidan exchanged a few words before Sean left, leaving Jessie alone with Aidan in the reception area. She fidgeted with her purse strap.

"Are you sure something else isn't bothering you? You seem edgy." He reached for her hand, and Jessie had to fight the urge to snatch it away.

"No, it's just that I have this headache," she insisted, unable to keep the stress out of her tone.

"Why don't we cancel dinner," Aidan suggested.

Jessie nearly sighed in relief. "That might be best. I'm not sure I could eat anything." She stood, eager to be gone.

"I'll drive you home. Wait here and I'll get my coat." He turned to go, but she stopped him.

"No! Please...don't fuss. I have my car. I'll be all right," she said shakily.

"Jess, I want to take you home. It's no problem. I'll drive you home in your car then take a cab back here to get mine."

"Don't be silly," she said a bit more caustically than she intended. "It'll cost you a small fortune in cab fare."

"It'll be worth it," he assured her.

Jessie could see the look of determination on his face and knew he wasn't going to take no for an answer. Reluctantly she agreed to his suggestion.

He gave her arm a gentle squeeze, then went to get his coat. However, as soon as he had disappeared around the corner she hurried past the receptionist to the elevator.

DEEP IN HER HEART Jessie knew Aidan was not a murderer. Every instinct she possessed told her he wasn't, yet the analytical part of her brain kept warning her emotional side that this was not a time to be trusting instincts.

She had left McCullough Enterprises thinking that once she reached home she'd be able to find some peace of mind. However, as soon as she walked into Gran's kitchen the phone rang. She knew it would be Aidan.

She was tempted not to answer it, but her mother's words echoed in her ear. *Never let a phone go unanswered. It could be an emergency.* Worried it might be news regarding Melissa, she picked it up.

Jessie's fingers tightened around the receiver when she heard Aidan's voice.

"Why did you leave without me?" he demanded.

"Because I told you it wasn't necessary for you to bring me home. I'm fine." She tried to make her voice sound assuring, but it was more defensive than assertive.

He sighed. "I was worried about you."

And just a little bit irritated, judging by the tone of his voice, Jessie thought.

When she didn't answer, he said, "I was thinking about coming over...maybe bringing you some chicken soup or something."

The thought of seeing him made Jessie's insides twist and turn. "No, please. I'd rather you didn't. I'm really not very good company, and it's probably best just to leave me alone," she said discouragingly.

"You could never be bad company for me." His voice was seductively warm and Jessie's discomfort grew.

She almost blurted out, "I don't want you to come over," but managed to say, "not tonight, please."

"All right," he said, disappointed. "But promise me you'll call if you need anything."

"I will," she replied quickly, hoping to get him off the phone. "I'd better go."

"I'd feel better if your grandmother was home with you."

"I don't need my grandmother, Aidan," she said a bit impatiently.

"Jessie, what's really wrong? What aren't you telling me?" he asked, his tone becoming suspicious.

"Nothing's wrong except I have a headache and I don't feel like being around people. Now, please hang up and let me go to bed." She didn't mean to snap at him, but her nerves were shot. "I'm sorry. I don't want to sound like a

rab, but I really need to get some rest," she murmured,
ating the doubts that were causing her to treat him with
uch disdain.

"Then it's probably best that I don't come over." She
ould tell by his tone that he was trying to convince him-
elf as much as her. When he closed with "I love you,
ess," her throat constricted.

She knew he was waiting for her to say the same thing to
im. She opened her mouth, but the words wouldn't come
ut. "I'll talk to you tomorrow" was all she said before
anging up.

Immediately Jessie was swamped with guilt. How could
she have allowed Lenore Green to plant such doubts in her
mind about a man she loved? She didn't want to think the
worst of Aidan, yet...

She pressed fingers to her forehead, wishing she could
think of a way to stop the conflicting emotions causing her
such pain. If only he had told her about his relationship
with Kathleen Daniels. If he wasn't so determined to see
that his father stay in prison....

Too restless to sleep, Jessie slipped her quilted robe over
her satin pajamas and went downstairs. Unable to interest
herself in any of the programs on TV, she decided to make
herself useful in the kitchen. She pulled out her grandmother's slow cooker and started chopping up vegetables.
At least when she came home from work tomorrow night
she'd have something warm for dinner, for it looked as if
she would be eating alone.

AIDAN DIDN'T LIKE the feeling he had in the pit of his
stomach as he pulled off the main highway and onto the
quiet residential street in Delano. It was a sinking feeling
that had been there ever since he had heard from Sean that
Jessie had been to see his father in prison. Although Sean

had assured him that nothing unusual had happened during their visit, Aidan couldn't help but wonder if something hadn't been said that had upset Jessie.

He'd seen a flash of some unknown emotion in her eye
when she had glanced at him at the office earlier this evening—something he thought had looked like fear. And despite her assertions that she simply wasn't feeling well,
Aidan could see there was something else troubling her, and
he had the uncomfortable suspicion that it was him.

Just what was it that had caused her to retreat emotionally? Had he rushed her with his talk about the two of them
having a future together? Was she having second thoughts
about their relationship? Or was it something his father had
said to her?

He had the uneasy feeling that it had to do with his father, as that was the only subject that had ever caused any
problems between them.

The closer the car got to the house, the more anxious he
became about what he would say to her. From the way their
conversation had ended, he knew she wouldn't be expecting him, and it was important that he not put her on the
defensive. If ever there was a time when he needed to keep
a tight rein on his emotions, it was now.

But the minute she opened the door to him and he saw
the startled look on her face, he knew it would be difficult
to stay calm.

"Aidan, what are you doing here?" she asked, staring at
him as though he were a ghost.

In her hand she held a vegetable peeler, her fingers
clinging to it almost as if it were a weapon, Aidan thought
as he stepped into the warm kitchen. Without any makeup
her cheeks were pale, her eyes wide as they stared at him
with an expression he couldn't quite identify.

He closed the door behind him, then stomped the snow om his leather shoes, carefully wiping his feet on the raided rag rug in front of the door. "I came to see you. I as worried."

She was not happy to see him, that much was evident by ie way her hands were clenched. He could see now that the ook in her eyes was one of apprehension.

"Jessie, will you please tell me what's going on?" he lurted out.

"What do you mean?" She went back to peeling vege-ibles at the kitchen sink. There had been no kiss, no ug . . . not even a welcoming smile. Only that look of ap-rehension.

"You don't show up for lunch, you tell me we can't have inner because you have a headache and now you're act-ıg as though I'm a neighbor who's stopped in to borrow a up of sugar."

"I'm sorry. I haven't felt like myself today," she told im, the vegetable peeler moving with a precise swift mo-on. "I've had a lot on my mind lately. I guess my niece 1elissa's illness has bothered me more than I wanted to dmit, and I guess I simply needed some time to sort nrough some of the problems my family's been having. nstead of going out I thought it would be better if I read he books my sister had given me on the subject of bu-mia."

She was rambling, talking faster than normal, her eyes ocused on the carrots. When she finally ran out of words, e moved closer to her and said, "Sean told me you went o see my father."

A big round chunk of carrot went skittering off the cut-ing board onto the floor. Jessica's hands stopped moving nd her eyes were downcast. There was silence, the only

sound in the room coming from the refrigerator motor th
was humming quietly in the corner.

"Is there any reason why I shouldn't have?" she aske
her chin lifting in an almost challenging way.

"None that I can think of," he answered, his gaze hol
ing hers. She didn't say anything and he added, "Is th
why you're angry with me? Because of my father?"

There were several moments of silence before she final
told him exactly what was bothering her. "Why didn't yo
tell me about you and *Kate?*" Her voice was barely abov
a whisper.

Aidan's mouth suddenly went dry. "Because I didn
want you to get involved in the problems between me ar
my father," he answered, hating the wounded look th
shadowed her eyes.

"Involved? Aidan, I *am* involved. I was on the jury th
convicted him," she said emotionally, slamming the peel
down on the cutting board.

"Yes, and because I knew what a difficult position th
was for you, I've tried to keep our relationship separa
from the mess my family is in. Kate was part of that mes
and I thought that if I told you about her, she would a
ways be there between us. It was a can of worms I didn
want to open."

"For my sake?" she asked in disbelief.

"Yes, for your sake, but also for mine. What good wou
it have done for me to tell you? She's a part of my past
want to forget."

"Well, sometimes we can't just shove things into the pa
and forget them," she said abruptly, her words slicir
through the air. "Especially not dead women with who
you've had an affair."

Aidan raked a hand through his hair, trying to keep imself under control. "This is exactly the reason why I idn't tell you about her. I knew you'd get upset."

"And you've been doing your best not to upset me, aven't you," she shot back at him.

"What's that supposed to mean?" he asked, annoyed by er smug tone.

"Every time I tried to find out any information about our 'Kate' you did your best to discourage me. You didn't vant me to know the truth." Her voice was a mixture of ccusation and sarcasm.

"And just what truth is it you think you've found?" he hallenged, his own anger rising.

"You were lovers." She spat the words out as if they were itter herbs irritating her taste buds.

"We had a brief affair," he admitted quietly, wishing he ould deny the accusation.

She shuddered, then asked, "While she was dating your ather?"

"No!" he denied angrily. "Is that what kind of man you hink I am? That I would share a woman with my fa- her?" This time it was his face that wrinkled with dis- aste. "I don't know what my father told you, but for your nformation, I had stopped seeing Kate long before he be- ;an his sordid little affair with her," he protested, stab- ing at the air with his finger. "And if he said anything lifferent, he's lying."

"It wasn't your father who told me about your relation- hip with Kathleen Daniels," she said, quickly correcting is false assumption.

"Then who did?"

"I spoke to Lenore Green."

"Lenore Green?" He threw up his hands in exaspera- ion. "Good grief, Jessie. That woman wouldn't know the truth if it jumped up and bit her in the face. I hope you didn't believe everything she said."

"Are you saying she lied?"

The distrust in her voice made Aidan wince. "I'm saying the woman hates men, and she thinks every one of us is dumping on some poor unsuspecting female," he said in disgust. "Well, I'll tell you something about Kate Daniels I'm sure Lenore Green didn't mention. She was the kind of woman who was in love with a man until a richer one came along."

"Is that what happened to you? A richer man came along?"

He eyed her shrewdly. "What are you thinking? That she threw me over for my father?"

"Did she?"

"I don't think you'd believe me if I said no, would you?" She shot him a dubious look. "I can tell by the way you're looking at me that you think you have it all figured out. You think we both wanted her, he won, so I left for California."

"I don't know what to think because you haven't told me anything," she said in frustration. "All I know is that you have all this anger inside you toward your father. For months you've led me to believe that anger was because of your mother. Now I find out that it was because you were in love with the same woman as your father." Her eyes misted at the agonizing thought.

"I was never in love with Kathleen Daniels," he declared adamantly.

Again, the look of apprehension gave her eyes a haunted look. He wanted to hold her, to comfort her, but she bristled whenever he got too close to her.

"I wish I could believe that," she said, her voice breaking with emotion.

"Of course you can believe it." Again he tried to take her
his arms, but she wouldn't let him.

"Your father told me you think I look like her."

This time there was no mistaking the hurt in her voice.
No!" The word was sharply delivered. "No, you're not
ke her at all." He could see that she didn't believe him.
Maybe at first I thought you resembled her, but there is
othing about you that reminds me of her," he said reas-
iringly.

She didn't say anything for several moments and appre-
ension began to torment him. "You don't think I was at-
acted to you because I thought you looked like her?" he
sked in disbelief.

"I told you. I don't know what to think," she said, tak-
ig a step backward. "You've kept so much stuff from
ie...." She trailed off in confusion.

"That's because I thought the fewer people who knew
bout me and Kate, the better. My mother doesn't know
hat I was the one who introduced her to my dad, that she
vas my girlfriend before she was his."

"So you kept your relationship secret because you
wanted to protect your mother?"

"Yes. I'd do anything to keep her from being hurt."

"Anything?" she repeated in a near whisper, shrinking
ack from him even farther.

She gave a shrug, a nervous little hunching of her shoul-
lers that alone wouldn't have meant much. However,
ombined with the apprehension in her eyes it made Aidan
ware that there was more on her mind than his relation-
hip with Kate Daniels.

"Why are you looking at me like that?" he asked, his
ieart thumping out of rhythm. "You can't possibly think
had anything to do with Kate's death."

Several moments passed without Jessie denying h statement.

"You can't think I had anything to do with it," he re peated on a note of desperation. Again she didn't answe and Aidan murmured, "Oh, my God, you do."

All he could do was stare at her. How could she possibl think he was capable of something so awful as murder?

Something of his anguish must have shown on his face for she became defensive. "Why didn't you tell me yo were in Minnesota the night she was killed?"

"I never said I wasn't," he replied, shaking his head i disbelief. "My God, Jessie. I'm not a murderer!" he ex claimed desperately.

"I don't want to believe it...."

"So why do you?" he interrupted angrily, then befor she could answer said, "Let me guess. You had one of you feelings. Is that it? Some greater power sent a message t you that told you my dad's not responsible for Kate' death, but I am. Is that it?"

She pressed fingers to her temples and squeezed her eye shut. "Stop it!" she cried out. "This has nothing to do wit my feelings."

"Oh, yes it does. For months you've told me you had feeling my father was innocent. My father—a man who ha meant nothing to you, a man who has admitted to hurtin people he loved, a man who was found guilty of murder b twelve people."

He paced as he talked, moving back and forth across th kitchen floor. "Now your 'feelings' are telling you that I ar guilty. Me—" he patted his chest with his fist "—the ma who has done everything he can to protect the women h loves, the man *you* say you love."

He took a step toward her and she flinched. He chuck led sardonically and shook his head in regret. "I can't eve get near you without your skin wanting to crawl right off your body, can I?''

"It's not what you're thinking," she said, trying to explain to him, but he wouldn't listen.

"No, it certainly isn't. Until a few minutes ago I was thinking that I had found a woman I could share my life with, someone who could see inside my very soul, someone I wanted to be everything for—lover, friend, hero.'' He stared at her, his eyes reflecting the anguish he was feeling. 'What a mistake.''

He turned and walked toward the door.

"Aidan, wait!'' she called after his retreating body, but he didn't so much as glance back. He kept right on walking until he was through the door and out in the cold.

THE FOLLOWING MORNING Jessie stood by the kitchen window, staring out at the bleak winter landscape. It was gray and cold and lonely, as if Mother Nature was putting her stamp of approval on Jessie's melancholy.

The once soft, white snow was now crusted over with a dingy covering of hardened ice and dirt. Instead of brightening the landscape, it made everything look dull and dirty beneath the ominous gray clouds gathering in the sky.

As she drove to work, the scene with Aidan played over and over in her head, just as it had done during the night when she had lain awake, tossing and turning. She kept seeing the look of total disbelief that had been in his eyes when he had realized she was suspicious of him. After the disbelief had come hurt and disillusionment. She closed her eyes to shut out his face, but it was useless. She would never be able to erase his image from her memory. The tears she had fought all morning began to fall.

She hoped that he'd show up at the window of Renae's Bridal Salon, but when her shift ended that evening and there had been no sign of him, she could only accept that he was gone from her life. As she drove back to Delano a sudden feeling of homesickness swept over her. Until their fight last night, she and Aidan had planned on spending the weekend attending the many events of St. Paul's winter carnival. Now the weekend promised to be a lonely few days.

When she stepped inside the front door, she headed directly for her bedroom closet and pulled out a suitcase. She quickly threw in enough clothes for the weekend, then picked up the phone and punched in eleven digits.

"Hi, Mom. I'm off this weekend so I thought I'd come home for a few days."

IT WAS LATE BY THE TIME she arrived in Harding. Fatigued from both emotional stress and the long drive on dark roads, Jessie felt tears mist her eyes at the scene that greeted her when she climbed the porch steps and peeked through the front window. Her mother sat on the brown tweed sofa, her embroidery in her lap. In the recliner to her right was her father, his feet propped up, his head back. The television was on, but she could see that he had fallen asleep, as usual.

They had waited up for her, just as they had done so often when she had been a teenager. Jessie swallowed back the lump of emotion in her throat and pushed open the door, determined not to show either of them how badly she was hurting.

Her facade of happiness worked with her father, but she was reasonably certain her mother guessed that there was something amiss. Jessie managed to maintain a cheerful disposition during a brief conversation, then she said goodnight.

Once she was up in her old room, she let the happy façade slip and sank onto the bed. The headache that had been with her ever since she had talked to Lenore Green still throbbed at her temples.

She quickly changed out of her clothes and into her flannel pajamas, then moved into a yoga position to meditate. When it was obvious she wasn't going to have any success, she climbed into the bed she had slept in as a teenager.

A soft light glowed from the porcelain lamp on the nightstand, creating shadows on the opposite wall. As she wriggled down into sheets warmed by an electric blanket, she remembered how when she was small she had hated having the light on because those shadowy shapes had a tendency to become monsters as she grew sleepy.

With a twist of her fingers she turned off the lamp so that the room was in total darkness. No slivers of moonlight peeking through the shades. No cracks of light slipping beneath the door. No monster shadows on the wall. Just darkness. Darkness and her thoughts of Aidan. As her head hit the pillow the tears fell once more.

CHAPTER FIFTEEN

"IS ANYTHING WRONG, DEAR? You don't seem yourself t[h]
morning," Eunice Paulson commented as she refilled J[e]
sie's coffee cup before sitting across from her daughter.

Jessie wrapped her hands around the deep green m[u]
appreciating the warmth of the steaming liquid. "I'm fi[n]
Mom. I'm just tired."

"You should have slept in," she said with maternal co[n]
cern.

Jessie smiled. "I don't get much time at home, and I l[i]
to spend as much of it with you as possible."

Eunice returned the smile, reaching across the table
pat her lovingly. "We love having you home. I can see w[hy]
Gran sings your praises so frequently."

"Has there been any news from Gran?" she asked.

"She called the other day from Florida and said t[he]
weather's been beautiful," Eunice answered as she add[ed]
cream and sugar to her own coffee. "She seems to be ha[v]
ing a great time."

Jessie smiled weakly. "I've missed her. The house j[ust]
isn't the same without her."

"I didn't think you'd have time to be lonely—not wi[th]
that new boyfriend of yours always around," her moth[er]
teased lightly.

"Since Gran's away, it must be Carla who's been telli[ng]
tales," Jessie answered, wishing the thought of Aid[en]
didn't hurt so badly.

"Any news I have came directly from the source."

Puzzled, Jessie looked at her over the rim of her cup. You spoke to Aidan?"

"Mmm-hmm. He was here a few days ago," her mother id smugly, obviously pleased with the thought.

"Aidan was here?" Jessie's mind searched its files until e came up with the memory bank holding Wednesday. idan had gone to St. Cloud on McCullough business. He ust have stopped in at the farm, as well.

"Yes, dear. He came to see your father," Eunice told her. Jessie couldn't imagine what Aidan would have to dis- ss with her father. Surely he wasn't old-fashioned enough state his intentions toward her to her father?

"Why?" she asked cautiously.

"Apparently he had some suggestions concerning run- ng the farm. Dad showed him the books and called Jim so the three of them could have a conference," Eunice swered.

"He wanted to talk to Dad and Jim about the farm?" ssie felt a twinge of disappointment that was quickly fol- wed by curiosity.

"Yes. He's an expert at managing businesses," she ex- ained, then chuckled and said, "Well, you know all about at. Anyway, he sat down with Jim and your father and me up with an operating plan for the farm."

"What did Dad think of all this?"

"You know how your father is with outsiders who try to l him how to run the farm," Eunice said with a lift of her ebrows.

"Oh, Mom, he didn't say anything he shouldn't have, did ?"

"Who? Your father or Aidan?" she said with a straight ce.

"Mom!" Jessie protested, unable to suppress her grin.

"You really care about him, don't you?" her mother sa
in understanding.

Jessie didn't see any reason to pretend she didn't. "Ye
I do. So tell me what Dad's reaction was."

"He said Aidan made a lot of sense, and even though I
knows there's no guarantee that his suggestions will worl
it's worth a try. If his plan does work, Jim won't have to g
looking for a job."

Jessie was at a loss for words. Why hadn't Aidan told h
this? Then she realized that he hadn't had a chance. TI
minute he had returned she had confronted him with h
fears and doubts.

"He's a good man, Jessie. Do you know he wouldn
even let Dad pay him for the advice? He said he unde
stood the plight of the farmer and wanted to do his part t
help out." The look on her mother's face was a combina
tion of amazement and respect.

Jessie's breakfast sat like a lump of clay in her stomacl
Aidan *was* a good man. Good and honest and caring. Ar
a man she must have hurt terribly with her accusation
Deep in her heart she knew he could never have murdere
anyone, yet she had allowed suspicions and jealousy
distort her judgment.

The remainder of the weekend she spent helping arour
the farm, sorting through her emotions and wondering
there was a way to save her relationship with Aidan. C
Sunday night she returned to Delano knowing there w
only one thing she could do. She needed to talk to him ar
explain to him why she had reacted the way she had.

Only come Monday, Aidan was nowhere to be foun
After several unsuccessful attempts to reach him, Jess
called Sean, who told her his brother had gone back
California. Anxiety turned into depression when Sean sa
he wasn't sure when Aidan was planning to return.

Jessie tried to be optimistic about his departure. If nothing else, the time apart would give each of them a chance to think about their relationship. But the longer she was away from him, the bigger her doubts grew. Was their love strong enough to withstand the turmoil that had torn them apart?

After only a couple of days of not knowing whether Aidan was even coming back, Jessie swallowed her pride and called Mrs. McCullough to ask for his California phone number. When she finally did work up the courage to call him, there was no answer. She could only hope that his mother would tell him she had been trying to reach him and that he would call her.

He didn't.

For Jessie, each day passed with agonizing slowness. It was hard not to dwell on her misery, especially when she was pretending to be a model bride during the day and going home to an empty house at night. The highlight of each day became the moment when she saw the blinking light on her phone answering machine. However, as soon as she had played the recordings and found that none of them was from Aidan, the misery returned. She didn't realize just how lonely she had been until she came home from work one day and the aroma of freshly baked bread greeted her.

"Gran!" Jessie called out in delight.

Her grandmother came bustling through the doorway, her apron wrapped around her middle.

"Did you have a good trip?" Jessie asked, welcoming her with a hug.

"Yes, it was nice, but it's always good to come home." She immediately picked up the teakettle. "Shall we have tea and catch up on all our news?"

Jessie smiled and nodded enthusiastically. She couldn'
resist giving her grandmother another affectionate squeeze
saying, "It's good to have you back. I've missed you."

Unlike the past two weeks, the following hour passed
quickly as Jessie filled her grandmother in on family news
and Gran entertained her with anecdotes from her travels
For the first time in weeks Jessie found herself laughing
and it felt good.

"By the way, Jessie, before I forget. Mr. McCullough'
been trying to reach you," her grandmother said as she go
up to check on the bread that was in the oven. "He called
earlier today... around noon, I think."

Jessie's heart fluttered. "Aidan called?"

Hope rose in her chest, but it was quickly dashed when
her grandmother said, "Not Aidan, dear. His brother
Sean."

"Oh." Jessie tried to hide her disappointment, but she
couldn't stop her face from falling.

"Is there something wrong with Aidan? Is that why his
brother called?" Gran asked, eyeing Jessie carefully as she
sat back down at the table.

"I haven't seen Aidan lately." Jessie couldn't see any use
in keeping the truth from her grandmother. "While you
were gone we had a disagreement."

"Oh, dear. I'm so sorry." She put her hand over Jessie's. "Surely it's nothing you can't put right again?"

Jessie shrugged. "I'm not sure about that, either, Gran."
This time she had to swallow to stop the lump threatening
to block her throat. "I let him down, Gran, and I don'
know how to make it up to him."

"Have you tried talking to him?"

She nodded. "I've called several times, but there's never
any answer." She sniffled, unable to stem the tears. "I need
to convince him that I believe in him."

Again Gran patted her hand. "If it's meant to be, it'll be," she said pragmatically. "If not..." She shrugged. "You're a lovely girl. You'll find another man."

"But I don't want any other man, Gran. I want him," Jessie said emotionally, surprising her grandmother.

"Then maybe you'd better go call his brother and see what he wants."

BEING THE LOVESICK FOOL that she was, Jessie thought up all sorts of reasons for Sean to be calling her. One was that he had seen how miserable Aidan was without her and had called to plead with Jessie to go to Aidan and patch things up.

Another was that Aidan had enlisted his brother to play Cupid and arrange a meeting between the two of them. This way neither would have to make the first move. They could forget everything that had happened and start fresh.

In Jessie's fantasy, all of the explanations for Sean calling had to do with Aidan. As it turned out, Sean hadn't called to talk about Aidan at all, but his father.

When she phoned him at McCullough Enterprises the following morning, his secretary informed her that he was out of the office but had left instructions that should Jessie call, he wanted to see her as soon as possible. Jessie told the secretary she would stop by the downtown firm on her way home from work.

As she walked into the reception area of McCullough Enterprises, her heart rate accelerated. What if Aidan was back? The thought of running into him made her palms moist and her knees unsteady.

But Aidan was nowhere in sight. When Sean stepped out of his office he was alone. He smiled at Jessie and she could feel some of the tension easing.

"You made it." Excitement was written all over his face, and they had barely stepped inside his office when she heard why.

"Will Lepley says the governor is going to pardon Dad this week. He's been cleared of all charges," he told her.

"What?" Surprise held Jessie speechless.

"It's true. Dad is innocent. He didn't kill Kathleen Daniels," he said simply. "He's going to be a free man again."

"But that's wonderful!" Jessie reached out and gave him a hug. "You must be relieved."

"I am. We all are. This past year has been a nightmare." He indicated she should sit down, then went around to the other side of the desk and dropped into the leather chair.

"Does this mean they found the real murderer?"

Sean leaned forward, his elbows on his desk. "Kathleen Daniels wasn't exactly murdered...at least, not the way everyone thought she was."

Puzzled, Jessie said, "I don't understand."

"The cause of death wasn't suffocation, but an overdose of cocaine."

"So it was drug related," she commented pensively. "If that was the case, why did the medical examiner testify that there was no sign of drugs in her system?"

"Because that's what he found—nothing. The initial toxicology tests were negative. It was only because we were able to get a second analysis that we learned the truth."

Jessie leaned forward. "Are you saying there was an error in the original report?"

"It wasn't exactly an error, although the medical examiner was to blame for the inaccuracy of the autopsy report."

"What do you mean?"

"He was working in a small lab with limited facilities. ormally, urinalysis is the method for detecting drug use, d in this case that's what the medical examiner followed r his report."

"So why wasn't it accurate in this case?"

"Because when a body starts to decompose, enzymes reak down the cocaine that is in the system. Once that appens, chances are a urinalysis won't detect them. You ed high-tech equipment to analyze the autopsy tissues."

"So the medical examiner wasn't exactly wrong in his port, he simply hadn't done enough testing." She looked him for confirmation.

"Exactly."

"So why didn't he send the tissues to another lab?"

Sean lifted his eyebrows. "I suppose it was a combina-on of inexperience and expediency. Murder is a pretty rare ccurrence in Wright County, and judging by this guy's at-tude I'd say he didn't want to take the time to send it out."

The image of the pompous coroner came to Jessie's ind. "When I saw him on the witness stand there was mething about that man that bothered me, but I couldn't uite figure out what it was."

"I'm sure he resented the fact that Will Lepley arranged have a forensics expert from a private lab do a second alysis. A man like that doesn't like to be second-essed."

"I'm surprised they could still do the tests. It's been over year since she died."

"That's where we got lucky. Fortunately for us, the edical examiner didn't throw anything away. Because urder cases are rare, he figured it might be an opportu-ity for others to study the decomposed tissues from such case. It was probably the one thing he did that we can ank him for."

Jessie shook her head in amazement as the informatio he told her sank in. "But he testified she had suffocat ed."

"Without the accurate drug test, he could only work wit the information he had. There was no sign of disease or in jury, no drug or alcohol use according to his toxicology re ports. All that he had to work with was the fact that she ha had sex with someone and she was found with a bag ove her head."

"If she died from a drug overdose, why was there plastic bag on her head?"

"That's where this gets even more interesting," Sean tol her. "It seems that just as we suspected, Kathleen was at party that night. A very private party with some ver prominent members of society."

"You mean people who wouldn't want it known tha they were using drugs?"

"Especially the host, Drake Lawton."

"The shopping mall developer?"

"That's him. Apparently he often held small, intimat parties where sex and drugs were freely exchanged."

"And that's where Kathleen went after she left your fa ther? To his home?"

He nodded. "And when she overdid it on the cocaine her host panicked. Not wanting the police to find her dea in his place, Drake decided it was in his best interest t dump the body far away. He got rid of her purse and wa let, hoping to make it look as though she had been as saulted and robbed by some drifter. Then he tied the plasti bag over her head to make it look as if she had suffo cated."

"It's hard to believe that a man in his position would d such a thing," Jessie said in amazement.

"There was a rumor he was interested in running for ublic office. Having the police find a woman overdosed on ocaine at his home would have put an end to that aspiraon."

"So instead he allowed an innocent man to take the lame." Jessie could only shake her head in disbelief. You'd think he would have come forward when they arsted your father. Doesn't the man have a concience?"

"If he did, his instinct for self-preservation was ronger," he replied bitterly. "He may not have murdered athleen, but he did violate the federal narcotics law. He upplied her with the drugs that killed her. Add to that the amage to his professional reputation and you have enough eason for him to keep quiet."

"How awful... for everyone involved."

He leaned back and sighed. "It's been a nightmare, Jesie. That's for sure."

"Did your father have any idea Kathleen was involved ith these people?"

Sean shook his head. "She kept that part of her life very rivate, and with good reason. He knew that she had another man—someone who was prominent in the public eye, ut he was never able to find out who it was."

Curious, she asked, "How *did* you find out his name?"

"Aidan's the one who deserves the credit. He did some igging on his own and the next thing we knew, the police ere questioning Drake Lawton."

"It was Aidan?" she repeated in bewilderment.

"He went to see some woman by the name of Lenore Green. Apparently she had been a friend of Kathleen's."

"And she knew about Drake Lawton?"

"No, but she was able to give him the information that ed to piecing together a picture of where Kathleen had been

that night." He shook his head in admiration. "I don'
know how he did it. When Will sent the private investiga
tor to talk to this Lenore Green, she wouldn't give him th
time of day."

Jessie didn't say anything. She couldn't. She was to
filled with regret over having ever even considered the pos
sibility that Aidan could have been responsible for Kath
leen's death.

"According to Will, Dad should be pardoned any da
now. And I have instructions that I am to thank you per
sonally for the help you gave us in getting the informatio
that kept this case open."

Suddenly the hair on the back of Jessie's neck began t
tingle. She heard the door open, and without turnin
around she knew it was Aidan. A strong sense of his pres
ence filled the room, just as it always did whenever she wa
with him.

"Well, if it isn't my little brother now," Sean said, get
ting up from his chair and coming around the front of hi
desk. "Come on in. I was just telling Jessie the news."

Jessie slowly turned around, watching Aidan's face fo
some sign of what he was feeling toward her. Usually h
wore his emotions on his face, but today his look wa
guarded.

"Hello, Aidan," she said softly, surprised that her voic
sounded so normal.

"Jessie." His voice was as guarded as his eyes.

Sean was talking about his father's impending freedom
but Jessie was only half listening to what he was saying, fo
she was wondering what Aidan must be thinking. When th
phone on the desk rang, conversation ceased as Sean wen
to answer it.

"That was accounting," Sean announced after a very brief conversation during which Jessie and Aidan said nothing. "The report I've been waiting for all day is finally finished. I'm going to go pick it up, if you don't mind?" He looked at Jessie for permission.

"No, go ahead. It's all right. I should be going, anyway." She gathered her things together and stood.

Sean took Jessie's hands in his and squeezed them gratefully as he said goodbye. As he disappeared out the door, Jessie felt like bolting out after him, for Aidan was almost scowling at her. However, she took a deep breath and turned to face him.

"Sean told me everything," she said uneasily.

He nodded in understanding. "It's a relief to have it over."

"Sean says it's because of you that your father's free," she remarked, hoping to slice through the tension that hung in the air.

He shrugged. "It was only a matter of time before the police would have solved the case," he said modestly.

He wasn't going to make it any easier for her. She had no choice but to jump right in and say what she was feeling. "I'm sorry, Aidan...about ever suspecting that you could have had anything to do with Kathleen's death," she said quietly.

He didn't speak for the longest moment. He just stood there staring at her with eyes as dark as the winter sky. "Apology accepted," he finally said coolly.

Jessie thought she would go crazy if he didn't say something else. Unable to stand his silence, she asked, "What happens next, Aidan?"

"The governor's going to pardon—"

"I'm not talking about your father, I'm talking about us," she interrupted in a rare show of emotion.

"Us, Jessie?" Again there was that mask of indifference.

"Aidan, I know I've hurt you and I'm sorry. I should never have accused you of being involved with Kathleen's murder, but I wasn't thinking clearly at the time."

"And you didn't know who the real murderer was, did you?" he said in a silky-smooth voice.

She stared at him, horrified. "You think I'm only saying this now because the case has been solved?"

"Aren't you?"

"No!" she vehemently denied. "I never really believed you were connected in any way to her death. Maybe the thought did cross my mind, but deep in my heart I knew it wasn't possible," she pleaded.

"You just needed time to 'logically' sort through all this confusion you were in, right?" he said sardonically.

Aidan's anger, hurt and disillusionment were all still there. Jessie's shoulders sagged at the realization.

She made one last effort to reach out to him. "I tried to call you."

"Why? Were you going to tell me that you believed in my innocence despite all the evidence against me?" he asked with a humorless grin.

Jessie was the one now who remained silent. Even if she were to tell him the truth, she doubted he would believe her. Not wanting to make an undignified exit, she called upon all of her resolve not to cry and to make one last plea.

"I can't change the past, Aidan. All I can say is I'm sorry."

"As I said, apology accepted." This time his voice was

downright cold. There was a finality in it that made Jessie shiver.

"It's really over between us, isn't it?" Her eyes pleaded with him to disagree, but he didn't. "I don't know why I expected it to last.... Look at the way we began...." And before he had a chance to see her cry, she hurried out of the room.

CHAPTER SIXTEEN

TELEVISION CAMERAS and reporters were at the prison the day Tom McCullough became a free man. When Jessie saw the taped report on the ten o'clock news that night she couldn't help but wonder if anything had changed between Aidan and his father.

Although Tom McCullough was interviewed briefly, no mention was made of his family or where he was going. Jessie knew the difficult times were not over for him simply because he had been pardoned.

Helen McCullough had stood by her husband's side throughout the entire ordeal, yet Jessie wondered what lay ahead for the couple. Certainly it would be easier to heal the wounds that had divided their family now that Tom was free, but there was more than criminal charges keeping the family apart.

Serious damage had been done to the foundation of his marriage. And the McCullough name had been sullied when personal business had been made public knowledge.

As Tom McCullough climbed into the family car, Jessie caught a glimpse of his wife, Helen. Despite all the evidence and the pain she had suffered, she had shown a loyalty not many women would have been capable of giving.

Jessie felt a stab of guilt. All it had taken was for one woman to implicate Aidan in the Kathleen Daniels case and she had been filled with doubts.

ssie wondered where she would be today if she had had a faith in Aidan. She deliberately pushed the thought n her mind. It was no use crying over what might have 1. As her mother had always said to her when she was a e girl, all the crying in the world wasn't going to change t had happened.

Vhen the taped report was over, Jessie turned off the vision with a decisive snap. Staring at the dark screen, wished it was as easy to erase the memories from her d. Although Tom McCullough had been pardoned, ie's posttrial stress was not over. She still suffered anx- over the role she had played in convicting an innocent 1, and she hadn't been able to forget the effect her de- on had played in the McCulloughs' lives.

after much thought, Jessie decided there was only one to resolve her feelings of guilt. She needed to see Tom Helen McCullough, to talk to them about everything t had happened, to close that part of her life once and all. She waited a week to make certain Aidan would e returned to California, then she went to see them.

"Come in, Jessie. It's nice to see you again," Helen said mly when she was shown into the sitting room at the Cullough home. She patted the brocade sofa invitingly. lease, come sit beside me. You're just in time for cof-
"

"I hope I'm not intruding," Jessie said apologetically, itating before sitting down.

"Not at all," Mrs. McCullough said graciously. "In fact, e been wanting to call you."

essie sat beside her on the sofa, appreciating the warmth l understanding in her eyes.

"You were so helpful in getting Tom's case resolved, yet ever had a chance to thank you properly," Helen told , reaching over to pour the coffee from the silver server.

"You don't need to thank me, Mrs. McCullough. I did do much of anything," Jessie answered, uncomforta with her gratitude.

"Yes, you did, and I'm glad I have this opportunity tell you how grateful all of us are." She paused with dainty china cup in her hand. "Cream or sugar?"

"Both," Jessie replied, noticing how bony the ol woman's hands were. Actually, all of Helen McCullou was thin, a fact Jessie attributed to the stress she had be under the past year.

"Sean told me he explained to you how Tom's rele came about," Helen commented as she handed Jessie cup.

"Mmm-hmm." She took a sip of coffee, then set the down. "When I heard the good news I almost came to you, but I thought it might be awkward."

"Because of Aidan?"

Jessie nodded, her throat tightening at the mention Aidan's name. "He would have been uncomfortable i had come here." She tried to state it simply, but her vo broke and moisture filled her eyes.

"Then it's true? You're no longer seeing each other There was concern in Helen's gentle eyes.

Jessie simply shook her head, unable to speak.

Helen poured a second cup of coffee, saying, "I ha hunch something was wrong from the way he was beh: ing."

Jessie took another sip of the coffee, hoping to swall the emotion that threatened to overwhelm her. She did want to talk about Aidan, but his mother was looking at I with such sympathy in her eyes she blurted out, " doesn't want to see me anymore." Then she started to c

Helen set down her coffee cup and slid closer to her. "There, now," she comforted her, placing her arm around shoulder. "It's all right."

"No, it's not." Jessie looked up, alarmed that she had broken down in front of Mrs. McCullough.

"If it's any comfort to you, Aidan's miserable, too."

Jessie dabbed at her eyes with a tissue. "He is?"

"Mmm-hmm. He went off in a snit as soon as Tom was released. Said he was going back to California for good," Helen told her with a sigh.

Before Jessie could ask any more questions, Tom Mc-Cullough entered the room, the lines on his face a little less lined than they had been the last time she had seen him. Jessie quickly wiped away the tears and forced a smile to her face.

"Am I interrupting?" he asked, hesitating in the doorway.

"It might be better if you gave us a few minutes alone," Helen suggested.

"No, please. It's all right," Jessie insisted, rising to her feet. "I came because I wanted to talk to both of you." She extended her hand to Tom, saying, "I wanted to tell you how happy I am that everything worked out for you."

Tom McCullough wrapped her hand in both of his and pumped it gently. "Thank you, Jessie. I appreciate your good wishes and I'm grateful for the information you uncovered that led police to the truth." He gestured for her to be seated again.

"I only wish I had followed my instincts during the trial. Then you wouldn't have been imprisoned at all," Jessie said regretfully.

"What's done is done, and there's no point in speculating, is there?" he said without any bitterness.

Helen poured a cup of coffee for her husband, and three of them talked politely of the trial and Tom's rele from prison.

When Helen was about to refill Jessie's cup, Jessie nounced it was time she leave. To her surprise it was T who insisted she stay.

To his wife he said, "If you don't mind, dear, I'd like speak to Jessie for a few minutes."

Helen simply nodded in understanding and said, " course. If you'll excuse me, Jessie?"

As soon as they were alone, Tom said, "I thought y should know that Aidan came to see me before he left California."

"I'm not sure we should be talking about Aidan, N McCullough," she cautioned him, but he paid no att tion to her warning.

"He's a man with a lot of pride, Jessie," he said, r bing his chin thoughtfully. "He's also fiercely loyal a very protective of those he cares about."

"You're talking about your wife?" she ventured to s

Admiration shone in his eyes at the mention of spouse. "She's an exceptional woman. As much as Aid and I have disagreed in the past, we agree on somethi very important. She must never know about Aidan's re tionship with Kathleen."

"You don't need to worry. I'd never mention it to her she assured him.

"I didn't think you would," he said with a gentle smi

"Then why did you bring it up?" She gave him a p zled look.

"Let me tell you something. When Aidan came to me, he talked not about his mother or the problems that and I have been having, but about you."

essie felt her face warm. "He's angry with me, isn't he." was a statement, not a question.

'Anger isn't such an unhealthy thing unless you let it p you from someone you love." He studied her ewdly. "And I do believe my son loves you, Jessie."

'It's not just a matter of loving someone, Mr. Mc-llough. There's so much stuff in our way," she said ubtfully.

'There are always things in the way, I'm afraid," he an-ered on a long, tired sigh. "If you love someone, you ve to work hard to shove all those things out of the way."

'I'm not sure our stuff will move."

'You'll never know unless you go find out." He handed a slip of paper he'd pulled from his pocket. "I'm afraid up to you, Jessie. I know my son. He can be very stub-rn."

essie looked at the scrap of paper. On it was Aidan's lifornia address. Did she dare make the first move?

ER SINCE MISSY HAD BEEN admitted to the hospital the ctor had recommended no visitors except for her imme-te family. When Carla called Jessie with the news that daughter was now ready to see other family members, ssie jumped in the car and drove to the Minneapolis nic.

Having been haunted by the memories of Missy's un-nourished body, Jessie was relieved to see her niece's alth had improved drastically. Although she still looked derweight, there was color back in her cheeks and a smile her face when she saw her aunt. She was also wearing a g-sleeved white blouse over a pair of jeans, instead of ck leather and metal.

"It's good to see you," Jessie told her, accepting her hug thusiastically.

"It's good to see you, too," Missy responded, maki their embrace last just a little longer than their usual hu "I'm glad you wanted to see me."

"Of course I wanted to see you," Jessie reassured h taking one of the vinyl chairs in the lounge. "I came soon as your mom said you could have visitors."

Missy looked down at her hands, fidgeting nervous "Well, I'm glad you did because I wanted to tell you I sorry about the way I yelled at you that day Mom and D had to bring me here."

"You weren't well, Missy. We all say things we do mean when we're not feeling good," Jessie said comp sionately.

Missy looked up and smiled weakly. "You're always nice to me and I don't know why. I've caused so ma problems." She looked away as emotion choked her voic

Jessie reached for her hands. They were trembling a moist as she took them in hers. "No one's perfect, Miss Everyone makes mistakes, everyone says things they do mean, everyone wishes they could change things they' done in the past."

"That's what they tell me in group...."

"But you don't believe them?" she probed carefully.

Missy shrugged. "I want to, but it's so hard."

Carla had told Jessie that Missy's need to be accept and liked by others had led her to believe she always had be happy and smiling. A lack of self-esteem had caused h to think that people around her looked at her with disa proving eyes, ready to criticize her if she wasn't perfect.

"How do you like your group therapy? Do you think i helping?" Jessie asked.

Missy started to say something then stopped. "I almc said it was fine, but then I remembered I'm supposed to l honest with my feelings."

'So how do you honestly feel about it?"

"I hate it," she said, then grinned. "There. I did a pretty od job, didn't I?"

Jessie smiled in understanding. "I bet it isn't easy open- ; up and talking to others about your problems."

"It's not. But I am getting better at it, and I guess if I'm lly honest about it, I have to admit I'm sort of getting d to it."

Jessie gave her hand an encouraging squeeze. "Good."

After catching up on family news and giving Jessie a tour the clinic's facilities, Missy said, "Mom says you have a w boyfriend."

Jessie sighed. "I'm afraid that's 'had' a new boy- end."

"You broke up?"

Jessie nodded. This time it was her voice that cracked th emotion. "I'm afraid I made a big mistake and said me really stupid things."

Missy lifted her eyebrows. "I know what that's like. Did u tell him you didn't mean them?"

"I was going to, but he didn't want to listen to me."

"And now you're miserable," Missy stated matter-of- ctly.

Surprised by her niece's perception, Jessie said, "Does show?"

"Not exactly. Mom told me you were pretty wiped out er this guy," she confessed with a half grin.

"And I thought I hid my feelings quite well," Jessie said htly.

"You know, you shouldn't try to suppress your feelings, untie Jess. It isn't good."

Jessie studied her niece for several moments before say- g, "No, you're right. It isn't."

Long after Jessie had left the clinic she thought abo
their conversation. Visiting Missy hadn't only eased l
mind concerning her niece's health, it had caused her
reflect on her own situation with Aidan. How would s
ever get over him if she didn't let out the feelings that w
causing her such misery?

Ever since her conversation with Tom and Helen M
Cullough she had been debating whether she should go
California. When Devony told her about several lo
models who were now working in the Los Angeles are
Jessie made up her mind.

With an uncustomary impulsiveness she called her age
to find out if she could be released from her contract wi
Renae's Bridal Salon. For someone who seldom took risl
the thought of packing up and moving to California wit
out having any job prospects was about as frightening
the thought of being pushed off a bungee jump. But Jess
knew that if she was to have any sort of chance with Aid;
she needed to be where she at least had the possibility
running into him. That was in Los Angeles.

Her booking agent, John Stockton, tried to talk her o
of leaving, but she refused to listen to his warning as to ho
difficult getting work in L.A. could be. After his initi
outburst of displeasure passed and he realized she was;
going to change her mind no matter how much persuadi;
he did, he made several phone calls that resulted in findi;
an apartment that could be subleased for a month and
couple of good leads for work in the Los Angeles area.

After the frigid temperatures of Minnesota, sixty d
grees felt almost tropical to Jessie as she stepped off t;
plane in L.A. A light drizzle had Californians scrambli;
to get indoors, but Jessie cavorted playfully in the rain, e;
joying the fresh smell of moisture and the freedom fro
down-filled coats and insulated boots.

However, had she known how homesick she would be all herself in a strange city, she probably wouldn't have been hasty in her decision. After only three days she was apted to get on a plane and return to Minnesota, but owing that Aidan was somewhere close by stopped her. e problem was getting him to see her without actually pping by his office uninvited.

Before she had left for California John Stockton had en her the name of a friend who would help her find rk should she decide to stay in L.A. After unsuccessly trying to find work on her own, she decided to give n a call. When she told him what she was looking for, he d the perfect answer to her dilemma.

TER SEVERAL DAYS of rain, the sun was finally shining ain as Aidan stared out his office window. The weather s rather mild for February, and normally he would have en planning a trip up the coast over the weekend, but ever ce he had returned from Minnesota he hadn't felt much e doing anything.

Just thinking about Minnesota caused him to chuckle to nself. He never thought he'd be saying that he missed the ow, but for some reason the rain seemed to bother him ore than any snow had done back home.

Home. Funny how easily that word had slipped out in ference to Minneapolis. He shook his head in regret. He uldn't think about it.

He wouldn't think about it. For two weeks he had been rking sixteen-hour days to keep from thinking about innesota, or more specifically, Jessie. The long hours dn't kept him from wondering where she was and what e was doing. She had really gotten under his skin.

"Mr. McCullough, will you be going out for lunch?" his cretary asked, interrupting his musings.

He was about to say no when the sunshine tempted hi
"I think I will, Janice. I could use a walk."

Hunger led Aidan to his favorite deli around the corn
where he gobbled down a pastrami sandwich. On his w
back to the office he walked past the same shops he h
walked past every day on his lunch hour for the past fo
years, only this time there was something different. Ped
trian traffic moved slowly in front of one particular sh
because of the small crowd outside its window display.

Curious, Aidan stepped out of the sunshine into t
shade beneath the striped awning and glanced through t
plate-glass window. He slowly removed his sunglasses a
stared, his mouth agape.

"Jessie?"

At first he thought he must have been confused, that
wasn't her but another model with similar features. H
moved closer to the window, unaware that he was rude
nudging people, stepping on toes.

She was the most beautiful model bride he had ever see
Standing perfectly still, staring out at the crowd, seein
everyone yet seeing no one. In her hand was a small pla
ard that read Wanted: One Groom.

"Jessie?" he repeated over and over. Yet she didn't s
much as twitch a muscle. Frustrated, he moved up to th
glass and again called out to her, ignoring the strange lool
he was drawing from the crowd.

Suddenly she made eye contact with him. A smile grac
ually creased her ruby red lips, then she slowly lifted he
right hand and blew him a kiss. The crowd cheered. Aida
grinned.

He disappeared, and when he returned he was carryin
an armful of long-stemmed roses. However, this time whe
Jessie saw him she did absolutely nothing. He waved, h

unded on the glass, he practically screamed at her, but
e didn't so much as flinch.

Aidan went storming inside to see the department store
anager, but by the time he found the woman his anger
d cooled. He simply gave her the roses and said, "These
e for the bride in the window."

Then he went back to his office and stared out the win-
w. From his spot on the third floor he could see the peo-
e on the sidewalk, but not the model in the window. He
zzed his secretary and asked her to bring him a pair of
noculars.

For the rest of the afternoon he monitored the window.
hen he saw the curtain close, he knew she was finished for
e day and quickly made his way down the stairs and out
ito the street. He hurried to the alley behind the shops,
irked himself outside the employee entrance and waited.

He didn't have to wait long. When Jessie stepped through
e door she was alone and not expecting anyone to be in
e alley. When she saw Aidan she gasped.

"You scared me!" she said, her hand fanning across her
iest.

"You had quite the same effect on me a few hours ago.
hat are you doing here?" he asked, his eyes hungrily de-
iuring her.

"Working."

"I thought you didn't like California."

"I thought I ought to experience it before I made that
idgment," she said saucily. "Just in case I end up living
ere."

His heart was beating faster. "Why would that hap-
en?"

She shrugged. "I might meet a man who wants me to
ay."

"Are you looking for a man?" he asked in a low, sex
voice.

"I thought I had found one, but I hurt him and I'm n
sure I can undo the damage I've done," she said quietly.

There was silence as they stood staring at each othe
"You thought I was a murderer," he finally said accu
ingly.

She shook her head. "No, I never thought that. I kno
it seemed as though I did, but I was so upset about yo
affair with Kathleen Daniels I couldn't think straight. Dee
in my heart I knew you could never hurt anyone, Aidan,
she said emotionally. "You left before I could tell yo
that."

He didn't say anything for several moments, but stoo
staring into her eyes, as though searching into her sou
When he spoke, it wasn't about the hurting. "Where are th
roses?"

"In here." She motioned to a shopping bag. "My bo:
packaged them up for me so I could get them home. D
you always give live mannequins roses?"

"Only those I happen to fall madly in love with," he sai
softly, catching her by the shoulders. He tipped her face u
with one hand. "Can I apply?"

"For what?"

"The position you were advertising for. Or do I need t
return tomorrow with this?" He pulled a printed résumé
from his pocket and held it up for her inspection. "I don'
mind wearing a tux, and I already have experience kissin
the bride."

She dropped the shopping bag and flung her arm
around him, raining kisses all over his face.

"You've got the job."